"I don't buy it." Crys seemed to be waiting
for his reply.

"Excuse me?" Luke's cheeks heated with
embarrassment. He wasn't sure he'd heard
everything she'd said. "You don't buy what exactly?"

Crys frowned. "That you're only here to help me with
my investigation. What do you really want?"

Studying her delicate features, being pulled into the
challenge glinting in her coffee-colored, long-lidded
eyes and tracing the curves of her heart-shaped lips,
Luke chose not to answer that question. "What do
you think I want?"

Crys kept her eyes on him as she settled back
against her seat. She regarded him in silence for a
beat before responding. "I believe you want to help
find this serial killer. Don't get me wrong. I appreciate
your help. But you have another agenda. What is it?"

Either she was scary insightful, or he'd lost his poker
face. "It's obvious I'll have to work hard to earn your
trust. I hope you'll give me that chance."

Dear Reader,

Have you ever felt so guilty about something that you were unable to talk about it even with the people you love most? Whether or not you were to blame, you allowed your guilt to propel you into actions that were unwarranted—maybe even dangerous.

That's one of the challenges my Crime Sisters—Crystal, a rookie homicide detective; Amber, a rising star in the city attorney's office; and Jade, a former crime beat reporter—are dealing with. They each blame themselves for the murder of their beloved aunt. But the shame of their guilt prevents them from sharing their secrets. Instead, they promise themselves and each other that they'll solve their aunt's cold case homicide—or die trying.

Fortunately, they don't have to walk their roads alone. Along their journeys, they each find someone who needs healing just as they need to be healed.

Thank you for taking a chance on my Crime Sisters trilogy. I hope you enjoy their journeys.

Happy reading!

Patricia Sargeant

BEHIND THE BADGE

PATRICIA SARGEANT

Harlequin

ROMANTIC SUSPENSE

MIX
Paper | Supporting responsible forestry
FSC® C021394
www.fsc.org

**Harlequin®
ROMANTIC
SUSPENSE™**

Recycling programs for this product may not exist in your area.

ISBN-13: 978-1-335-47182-6

Behind the Badge

Copyright © 2026 by Patricia Sargeant-Matthews

Harlequin Enterprises ULC
22 Adelaide St. West, 41st Floor
Toronto, Ontario M5H 4E3, Canada
www.Harlequin.com

HarperCollins Publishers
Macken House, 39/40 Mayor Street Upper,
Dublin 1, D01 C9W8, Ireland
www.HarperCollins.com

Printed in Lithuania

Nationally bestselling author **Patricia Sargeant** was drawn to write romance because she believes love is the greatest motivation. Her romantic suspense novels put ordinary people in extraordinary situations to have them find the Hero Inside. Her work has been reviewed in national publications such as *Publishers Weekly*, *USA TODAY*, *Kirkus Reviews*, *Suspense Magazine*, *Mystery Scene Magazine*, *Library Journal* and *RT Book Reviews*. For more information about Patricia and her work, visit patriciasargeant.com.

Books by Patricia Sargeant

Harlequin Romantic Suspense

Justice Hunters

Behind the Badge

The Touré Security Group

Down to the Wire
Her Private Security Detail
Second-Chance Bodyguard

The Coltons of Arizona

Colton's Deadly Trap

Visit the Author Profile page at Harlequin.com.

To My Dream Team:

* My sister, Bernadette, for giving me the dream.

* My husband, Michael, for supporting the dream.

* My brother Richard for believing in the dream.

* My brother Gideon for encouraging the dream.

And to Mom and Dad, always with love.

Chapter 1

"Detective Rashaad. I'm Special Agent Lucas Gilchrist." The conservatively dressed, thirty-something stranger swallowed Crystal Rashaad's outstretched hand in a firm grip. A warm grip that sent disturbing—though not unpleasant—currents up her arm.

Crystal slipped her hand free. Ignoring the echoes of his touch on her skin, she tipped back her head to meet his deep-set, black onyx eyes. "Agent Gilchrist—"

"Luke." He turned to escort her from the Ohio Bureau of Criminal Investigation's utilitarian lobby into a wide hallway early Wednesday morning.

Crystal's black, faux-leather loafers were nearly silent against the gleaming white-and-green-tiled flooring as she matched her strides to the agent's. The paper white walls added to the strict establishment vibe oozing from their surroundings. Luke pressed the Up button beside a black stainless-steel elevator.

The BCI was housed in a two-story building. Crystal was a fit five-nine with her loafers' two-inch heels. Luke had about five inches on her, not including his black oxfords' one-inch heels, and he was built like a tight end on a professional football team. So why were they waiting for an elevator?

"Let's take the stairs." She strode toward the staircase farther down the hall. Luke's footsteps sounded behind her. "I'd sent my case file to Special Agent Kim David. I was told I'd be meeting with *her* today."

Crystal had contacted the BCI's Special Investigations Unit almost a week earlier to request their assessment of her two homicide cases. SIU had assigned her to Special Agent David. They'd had a brief conversation before Crystal had hand delivered her files. Crystal was still grouchy over her clock tossing her an hour into the future ten days earlier with the Autumnal Equinox time change. Fatigue made her irritable and this game of Agent Musical Chairs made her crankier. Why hadn't anyone warned her about the switch?

As she mounted the stairs, Crystal assessed her new SIU contact. Everything about him bellowed "Conformist!" From his classic fit, navy-blue suit, matching tie and blinding-white shirt to his short, dark brown curls, clean-shaven brown face, square jaw and stubborn chin. He was trying hard to fade into the background, but Crystal saw through his subterfuge. His piercing eyes under thick, black, arched eyebrows, coupled with full, well-shaped lips, signaled this brother had hidden depths.

"Agent David has a full plate." Luke ascended the steps beside her. "I offered to take a few cases off her hands, including yours."

Crystal arched an eyebrow at the agent. "She doesn't let you call her Kim?" This dude was def uptight.

Luke's dark eyes gleamed with appreciation of her sarcastic wit. "I've reviewed your documents and can assure you I'm up to speed with your case."

"Good. Two people have already been murdered. I need to catch their killer yesterday." This was her first big case since she'd become a homicide detective eight months earlier. She was anxious to prove herself to her department—and to herself.

Luke stopped beside her. His eyes were inscrutable as he scanned her face. "I understand."

Why did she have the uneasy feeling his sentence was only half finished? What wasn't he saying to her?

Her thoughts scattered when he gestured toward the end of the bright hallway. She followed him into a small, sparse space that cried out for a personality, anyone's personality. Where were the little touches that gave visitors insight into the person who occupied the office forty-plus hours a week? The photos that reminded him of the people and places that mattered in his personal life? The knickknacks that kept treasured memories within arm's reach?

The lack of individual touches left a vacuum filled by beige walls and institutional furniture. *Ah.* Crystal corrected herself. Luke had mounted a large tan corkboard on the far wall and pinned neat rows of bureau memos and resource lists to it. *Fun.* His L-shaped, silver-and-white desk stood against the opposite wall with its requisite black computer, black phone, pens, pencils and notepads. She wanted to scribble a note across his black-and-white desk calendar: *Buy Toys!* Do something that would make him seem less like AI and more like a warm-blooded, three-dimensional human being.

"Please have a seat." He gestured to the black-vinyl-and-silver-metal visitor's chair.

"Thank you." Crystal lowered herself into the seat.

He had very nice manners. She liked that. Her eyes landed on the closed hutch above his desk. What was he hiding in there? Perhaps some personal touches?

"Would you like a cup of coffee?" Luke paused beside his black cushioned swivel chair.

Crystal glanced at his plain black coffee mug. "No, thank you. I'm fine." She opened her writing tablet on her lap and uncapped her pen.

Luke shed his jacket and hung it on the back of his wheeled chair before sitting. "How long have you been working this case?"

Crystal gestured toward the unopened manila folder centered on the desk in front of him. "As I noted in the files I shared with Special Agent David, my partner and I have been investigating these murders for a little more than a month." Five weeks and two days. "The first victim, Rita Gomez, was identified February 9."

"Why isn't your partner here with you?"

Crystal raised her eyes to meet Luke's enigmatic stare. "He's unavailable."

Her tone was flat and final. She didn't want to discuss the reason her partner, Victor Hansen, wasn't at this meeting. Not now. Crystal was grateful when Luke didn't push for an explanation.

"According to your case files, the victims don't appear to have any connections to each other." He opened the first folder on the stack. "Rita Gomez was a Hispanic woman in her early thirties. Your most recent victim, Alfred Murphy, a white man in his late fifties, was recovered fifteen days later, February 24. They worked for different companies, lived in different neighborhoods, had different hobbies and interests."

Crystal took over the review. "They attended different churches and graduated from different colleges. The only thing linking them is the method of murder and the recovery location. Both were found at Griggs Reservoir." The dam was constructed in northwest Columbus on the Scioto River. "The lack of blood or signs of a struggle indicate the area was a secondary crime scene. The suspect killed them at a separate location before bringing them to the reservoir."

Luke made a noncommittal hum. "The suspect used a knife and twisted it in the victim's back."

"That's right." Crystal found Luke's steady stare distracting. "We've identified the weapon as a straight, double-edged, eight-inch blade."

"Like a dagger." Luke finally dropped his eyes from Crystal, returning his attention to the folder and allowing her to breathe.

Crystal angled her head. "Why do you say it that way? As though using a dagger somehow makes sense to you?"

He looked up at her again. "These murders feel like revenge killings, a knife to the back with the blade being twisted."

His description gave Crystal chills. "I'd wondered about that. The phrase 'Twist the knife' kept playing in my head. But I thought I was being too literal."

"You have good instincts. Never second-guess yourself." Luke's crooked smile was both charming and very human. It gave her a glimpse into the man behind the virtual reality simulation.

Crystal's face heated, both from his appeal and his compliment. "Thank you. That means a lot."

Luke's expression sobered as though he regretted sharing that sexy smile. "Stabbing the victims in the back could indicate the suspect thinks the victims broke their trust." He flipped through the folder. "Your notes also mention a fishing lure."

"Yes. The killer left one fishing lure in each victim's mouth. It was a plastic silver minnow." Emboldened by his previous encouragement, Crystal shared her thoughts. "I wondered if there could be a connection to the phrase 'Taking the bait.'"

Luke nodded. "I think you're right. Again."

Crystal expelled a frustrated breath. "But who took the bait, the victim or the killer? And how did these victims break the killer's trust?"

Luke searched her features again with an intense, lingering scrutiny. "You sound very committed to this investigation."

What a strange comment, especially from another member of law enforcement. "Of course I'm committed to it. Someone is killing people in our community. Regardless of the reason, they have to be stopped."

"Of course." Luke closed the folder. He laid his hands on top of the stack of files. "As I said, I'm caught up on your case. I'd be happy to partner with you on it."

Warning sirens tripped in Crystal's brain. Why would a BCI special agent offer to partner with her to chase down a killer? The bureau offered its expertise to local, state and federal law enforcement agencies, including its laboratory services, DNA testing and background checks. Crystal wasn't aware of them partnering with detectives on their cases, though.

Then she remembered the intense looks the attractive agent had been giving her since they first met. Could that have anything to do with his interest in working with her? To tell the truth and shame the devil, the idea held some appeal. She wasn't going to lie. But Crystal didn't mix business with pleasure, not when her community's safety was at stake. Now, if he wanted to give her his number for later— once the suspect was caught—she wouldn't give it back.

She capped her pen and closed her writing pad. "Thank you for your offer, Special Agent Gilchrist—"

"Luke."

"—but my partner and I have this covered." She caught her breath at the thought of her partner. She forced herself past her grief and rose from the chair.

"Are you sure? I would be able to better assess the case if I were on-site with you." Luke's eyes cooled.

Had she offended him? Crystal didn't have time to worry about his ego. She had enough on her to-do list. More than enough. "I'm sure. Thanks, though."

Luke rose, pulling a business card from the holder on his desk. He handed it to her. "Let me know if you change your mind."

"I won't, but thank you." Crystal took his card, then raised her hand as Luke circled his desk. "I can find my way out. Thanks again for your time, Luke."

"Good luck, Crystal." Luke walked with her into the hallway. "I hope our paths cross again."

Perhaps. But if they did meet again, she hoped it was after she closed this case. Then she could focus on the pleasure and not worry about the business.

Crystal Rashaad was a beautiful woman. Luke could stare into her long-lidded eyes all day. They were the exact color of morning coffee. But it wasn't wise for him to become attracted to the target of his investigation.

He watched her stride down the hall to the staircase. She moved with a confidence, energy and grace he found hypnotic. Despite these distractions, he'd also noticed that her baggy gray blazer, tailored black slacks and polyester white blouse with red roses weren't out of reach of a detective's salary. Neither was her watch, which must have cost all of ten dollars. So what was she doing with the money she was allegedly collecting from bribes?

He waited until Crystal disappeared down the stairwell before returning to his office. He unlocked the hutch above his desk and removed his thick case file on Detective Crystal Rashaad before meeting with his boss.

Luke tapped his knuckles twice on her open door. "Do you have a minute?"

Special Agent in Charge Martina Monaco tapped a series of keys on her computer before swinging her wheeled black cloth executive chair to face him.

Martina was in her mid-fifties, average height and solidly built. She'd accessorized her plain white scoop-neck blouse with a collar-length, thin copper necklace and matching earrings. Her makeup was heavily but expertly applied to her pale white features. Her chin-length, blond hair was salon styled in layers that framed her round face.

She gestured toward one of the two visitor's chairs in front of her large cherrywood desk. The scent of designer perfume asserted itself over the aroma of coffee rising from the large, rose-pink porcelain mug beside her keyboard. "How was your meeting with Detective Rashaad?"

"It was a good start." Luke lowered himself into the black-vinyl-and-silver seat. "But she didn't confess, of course."

The corner of Martina's thin pink lips curved in dry humor. Behind her rimless glasses, her brown eyes glinted. "You'll have to work a little harder if you want the detective to admit she and her partner have been accepting bribes to tamper with criminal investigations."

When Martina had approached him about looking into allegations of corruption against Crystal and her partner, Luke had jumped at the opportunity. He couldn't stand the idea of illegal activities of any kind, either in the private or public sector. He especially abhorred criminality by public officials. Luke's temper stirred thinking about it. Those acts betrayed the community's trust and reflected badly on all public servants. The deception also made it harder for honest officials to do their jobs of protecting neighbors' lives and property.

However, other than the complaint filed by the anonymous source Martina had interviewed a little more than two months ago today, Luke didn't have any indication Crystal wasn't an honest broker of the public's trust.

"I reviewed Detective Rashaad's personnel file before meeting with her." Luke put his right ankle on his left knee. "It's impressive. Her evaluations are excellent. She's received commendations from supervisors as well as members of the community. Based on those reports, it's hard to imagine her being involved in anything illegal."

Martina started shaking her head before he'd finished speaking. "Rashaad may look squeaky-clean, but that doesn't mean she is. Remember that." She waited for his nod of agreement. "You'll have to work harder to build a case against her. You'll also have to be careful. If she knows you're investigating her, she'll destroy any evidence against her."

His supervisor sounded confident of Crystal's guilt. The unidentified complainant must have been convincing.

Luke's eyes roamed over the familiar framed service awards and pictures of Martina with statewide movers and shakers, including local and state government officials, lobbyists, captains of industry and celebrities. The images hung on her office walls like a photographic parade of who's-who. She'd lined her desk and bookcase with additional event pictures and awards. Luke wondered about the absence of photos with family members. Didn't she have any, living or deceased?

"I need to get close to her." An image of the attractive detective flashed into his mind. *Not that way.* Luke shook his head to clear it. "I offered to help with her investigation. Working with her would let me observe her actions and meet some of her associates. But she turned me down."

Partnering with Crystal would give him the opportunity to gather the evidence he needed to either charge her, if she was guilty, or clear her name. It also could test his professionalism. In the brief time they'd spent together, Luke had enjoyed her dry sense of humor, sharp mind and directness. She was also unpredictable. Her abrupt decision to take the stairs after Luke had summoned the elevator had forced him to scramble to catch up with her.

"She declined your offer to help her?" Martina stroked her chin in thought. "Now that's interesting. Did she give a reason?"

He shrugged his eyebrows. "She said she and her partner had it covered. As we both know, her partner, Victor Hansen, is dead."

Martina raised her thin blond eyebrows. "She lied to you. Why do you think she did that?"

"I don't know." Luke moved his shoulders restlessly. "I didn't challenge her on it, though. It would have looked suspicious. She may have wanted to know why I'd researched her before our meeting."

Crystal would have confronted him. He was sure of it. She'd been wary of him from the moment they'd met. Several times during their meeting, Luke had caught her looking at him as though she sensed he was hiding something, which he was. Her suspicions were reminders not to underestimate the rookie detective.

Martina spun to her computer and entered a command. "I'm not going to let Detective Rashaad's refusal of your offer stand in the way of our investigation."

"What are you going to do?"

Martina kept her attention on her computer as though she was searching for information on the screen. "I've got some pull with the chief of police. I'll have his office contact Rashaad's superior to convince him to assign her to work with you."

"I'll wait to hear from you." Luke stood to leave.

He had an uneasy feeling about Martina's plan. Crystal probably wouldn't react well to strong-arm tactics. She'd been clear about not wanting to work with him. But Luke couldn't worry about that. His objective was to get to the truth, wherever that truth might take him.

"How was your meeting with Special Agent David?" Lieutenant Jasper Bright waved Crystal into his office. The space was small but filled with natural light, photos, knick-knacks and file folders, most of which were on his desk.

Tall and slim, with sharp gray eyes, Jasper had been leading the department for seven years. His smooth white skin and clean-shaven head made it difficult to pinpoint his age. If Crystal had to guess, she'd say her new boss could count the years to his retirement on both hands.

"My request was reassigned." Crystal settled into the thinly padded and heavily worn gray chair in front of Jasper's scarred and battered faux mahogany desk. "Special Agent David had too many projects on her list. I met with Special Agent Gilchrist instead."

Jasper looked as though he was making a mental note of the switch for future reference. "Was Gilchrist helpful?"

"Actually, yes." Crystal had mulled over Luke's input

on the drive back to her department. "I have an idea for a new approach. Luke believes the killer's actions—using a dagger, twisting a knife in the victims' backs and leaving the fishing lure in their mouths—are signs the killer's motivation is revenge."

"Makes sense." Jasper settled back against his chair. His pale gray shirt made his eyes seem cooler.

"You've heard the saying 'Revenge is a dish best served cold'?"

"Of course." His scratchy voice held a hint of a Southern Ohio accent. "Who hasn't?"

"We think that's what our killer's doing, serving a cold dish of revenge." Crystal stood to pace the tight confines of her boss's office.

She started toward the mini silver filing cabinet on his south wall. Since most of the lieutenant's files sat on or around his desk, Crystal suspected the cabinet's sole purpose was to support Jasper's personal coffee station. The beans' bold, smoky aroma filled the space.

Crystal breathed in the scent before continuing. "The murderer could have been planning these attacks for months or even years. Vic and I don't think Rita and Alfred were chosen at random." She paced back to Jasper's desk and stood behind her chair. "The suspect has a personal connection to them, which means Rita and Alfred are somehow connected to each other. I need to dig deeper into their backgrounds to find that link. Once I do, I'll find their killer."

Jasper's expressionless eyes searched her face in silence while she returned his scrutiny with confidence. She must be right. She needed to be right. Rita and Alfred deserved justice. Every victim did, sooner rather than later.

Crystal held on to the back of the visitor's chair and her

patience. She didn't like waiting. She needed to be doing something. But during the eight months she'd worked for Jasper, she'd come to understand he worked at his own pace. She'd get used to it. Eventually.

"Good. Keep me apprised of your progress." Jasper straightened in his chair and smoothed his thin black tie. "Vic's death has knocked everyone in the department off stride, but you were his partner. I'm sure it hit you hardest. How are you holding up?"

"I'm OK." That sounded better than admitting she wasn't sure.

Vic had been a messy, irreverent, thoughtful man with a weakness for junk food. He'd been her partner for eight months, but Crystal felt as though they'd known each other for years. She'd been devastated by his murder almost two weeks ago during a break-in at his home. Shot to death with no witnesses. Crystal shivered. It was a chilling reminder of another heartbreaking loss much closer to home.

"Do you need time off?" Jasper's laser-like stare tried to work its way into her mind as though he wanted to discover the truth for himself.

"My cases can't wait." Crystal resumed her seat, crossing her right leg over her left. She rested her hands loosely on the chair's arms, afraid Jasper might interpret any restless movement as uncertainty. "Besides, work keeps me focused on something other than losing Vic. Has the team assigned to his case learned anything more?"

"Nothing that gives us a better idea of the identity of the killer—or killers." Jasper's voice held a hint of frustration. "Their theory is Vic got home late. Surprised a burglar. There was a struggle and he took a bullet to his chest."

Crystal flinched. The circumstances of Vic's murder were so similar to her aunt's. Kendra Chapel, Crystal's

mother's younger sister, had returned home one evening
late from work and surprised an intruder. The burglar had
shot Aunt K at point-blank range in the chest, killing her
instantly. This upcoming Saturday would mark the one-
year observance of her aunt's murder. Crystal pushed past
the pain and anger that the killer was still walking free.
She hoped the detectives assigned to Vic's case would have
more success.

"Fortunately, no one else was hurt." Her partner had
been a recent widower, and his three adult children no longer lived at home.

"You can't continue to work these cases alone." Jasper's
hands waded through the sea of folders across his desk before fishing one out. "You're doing well, but you're still new
to the position and the department. You need a veteran to
show you the ropes and get you acclimated. I'm hoping we
can get one for you soon, if only on a temporary basis."

"I understand." Crystal uncrossed her legs and set both
feet on the ground. "Luke offered to help with the case."
Even though she didn't want to work with the special agent,
she didn't want her new supervisor to think she was in the
habit of withholding information.

Jasper's expression was skeptical. "Don't they have
enough cases at the SIU?"

Crystal's lips curved into a smile before she realized
Jasper was serious. "I can't answer that, but I wanted you
to know about his offer and that I'd declined it. I told him
I had it covered."

"You *do* have it covered. For now." Jasper gave a deci-
sive nod. "In the meantime, I've got several possibilities
for your new partner. We'll have someone to help you by
the end of next week."

Music to Crystal's ears. She was confident in her investigative skills, and she had her lieutenant's support. But she could use a partner as a sounding board and to help with the heavy lifting.

"Thanks, Lieutenant." Crystal pushed herself to her feet. "I'll get back to it. I'm also going to check on Abby tonight."

Abigail Hansen Tiller was Vic's oldest child. The department had had a strong presence at Vic's wake and funeral—everyone from patrol officers to detectives and leadership had shown their support for a member of their community who'd been taken too soon by criminal violence.

Jasper inclined his head. "Thanks, Rashaad. Let her know if she or her siblings need anything, they can call me."

"I will." Crystal turned to leave.

She hadn't had the opportunity to express her condolences or voice her appreciation for everything Vic had done to welcome her and help her settle into her new role. It was important to Crystal that she share those feelings with her deceased partner's family. She knew how comforting such sentiments could be when grieving the loss of a loved one, especially when they'd been taken unexpectedly—and their killer still hadn't been brought to justice.

Chapter 2

"Two things were so very, very important to my dad." Abigail Hansen Tiller offered Crys a mug of hot tea before taking her seat on the other side of the maple wood dining table. "His career in law enforcement and his family. He'd wanted to be a police officer all his life."

Crys wrapped her hands around the mug, letting its warmth chase away the chill of her grief. "It's a huge responsibility and also a great honor to protect the people in our community, to keep our neighbors and neighborhoods safe."

She'd met her deceased partner's children for the first time at his wake. She wished it had been under happier circumstances. Since Vic had talked about his kids *a lot*, Crys had felt like she'd known them. Abby, his eldest, was Crys's age, thirty, and a nurse. She was pretty with blue eyes that reminded Crys of Vic's. She was a few inches shorter than Crys with full curves. Her peaches-and-cream features were devoid of makeup. She'd gathered her bone-straight, strawberry blond hair in a knot on the crown of her head as though she'd been more interested in getting it out of the way than in how it looked.

"That's how Dad felt, too. He always said it was an honor to play a part in keeping the community safe." Abby watched Crys closely as though she was trying to probe her thoughts.

Why were people looking at her like that today? First Luke, then Jasper and now Abby. Well, maybe Jasper didn't count. He looked at everyone like that all the time. Still, did they know something she didn't?

Crys sipped her tea and focused on the reason she was there—to give Abby comfort and support in her time of grief. "It was a great acknowledgment of his service that so many friends, colleagues and brass paid their respects at his wake and funeral."

Abby nodded, her eyes still locked on Crys's face. "That meant a lot to me and my family just as it means a lot that you're here today. My father thought very highly of you, Crys. He said a lot of nice things about you, including that you're a great detective. It's important you know that."

Crys's face warmed with pride. "That means a lot. Thank you for telling me. Your father had been a detective for decades. I'd be honored to have a career as long as his."

A small smile eased the intensity of Abby's stare. "I'm sure you will."

"Thank you." Crys cast her eyes around Abby's dining room.

It was spacious, allowing Abby's young family of six to enjoy each other's company as they shared their meals. The cool green walls complemented the warm maple wood hutch serving table and hardwood flooring. Pale green curtains waved in the cool breeze that slipped through the window behind the table. Family photos covered the opposite wall.

Beneath the hot tea's herbal aroma, Crys smelled the cheese, tomato and oregano from the pasta heating on the stove in the nearby kitchen. She'd declined Abby's generous offer to join her family for dinner. She needed to leave soon if she intended to be on time for her weekly get together with her sisters.

"Have you heard anything more about the investigation into my dad's murder?" Abby's question caused Crys's stomach muscles to tangle. She didn't want another person she cared about to be the victim of an unsolved homicide.

"Not yet, but they just need a break in the case." Crys hoped that break came sooner rather than later.

Abby sipped her tea in silence for several seconds. "My father brought home the overprotective manner he had at work. Do you do that, too?"

Crys smiled. "My sisters would say yes. But then they've always accused me of smothering them."

"Maybe one has to be a little controlling to be a good police officer." Abby's tone was wry. "But being so protective of others is its own burden. You can't always keep the ones you love safe. When my mother was diagnosed with lung cancer four years ago, it tore my dad apart. He wanted so badly to take her place. It was hard for him to see her like that."

"I understand." Crys's muscles tensed as Abby's words brought back memories of her parents' battles with cancer.

Both illnesses had been difficult for Crys and her sisters. Their father had passed away less than two years before their mother's death. And as Abby had said, it's hard to watch loved ones suffer. By the time their mother's cancer had been diagnosed, all her doctor could do was try to make her comfortable. They hadn't been successful. Cancer was a curse.

Abby's eyes were clouded with painful memories. "Her treatments were expensive, but Dad had been desperate to try anything to help ease her pain. He didn't care about the cost. He ended up with a lot of debt."

Crys hurt for Abby and her family. "My sisters and I went through a similar experience with our parents."

Abby leaned into the kitchen table, closing the distance between them. "So you can understand the situation my dad was in. You know how he felt."

"Not exactly." Crys frowned. Abby was starting to make her uncomfortable. "I'm sure losing your spouse is different from losing a parent."

"Of course." Abby shook her head, dropping her eyes to her half-full mug. "But grief has a way of impairing your judgment."

Crys's confusion cleared. "I get that. Sometimes in an effort to escape their grief, people do things they can't explain even to themselves." She searched Abby's eyes, looking for the motive behind this odd conversation. "How are your siblings?"

Abby's brother, Laurence, taught high school English. Her sister, Rebecca, was the youngest and a pharmacist. The trio had seemed lost and almost confused during the wake and funeral.

Abby shrugged restlessly. "Larry and Becca are as well as can be expected, I suppose."

"Grief is very personal. Everyone deals with it in different ways."

Abby's capable shoulders lifted with a deep sigh. "My dad didn't deal well with his grief over my mother's passing. And now he's gone." She gave Crys a searching look. "Does it seem as strange to you as it does to me how similar the circumstances of my dad's death are to your aunt's?"

Startled, Crys blinked. "How do you know about my aunt's murder?"

Abby straightened in her chair. "Dad told me, but I didn't mean to upset you."

"You didn't. I was just surprised." And a little wary. Suspicion was a family trait, though.

Crys tried but couldn't remember sharing the details of her aunt's murder with Vic. She tightened her grip around the cooling mug. What was happening right now? Was she being paranoid? Or was she being played?

Dealing with her grief over Vic's death so close to the one-year observation of her aunt's unsolved homicide was hard, especially given their similarities. Unfortunately, home burglaries happened too often. The fact two people she was close to died during such a crime could be a co-incidence.

Crys was beginning to have her doubts.

"Sorry to keep you waiting." Crys slid into the hardwood bench seating beside her youngest sister, Jade Rashaad. "I checked on Vic's daughter, Abby, on my way over."

Jade and their middle sister, Amber Rashaad, had claimed a booth in the center of the sports bar Wednesday evening.

"We haven't been here long." Amber waved a dismissive hand. "Besides we were early. We ordered your soda."

The three of them always arrived several minutes before their agreed-upon meeting time. Was it healthy to be so competitive?

"How's Abby?" Jade sipped her ice water. Her attention was riveted to one of the three televisions mounted to the oak wall across the dining room.

The NBA's Cleveland Cavaliers were playing, which explained why the bar was so crowded. With multiple monitors suspended from every wall, there wasn't a bad seat in the house for patrons interested in the game. Due to its location downtown between the police headquarters and the Franklin County courthouses, most of the bar's clientele worked in law enforcement: officers, detectives, judges and lawyers. Crime beat reporters were also regulars.

"She's still processing her grief." Crys pitched her voice to be heard above nearby conversations and cheers from the Cavs faithful. "Fortunately, she and her siblings are close, so they'll get through this together just like we did."

The bar was cool, perhaps a little cold. Crys pulled her dark blue, classic bomber jacket closer around her. The dining area was thick with the scents of spicy buffalo wings, greasy fries and cheesy loaded potatoes. When their server came, Crys and her sisters ordered their usual wings and salad.

"Have there been any developments in the investigation into Vic's death?" Jade had been a crime beat reporter with the *Capital Daily News* until she'd been laid off from the newspaper last month. Now she was preparing to launch a true crime podcast while sending out résumés.

Her youngest sister was struggling with anger and disappointment at having to start the New Year unemployed. Crys could understand that. She was angry and disappointed for her.

"No." Crys shook her head. "Jasper said he'd update me when the detectives assigned to Vic's case make progress." She'd never handled waiting well.

Amber squeezed her lemon, letting its juice spill into her tempered glass of iced tea. "I can't get past the similarities between Aunt Kendra's and Vic's murders. That can't be a coincidence." She set the lemon rind on the napkin that served as its coaster. "And since Vic and Aunt Kendra lived in different parts of the city, this could be an indication that the burglary ring has expanded."

After graduating from New York University's School of Law three years ago, Amber had accepted a job with the Columbus City Attorney's Office in its Prosecution Division. Rumor had it she was a rising star in the office. That was a rumor Crys enjoyed spreading.

Crys took a drink of her soda. "I've mentioned that to the detectives assigned to Vic's case. They don't have much to go on, though, since several documents from Aunt K's case files disappeared early in the investigation."

"I still can't get over that." Jade's voice was rough with frustration. It was a feeling they all shared.

Crys's eyes were on the Cavs game, but her mind superimposed images of their aunt over the TV: her thick, dark curls, smooth brown skin and quick, warm, infectious smile.

She fought the grief and anger that tried to sap her hope and shared a look between her younger sisters. "We're not giving up on our search for Aunt K's killer. We owe it to Mom, Aunt K and ourselves to get justice for her. But it will be hard without the complete file."

Amber's cocoa eyes glinted with determination. "Then we'll start from scratch with our own investigation."

"Do you two have time?" Jade drew Crys's attention from the Cavs game. Her espresso-colored eyes were inscrutable. Her tone was difficult to interpret. "You're both always so busy with work."

Was there a hint of criticism in Jade's voice? Before she could follow up with her sister, the server arrived with their small garden salads. The moment was lost. The harried young woman's pink T-shirt bore the business's logo and clashed with her bright red hair.

Amber waited until the server left before continuing their conversation. She drizzled balsamic vinaigrette dressing over the bed of lettuce, sprinkling of cheddar cheese and diced cucumbers, tomatoes and onions. "We want Aunt Kendra's killer brought to justice. If we need to start the investigation from scratch, I'll make the time."

"So will I." Jade stabbed a forkful of her salad before dipping it into her container of zesty Italian dressing. Hostility radiated from her.

"Then it's unanimous." Crys looked from Jade beside her to Amber across the table. "We'll reinterview her neighbors. I'll speak with the patrol officers who were the first to arrive at the scene. One of the detectives who worked the case is dead, but the other retired to North Carolina. I'll get his contact information."

Amber gestured toward Crys and Jade. "We all spoke with her that day. Let's write down what we remember of those conversations for the record."

Crys narrowed her eyes at Amber. She sounded less than enthusiastic about the idea she'd just pitched. Then why had she suggested it? Crys lowered her eyes. Perhaps the memory of that final phone call with their aunt brought as much pain to Amber as the echoes of Crys's last exchange caused her.

The server returned with their buffalo wing orders. Amber had requested teriyaki sauce. Jade had asked for hot wings and Crys had chosen medium.

"Then we have a plan. Tonight, I'll do an internet—" Jade cut herself off and slapped Crys's shoulder. Her voice was sharp with urgency. "Get up. Get up."

Confused, Crys hurried out of the booth. "What's going on? What are you doing?"

Ignoring her, Jade moved to sit beside Amber. "Scooch over."

"Why? I thought you didn't like sitting with your back to the room, Ms. Paranoia." Despite her protests, Amber gave Jade space on the bench setting.

Standing beside her younger siblings, ready to shield them from danger, Crys scanned the room. She couldn't identify any threats. "J, what's wrong?"

Jade balanced her right elbow on the table in front of her and braced her forehead in her palm. "The guy who took the booth across the room. The one in the dark gray suit with the purple shirt. He's The Enemy."

"Which guy? What enemy?" Crys located the topic of their heated whispers. He sat alone at the booth beneath the only TV not streaming the Cavs game.

In the bar's dim lighting, she couldn't see him well, but he appeared to be an attractive Black man in his early thirties with a natural fade and sharp cheekbones.

Amber twisted around to see for herself. "He's handsome."

"Don't look." Jade smacked Amber's upper arm. "Why are you looking? Can't you at least feign subtlety?"

Realization was like a bucket of cold water in Crys's face. "Is he *Capital Daily*'s new executive editor?"

Jade's eyes gleamed with anger. "Yes. He's Caleb Brunson—the reason I was fired."

Crys returned her attention to The Enemy, only to discover he'd also noticed them. He had a very attractive smile. But her resentment over Jade's situation made her want to punch him.

"Ignore him." Crys sat and selected a wing from her plate. "Don't let him ruin our dinner."

Jade moved her empty salad bowl to the edge of the table

and drew her plate of wings closer. "Speaking of ruining dinner, Am, did you hear The Cad is back in Columbus?"

"What?" Crys stilled with a wing halfway to her mouth. "Trent's back?"

Trent Mitchell was Amber's ex-fiancé. He'd broken her heart a year ago. Hearing his name again sparked an explosion of anger inside Crys. She could only imagine how upset Amber must be.

"Yes, I heard Trent was back." Amber's hesitation was almost imperceptible. Almost. "He's working in the public defender's office."

Jade drank her water. "He's such a bleeping cad." She blinked when Amber extended her hand palm up almost under her nose. "What?"

Amber sighed. "If you want to clean up your language, you can't just substitute swear words for other words."

Jade scowled. "Says who?"

Crys hid a smile behind her glass of diet soda. Her youngest sister had a potty mouth. No one could deny that. Recently, she'd decided to reinvent herself, starting with cleaning up her language. Part of her motivation was not wanting to drop obscenities into her podcast, which she'd then have to edit out.

She'd enlisted Amber as her human swear jar. Crys had no idea what Jade planned to do with all that loot, but at the rate she was going, she should be able to take a Caribbean cruise by Christmas.

"Do you want me to hold you accountable or not?" Amber wiggled her fingers. "Pay up."

"Urgh." Jade pulled her wallet from her purse. She fished out a quarter and slapped it into Amber's hand. "Anyway." She softened her tone. "How are you handling The Cad's return?"

Amber pocketed the coin. "It's been a year—or so." She paused again as though the words didn't want to come out. "The scar's still scabbing over. I've been trying not to think about him and instead throwing myself into my work. Maybe that's been a mistake, too."

Jade squeezed Amber's hand as it lay on the table between them. "I'm so sorry, Am."

"So am I." Crys's heart tightened with pain and anger for her sister. "If you need to talk, let us—"

"Excuse me." Their overworked server returned, placing a mug of beer in front of each of them.

"These aren't ours." Bewildered, Crys looked up at the young woman.

Their server smiled. Tucking her now-empty tray under her right arm, she pointed across the dining area with her left. "The good-looking man over there paid for them. Isn't that nice of him?" Without waiting for their response, the frazzled young woman again hustled from the dining area.

"He's a tad clueless." Amber's voice was dry. "None of us is drinking beer."

Crys looked to Jade. "What are you going to do?"

"Watch." Jade lifted a mug with one hand and her mostly empty salad bowl with the other. She shifted in her seat until she drew Caleb's attention. Once he was looking, she poured the contents of her mug into the bowl.

Crys's eyebrows climbed up her forehead. *Oh, no.* Her baby sister had a temper. Being fired from a job she loved and having her dream career derailed had put her in a permanent funk. She and Amber had been tiptoeing around Jade since that fateful day a month ago. Caleb Brunson didn't know about that. Like their server, he probably thought he was making a generous gesture, a friendly overture. Instead, he'd tap-danced across a minefield. *Ouch.*

With dread, Crys looked over at Caleb. To his credit, the executive editor didn't flinch. He smiled and inclined his head as though acknowledging his olive branch hadn't gone over well. Crys was impressed. Caleb turned to study his menu. Crys noticed a second menu on the other side of the table. Who was Jade's enemy waiting for?

"Does he even know why you're angry with him?" Amber's question drew Crys's regard to her. She wanted to know, too.

"Of course. I told him." Jade took a deep drink of her ice water, then set the glass down with a snap. "I was fired to make room for his salary."

"You said that to him?" Amber's eyes widened. She threw a look at Crys before turning back to Jade. "How did he—"

"Oh. My. Goodness." Stunned, Crys stared at the tall, lean, broad-shouldered man in a conservative navy-blue suit who walked across her line of vision.

He'd come into view from around the partition that separated the bar from the dining room and crossed without hesitation to Caleb's table. What was going on there?

"What is it? What's wrong?" Jade started to turn around, then stopped herself. "Is it The Enemy?"

Amber didn't have Jade's self-control. She looked over her shoulder and found the new arrival right away. "Do you know that guy? He's handsome."

Apparently throwing restraint to the winds, Jade shifted on the bench seating to see who Crys and Amber were talking about. "Ooh. Yes. Who is he?"

Crys was speechless. Luke seemed to know Caleb well. They greeted each other with warm handshakes and a man hug. Was it a coincidence that the person who'd forced her sister out of a job was good friends with the man who'd tried to force his way into her investigation? Perhaps, if she believed in coincidences. She didn't.

"Crys?" Jade prompted her when she remained silent. "Who is that?"

She shook herself free of the puzzle. "That's Special Agent Lucas Gilchrist. He's with the Bureau of Criminal Investigation's Special Investigations Unit. I consulted with him this morning about my case."

Suddenly, Luke looked over as though he knew she was watching him. He nodded his greeting. She returned the gesture, then watched as Luke settled into the bench seat opposite Caleb.

Amber plucked a wing from her plate. "I wonder how they know each other?"

"And for how long?" Jade asked.

"I'm wondering the same things." What was the connection between the newspaper's executive editor and the special agent?

Chapter 3

"You wanted to speak with me, Lieutenant?" Crys pushed Jasper's door wider—and found Luke sitting in one of the two visitor's chairs in front of her boss's desk. A current of shock sped down her spine. "What are you doing here?"

Luke stood, turning to face her. Crys regretted her question as soon as she'd asked it. It was unprofessional—and revealing. But Luke had caught her off guard.

Jasper answered before Luke could speak. "BCI believes Special Agent Gilchrist has something to add to our investigation. They've offered to let him work with us on a temporary, one-time-only condition."

Crys struggled to keep her jaw from dropping. She turned to Luke. Her confusion followed. A torrent of questions flooded her mind—none of them kind—starting with why? Why, when she'd already rejected his offer to work the case with her, was he standing here this morning?

Luke's onyx eyes were unreadable. "I look forward to working with you, Detective Rashaad."

I wouldn't be so sure about that.

Crys found her voice. "Special Agent Gilchrist, could you give Lieutenant Bright and me a moment?"

"Of course. I'll wait for you in the hallway." Luke stepped forward. He took the door handle from her. Crys had forgotten she'd been using it to hold herself up. His palm brushed the top of her hand, sending a current up her arm and across her breasts. She waited for Luke to pull the office door closed before facing her boss, seated behind his desk.

She lowered her voice. "Why is he here?"

Jasper gestured for Crys to take the chair Luke had vacated. "I got a call last night from the chief's office. Leadership has become impatient. They want this case solved and a suspect prosecuted yesterday. People are afraid to go to the reservoir. Nearby businesses are seeing a drop in customer traffic."

Meanwhile, her fifty-eight-year-old aunt's murder remained unsolved after almost a year. Perhaps if there'd been an economic downturn connected to her killing, the brass would have made a few calls. Situations like these were so unfair. The social status of the constituents involved shouldn't matter. Leadership should pull strings for all investigations or none. Crys closed her eyes briefly and drew a calming breath. The bold aroma of Jasper's coffee helped clear her head.

Struggling to keep her voice down, Crys swung an arm toward the door. "That doesn't explain why they're sticking me with someone from SIU rather than another detective."

Amusement flared in Jasper's cool gray eyes before winking out. "The chief doesn't need to explain. They tell us what needs to be done and we jump."

Crys expelled a sigh of frustration as she rose from the chair. She glanced toward the door, imagining Luke standing on the other side. Could he hear them? "Are you still planning on getting a new partner for me by next week?"

"That plan is on hold for now." Jasper leaned into his desk and held Crys's eyes. "Focus on solving the case, Rashaad. That's our priority. Everything else is noise."

Her boss had a point. Still… "Is Special Agent Gilchrist the right person to work this case with me?"

Jasper's eyes narrowed. "Do you know something about Gilchrist that I don't?"

Crys started to say she didn't trust him. She sensed he was hiding something. But without proof to back up her feelings, her new boss would think she was paranoid. Crys was trapped. "I don't know him."

"You didn't know Hansen when you started, either." Jasper sat back against his chair. "I've reviewed his record. He has an impressive closure rate. His last couple of performance reviews are excellent. He should be an asset—"

Crys's work cell phone buzzed, alerting her to a text. She scanned the message on the screen. Her heart sank. Her blood ran cold. "Another body was found at the reservoir."

"Go." Jasper jerked his head toward the door. "The sooner you close this case, the sooner you can send Gilchrist home."

Crys held tight to that promise. She jerked the door open. Luke was waiting in the hallway as promised. "There's another body at the reservoir."

She continued down the hall without waiting to see whether he'd follow. If he was going to work with her, he'd have to keep up or be left behind. She'd rather the latter.

"I know you don't want my help on your case." Luke's voice came from her left as he easily kept pace with her. "But I believe my experience and insights could be a benefit to your investigation."

Irritated, Crys stopped. She met his eyes, ignoring the bubbles popping in her belly. "You don't have to work with me to share your opinions on the case. I gave you—or rather, I gave Special Agent David—my case files before.

I can do it again. So I don't think this is about the case. Why are you really here?"

She wanted to accuse him of using her investigation as a form of speed dating, but she was too self-conscious.

A flash of what seemed like surprise jumped from the depths of his piercing eyes. The reaction happened too quickly for Crys to be sure it wasn't some other emotion. Panic? Fear?

Whatever the reaction was, Luke masked it before responding. "This *is* about the case. I want to help."

"Try again." Crys spun on her heels and continued down the hall.

A small part of her—teeny, tiny—was flattered. She would be lying if she denied it. Luke was attractive, successful and intelligent. Who wouldn't want someone like that to be interested in them?

But another part—a much larger part—was offended. That he would think so little of her professionalism that he'd assume she'd pursue a romantic relationship with him while searching for a killer. Make that a serial killer, if this latest victim was connected to the first two.

"Why don't you believe me?"

Crys felt Luke's eyes searching her face as though looking for answers when he wasn't willing to give any. The nerve. "Don't you have enough to do at SIU?"

"I can manage my caseload there and help you."

"Who are you, Superman?"

"More like I don't have a social life."

He wasn't going to tell her what he was up to. Crys's muscles tightened with exasperation.

She took a detour to her desk. Avoiding looking at Vic's, Crys grabbed her dark blue bomber jacket and navy-blue satchel.

"Fine, then help. That would be great." She shrugged her satchel onto her right shoulder. "But stay focused on this case. One misstep and I'll find a way to get you dropped from this investigation."

"You don't have to worry about me."

Crys was taking a wait-and-see approach. Without responding, she continued to the stairwell, then jogged down the two flights of stairs to the police department's black-and-white-tiled lobby.

Luke kept up with her as she strode to the door. "Were the two women with you at the bar last night your sisters?"

Crys slid him a look. So much for staying focused. "I think you know the answer to that. Here's a question for you: How do you know Caleb Brunson?"

Luke gave her a half smile. "We've been friends since college."

Crys arched an eyebrow but maintained her silence. Another strike against him.

Reaching past her, Luke pushed the glass-and-silver-metal entrance door open, allowing her to precede him from the building.

"Detective Rashaad. Crys."

Turning toward the woman's voice, Crys found Abby Hansen Tiller near the entrance to the police department. Dressed in blue tennis shoes, black yoga pants and a loose-fitting, lightweight gray sweater, her deceased partner's eldest child used both arms to clutch an oversize, thick manila envelope to her chest.

Abby's voice trembled. "May I speak with you, please?"

Crys was torn. The other woman looked to be in distress, but she'd just lectured Luke on focusing on the case. "I'm so sorry, Abby." She glanced at the special agent before continuing. "We're on our way to a crime scene. Could I—"

"This won't take long." Abby took a tentative step forward. "I promise."

She couldn't continue to ignore the pain in Abby's eyes. They were pink and swollen as though she'd been crying. Again.

Crys glanced back at Luke. "I'm sorry. Could you give me five minutes?"

"Of course." Luke's eyes were on Abby's envelope.

Crys drew the other woman aside. "What's wrong, Abby? How can I help?"

Abby glanced at the envelope. "My father left something for you."

"Me?" Shocked, Crys pressed her right palm to her chest. "We barely knew each other. Why would he do that?"

Abby continued. "He left me a message, telling me where to find this packet. I was to give it to you immediately upon his death. I know eleven days isn't immediate. I'm sorry. I read it first." She drew another deep breath as though trying to ease the pressure in her chest. "Crys, I need you to know my father was a *good* man."

"I know that." Crys reached out to rub Abby's arm, offering comfort. A cloud of misery surrounded her partner's daughter. Crys was hurting for her, for both of them.

"My dad loved being a detective." Abby's voice was husky. She squeezed her eyes closed. When she opened them again, tears poured down her cheeks. "Keeping people safe, protecting the community. But he loved his family, too. Is that so wrong? Everything he did was to try to protect us, to keep us safe. Do you understand that?"

Crys felt a chill of foreboding. "Abby, what's going on?"

The other woman hesitated before relinquishing the packet to Crys. "Please. Just try to understand."

Without another word, Abby spun toward the parking

lot and hurried to her car. Frowning, Crys watched her shrink into the distance. She looked at the thick, surprisingly heavy packet in her hands. The words *For Crys* were written in Vic's nearly illegible cursive. What was happening right now? What was in this envelope? She shifted the packet to open it.

No. Crys drew a steadying breath and focused on her primary responsibility: finding a serial killer. Keeping her community safe. She dropped the envelope into her satchel and pulled the keys to her department-issued tan, four-door sedan from her front pocket.

She turned to find Luke staring at her. "Let's go."

"What's in the envelope?" He strode beside her into the parking lot.

"None of your business, Nosy." Crys used the key fob to unlock the car, then dropped the satchel into the backseat. "Keep your mind on the case. Remember?"

Keeping my mind on the case, and not on the very large, very thick, mysterious mailer stashed in Crys's car.

Luke crouched closer to the corpse. The killer had left the body on the banks of the Scioto River at the Griggs Reservoir. This spot was popular for fishing as well as Frisbee golf. A quartet of players had found the body earlier this morning.

"The victim is Sally Stead." Crys's tone was somber as she went through the wallet found in the dead woman's purse. "According to her driver's license, she recently turned fifty-seven. Her address is on the southeast side."

"The exact opposite end of the city from this park." Luke looked up at her.

Crys stood on the other side of the corpse. She was tall with a dancer's well-toned figure. She'd paired her smoke-gray, tapered jeans with a black boatneck blouse that featured a pink rose-petal pattern. She'd wrestled her mass of brown curls into a ponytail that she'd secured at the crown of her head with a red, yellow and green polyester scarf. Her hair swung above her narrow shoulders as it danced with the wind. Her delicate golden-brown profile was marred by a slight frown. Luke's fingers itched to smooth it away.

Keeping my mind on the case.

He resumed his examination of the crime scene. Sally Stead's shoulder-length, ash-blond hair streamed behind her. It was tangled with leaves, grass and sticks as though she'd been dragged across the lawn to this spot. Dirt had burrowed into her pink coat and over her tan slacks. A stiletto was missing. Bruises at her neck and wrists stood out against her pale white skin. There were cuts on her small palms. Defensive wounds? There was very little blood at this site.

"She'd struggled with her assailant." Luke pressed against the victim's arm. "Rigor mortis has set in."

Crys's eyes were shadowed as she looked at the body. "The killer waits until the middle of the night to move the victim from the primary crime scene—which could be anywhere—to the river, which they've chosen as their secondary."

Was it his imagination or was there something about this scene that was affecting Crys? Luke dismissed his suspicions. He knew from her files that Crys had been in law enforcement for almost ten years. She'd worked other homicide cases as a patrol officer. She could handle scenes like this.

"Your report noted the bodies were found twelve or more hours after the estimated time of death. You're right. The murder may not happen at the same location each time." Luke straightened and studied their surroundings. "Are there any differences between this scene and the other two? Is the killer escalating, declining, maintaining?"

The Scioto River rolled north to south. The water was brown and swollen from the heavy rain earlier in the week. A thin, cool breeze whispered past him. It jostled the underbrush and shook the tiny spring buds that clung to the tree branches. Luke breathed in the moist air, laden with the scents of damp earth and wet grass. Nature's harmony was interrupted by the sounds of patrol car doors slamming, crime scene cameras clicking and voices calling up and down the riverbank. A beautiful spot for an ugly act. Was that deliberate, too?

"Each victim had been recovered from a different area of the reservoir. Otherwise, this scene matches the other two exactly." Crys paced around the body. "Bruising around her neck. Defensive wounds. The victim is posed on her left side. The knife has been twisted in her back." She stopped beside Luke and crouched down. Reaching out with her gloved right hand, Crys angled the deceased's chin toward her and revealed a plastic silver minnow hanging from the victim's mouth. Her voice was low. "Here's the fishing lure."

"There are also drag marks." Luke nodded toward the nearby parking lot where patrol cars and their sedan waited. "The killer must have parked over there, carried the body from the car to the hill, then positioned it. That explains the dirt and foliage in the vic's hair."

"In Sally Stead's hair." Crys straightened and stepped back from the body. The wind tossed her ponytail over her shoulder. "Let's notify Ms. Stead's family."

Luke stripped off the blue latex gloves and followed Crys back up the incline to their parked car. It wasn't his imagination. This case was affecting her. Luke wanted to wrap her in his arms and reassure her they'd find Sally Stead's killer and bring that person—or people—to justice.

The reckless impulse stunned him. Where had it come from? He didn't know Detective Crystal Rashaad. Worse, she was the subject of his ethics investigation. Was she the dedicated civil servant her colleagues claimed her to be? Or, as the confidential complainant alleged, was she a corrupt officer—now detective—abusing her power for personal enrichment? Until he had answers to those questions, he had to walk a careful line between his two newest cases: the hunt for a serial killer and the search for the real Crys Rashaad.

Wylie Stead had almost collapsed after Crys had responded to his demands for information by explaining his wife, Sally, was dead.

Fortunately, Luke's swift reflexes had enabled him to catch the sixty-something-year-old before he crumpled to the floor. Tall and broad-shouldered, Wylie had been even heavier than he'd looked. Crys had directed Luke to help Wylie into a nearby seat at the dining table, while she went in search of the kitchen for water and napkins.

"Mr. Stead, we're so very sorry for your loss." Crys pressed a glass of water into the grieving man's hand.

Wylie's ruddy features were drawn and tight with stress. His thinning salt-and-pepper hair was tousled as though he'd been pulling at it in frustration for hours. When they'd identified themselves and explained what they were doing there, he'd gone into denial. He'd become angry, curling his hands into fists as though he'd wanted to fight them. Then Crys had shown him the photo of his wife's body at the reservoir.

"Where did you find her?" Wylie struggled to speak through his tears. "Where did you find my Sally?"

"At Griggs Reservoir." Crys sat across the table from

Wylie and Luke. The large, rectangular, white wooden piece accommodated six chairs with a section for expansion.

Wylie stiffened with shock. "Griggs? What the heck was she doing way the heck over there?"

"We were hoping you could tell us, sir." Crys's voice was as soft and gentle as a summer breeze. "When was the last time you saw your Sally?"

"Yesterday morning." Wylie collapsed back against his chair. He drained the tall, clear glass of water before elaborating. "I have the night shift. Sally's on—" His voice choked with fresh tears. "She was on days. I wake up and keep her company while she gets dressed for work. Then I call her when I get to work around five. She's usually getting ready to go home by then."

Luke saw the flash of pain in Crys's eyes. The older man's grief affected him, too. They would confirm Wylie's alibi as a matter of course, but Luke didn't think the new widower killed his wife. His distress was genuine and heartbreaking.

"When did you realize your wife was missing?" Luke tried to model his tone after Crys's.

"This morning." Wylie caught his breath, scrubbed his face. "I got home after midnight. She's usually in bed by then, but this time she wasn't. The bed didn't even look slept in." He tossed an arm ahead of him, presumably toward the bedroom. His voice was rising as emotions gripped him. "I texted and called a couple of times. Nothing. I called her friends. They'd seen her at work, but she didn't tell them if she was going somewhere afterward. Heck, she didn't tell me she was going anywhere, either."

Luke frowned his concern. "Why didn't you report her missing?"

Wylie's swollen brown eyes widened. His voice edged

ever closer toward hysteria. "You're supposed to wait twenty-four hours before filing a report. Everybody knows that."

Crys reached across the table and squeezed his upper arm. "We understand, Mr. Wylie. We're so sorry for your loss. Where did your Sally work?"

Wylie seemed to calm down under Crys's magic touch. "Coventry First Bank downtown." He looked lost. "My kids and I have been looking for her all day." He grabbed his head with his hands and pulled his hair. "What am I supposed to tell my kids?"

Crys leaned into the table. "Why don't you call them now, sir? Ask them to meet you here. We'll stay with you until they arrive."

While Crys watched Wylie text his children, Luke couldn't look away from her. The concern in her eyes moved him. The care in her voice made him want to be a better person. It also confused him. Her empathy was at odds with the type of person who'd extort tens of thousands of dollars in bribes from families whose loved ones were facing criminal trials.

Luke stood. "I'll make coffee while we wait."

Wylie's three adult children—two sons and a daughter—arrived within minutes of their father's summons. As promised, Crys helped him break the tragic news. She and Luke asked some preliminary questions about Sally's mood, state of mind and behavior before she and Luke left, giving the Stead family privacy to grieve.

"Let's return in the morning." Crys led the way back to the car she'd parked down the street. She depressed the key fob to unlock the sedan. "They aren't in any condition to answer our questions now."

"I agree." Luke waited for Crys to get in behind the

wheel before settling onto the passenger seat. "Based on what Wylie was able to share with us, it sounds as though Sally had a normal day until after work. The killer either took her during her commute or after she arrived home."

"We'll get some patrol officers to help us canvass the neighborhood." Crys checked traffic before pulling away from the curb. "Maybe we'll luck out and one of Wylie's neighbors will have security cameras that caught something—anything—about Sally's abduction. I'm going to stop for gas on the way to Coventry First Bank."

Luke gestured toward the windshield. "I saw a station around the corner."

Crys shook her head. "There's a station two blocks west that's cheaper."

Luke frowned at her profile, his eyes lingering on her lips. "Won't your department reimburse you? Why drive out of your way?"

Her voice cooled. "It doesn't matter whether it's coming out of my pocket or the department budget. A waste of money's still a waste of money."

Surprised, Luke turned his frown toward the passenger window. Nothing about Crys Rashaad made sense in the context of his investigation. He would have expected someone susceptible to bribery to be more cavalier toward their department's finances. Instead Crys had found the cheapest gas station in their area with which to fill up her city vehicle. Could this budget-conscious employee really be on the take?

Crys pulled herself through the connecting door off her garage Thursday evening. She was emotionally and mentally exhausted after interviewing Sally Stead's supervisor and several coworkers. No one had been able to provide any helpful information. Perhaps they were in shock, and something would come to them later. Crys held on to hope.

She crossed her entryway's cream laminate flooring. Kicking off her black loafers, she left them at the foot of the honey wood staircase, hooked her satchel onto the handrail and hung her bomber jacket in the coat closet. That's when she remembered the packet Abby had given her earlier that morning. It had been a long day.

Luke's presence had made it longer. It was hard keeping her guard up when she enjoyed watching him work, admired the way he assessed the case, lost herself in the warm notes of his voice.

Pull yourself together. Luke Gilchrist was a colleague. A colleague who kept secrets.

Crys pulled the envelope from her satchel, opening it as she walked in stocking feet into her kitchen. She withdrew its contents onto the blond wood table. Her mind went blank with disbelief. The packet contained the missing documents from her aunt's homicide cold case. Her eyes grew wider as she shifted through the stack of witness forms, forensic documents and interview notes. Her stomach dropped. Her muscles quaked with shock, confusion and anger. She collapsed into the blond wood chair beside her.

How? When? *Why?*

This must be how Abby had learned the circumstances of her aunt's murder. She'd admitted to reading these papers before relinquishing them. Crys's mind fired off obscenities that would have made Jade blush.

A plain white business envelope had risen to the top of the pile. Her name was on it. She recognized Vic's almost illegible cursive. Crys tore it open. Her hands shook with anger. "You'd better have an *awesome* explanation for this, Vic."

The letter began with an apology she wasn't ready to accept. Her late partner confessed to taking a bribe to destroy critical documents from her aunt's case file. Although he'd taken the money, he claimed he'd tried to protect her by safeguarding the paperwork instead. Did he think that absolved him of his criminal act? A fresh stream of swear words exploded in Crys's brain.

"Crys," the letter continued:

> I know you're going to work your aunt's cold case. I know how determined you are to bringing her killer to justice. I understand. I'd do the same thing. But, Crys, be careful. I mean it. By taking on this investigation, you're going up against some very bad people. Very powerful and dangerous people who have connections in very high places. I also understand you can't forgive me now, if ever, but I want to apologize for my role in causing you and your family pain. I'm so sorry.

Crys crushed Vic's note in her right fist. He was correct. She couldn't forgive him. Not yet. Maybe later. Maybe. But she wouldn't dwell on that now. She'd already lost too much time, an entire year. To find their aunt's killer, she and her sisters needed to get to work.

She found her cell phone and sent them a group text:

We need to meet. Now. Please.

Chapter 4

"Someone paid your partner to destroy the contents of Aunt Kenny's homicide case file?" Jade sat beside Amber on Crys's thick, floral-patterned, powder-blue sofa Thursday evening. Beneath her winged eyebrows, her long-lidded espresso eyes were wide with shock and turbulent with temper.

Crys leaned forward on the matching armchair to accept Vic's partially crumpled note from Jade. With her mind still reeling, she'd given her sisters Vic's message to read themselves. Not only had the partner she'd trusted—her mentor—accepted a bribe to destroy police records, but those records were crucial to solving her aunt's murder. And he'd never said a word to her about it.

If Fate hadn't intervened by making them partners, would she ever have learned what had happened to the missing documents? Would she have gotten these files back? She pushed those agonizing questions to the back of her mind. She couldn't think about that now. There was too much to do.

"Abby must have read the note before I visited her Wednesday." Crys returned the two-sided letter to its plain white envelope. Her movements were jerky with rage as she stuffed the envelope into the manila carrier. Rising, she put the packet on the honey wood coffee table centered between her chair and sofa, then turned to pace her family room. "That's why she wanted me to know her mother's illness had left Vic with a lot of debt. She's probably hoping I won't tell Jasper that Vic stole Aunt K's files."

"Do you think it's possible he's taken other bribes?" In her amethyst skirt suit and pale cream shell, Amber looked like she'd hurried to Crys's home straight from work. Her cocoa-colored eyes shimmered with restrained anger.

"Yes, I do." Crys's response was unforgiving. She stared blindly at the bay window in her north wall. Hanging leafy plants were suspended from hooks at the top. A collection of coleuses, African violets and Chinese evergreens sat on the ledge. "But I'll leave that to internal affairs to investigate. I want to focus on finding Aunt K's killer."

"So do I." Jade's voice was husky with grief. Her bronze, long-sleeved cotton pullover brought out the gold undertones of her complexion and warmed her eyes. "Now we know it wasn't a burglary gone wrong. Someone had planned to kill Aunt Kenny and made her murder look like a break-in."

Color drained from Amber's golden-brown skin. Her voice was paper-thin. "Why would anyone want to kill Aunt Kendra?"

Crys's anger turned inward as she paced past her white stone fireplace with its collection of photos and trinkets from family and friends.

And why hadn't I been with her, keeping her safe?

"Vic wrote that whoever's behind the cover-up is dangerous." Crys spoke over her shoulder. "They're also connected to people in positions of power."

"Hold on." Amber spread her hands. Her well-manicured nails were accented with amethyst polish. "Am I the only one having a hard time wrapping my mind around our aunt being involved in something that could put her on the wrong side of powerful people? Aunt Kendra was the administrative assistant to the CFO of a life insurance company. She didn't hobnob with captains of industry, political leaders or foreign dignitaries."

"I know, but Vic was clear. Prominent people set up Aunt K." Crys stopped pacing beside her black-and-silver entertainment center. She didn't mind that the honey wood coffee table didn't match anything else in the room. The table had sentimental value. Her parents had made it.

Jade's delicate oval face, framed by a cloud of ebony curls, seemed drawn as though she was reliving the grief and sorrow of their aunt's death. "Do you think Vic's murder is connected to Aunt Kenny's?"

Crys crossed her arms over her chest. She flexed her shoulders in a restless shrug. "Until we have concrete evidence, I'm just speculating. All we have right now are coincidences, but you know I don't believe in them."

"Neither do I." Amber crossed her right leg over her left, smoothing the hem of her skirt to her knee.

"Me, either." Jade rubbed her forehead.

Crys continued. "What made someone decide to kill Vic now?"

"He was a loose end." Amber's smooth brow wrinkled. "They must have suspected he was going to implicate them in Aunt Kendra's murder."

"But what made them think that?" Crys stood behind her armchair. "I can't imagine Vic would have warned them. He would've known they would kill him. Did he tip off someone else? Or were they keeping tabs on him?"

"If they were, then they could be keeping tabs on you, too." Jade stood to pace. "Vic's right. We have to be aware of the danger involved in investigating Aunt Kenny's murder."

"J has a point." Crys sighed, drumming her fingers on the back of her chair. "Maybe I should handle this investigation alone."

Jade spun to face her. "That's not what I was saying."

Amber spoke at the same time. "No, you should not."

Jade hooked her small hands on her slim hips. "We agreed we would work together to solve Aunt Kenny's murder. We owe that to her and to ourselves."

Amber nodded. "We know you can't share the reports with us, but this investigation is too big for one person."

Jade paced toward Crys's bay window. "All I'm saying is that we have to stay alert. If Vic's right, Aunt Kenny was involved in a very dangerous situation, one she probably wasn't even aware of."

Crys struggled to shake off her guilt. *And I should have protected her. Instead, I'd left her to fend for herself.* "Neither of you are trained law enforcement. I'm the only one who has a gun."

Amber's frown deepened. "J and I have taken self-defense courses for years. I know that doesn't make us immortal, but we're not completely vulnerable, either. We also have home security systems, thanks to your nagging."

Crys straightened her shoulders and pinned Amber with a scolding look. "I don't nag."

"You do a pretty good impersonation of it." Jade's tone was dry.

Amber ignored them both. "But J's right that we should be even more alert to any possible danger."

Crys shared a scowl between Amber and Jade. "I still think I should handle this investigation on my own. I'll keep you both informed every step of the way. But I don't think either of you should get involved. It's not safe. Two people have already been killed."

"Am and I have made our decision." Jade returned to her seat beside Amber.

Amber gave a short, sharp nod of agreement. "There's a lot to do and you're wasting time."

Crys considered her sisters. She couldn't risk anything happening to them. She didn't know the danger they were facing or who it was coming from. The one thing she was sure of was that whoever they were going up against had already killed people they considered a threat. Her palms started to sweat.

"All right." She spread her hands. "Now that we have the missing files, I'll review them and make a plan on how we should proceed."

And I'll do everything in my power to keep you safe in spite of yourselves.

"What am I missing?" Crys scowled at the plain white papers spread across her scarred, faux maple wood desk late Friday morning.

"What are *we* missing?" Luke didn't want her to forget he was part of this investigation, too.

His matching desk, formerly Victor Hansen's, faced hers. Crys sent him a sour look before rising from her chair. A cold breeze manifested above her workstation in the stuffy department and sliced through him. Obviously, Luke's efforts to remind her that they were a team weren't welcome. He wouldn't let her reaction hurt his feelings. But his temporary partner seemed more annoyed than usual today.

Did her aggravation have anything to do with the thick manila envelope Vic's daughter had given her yesterday?

She must have opened it last night. How could he convince her to tell him what it had contained?

Luke watched Crys gather the reports, leaving behind the usual desk supplies: stapler, pens, pencils, inbox. A pale pink coffee mug covered with watercolor images of long-stemmed, yellow sunflowers stood beside her black phone. A white daisy motif porcelain photo frame watched over her computer keyboard. It held a picture of her with her sisters. Their family resemblance was strong.

"Rita Gomez was a thirty-two-year-old woman." Crys taped the informational sheet on their first victim to the crime scene board, a steel mobile dry erase panel beside their desks. "She was born and raised in Columbus. Rita and her husband had been married for six years. They have a four-year-old daughter, Nelly."

Luke studied her slender back and the riot of brown curls that tumbled past her shoulders. "I can hear the grief in your voice." Which was not something he'd expected from a detective who allegedly extorted bribes from victims' families.

"It doesn't bother you that Nelly's been robbed of the opportunity to grow up with her mother?" Crys threw the irritable reply over her shoulder. "And that Fredo is a widower after only six years of marriage?"

"It does. I also noticed you used Sally Stead's name when we were examining the crime scene." A corrupt detective with a heart? That didn't make sense.

"Are you searching for a point?" She still wouldn't look at him.

"This job will eat you alive if you don't learn to separate your emotions from your cases." He considered her with narrowed eyes. Her long-sleeved, cream shirt was covered with oval green patterns that looked like dots but were images of unopened rosebuds. Interesting. The testy detective had a thing for flowers and roses.

Crys snorted. "I've been in law enforcement for eight years. I can handle my emotions. Thanks anyway."

Definitely testy, even more so than yesterday. What had been in that envelope?

Luke stood, raising his hands, palms out although she couldn't see him. "Just trying to help."

Crys didn't acknowledge his comment. She cleared her throat. "Rita graduated from Centennial High school, which is in northwest Columbus. She received her Bachelor of Science degree in computer engineering and her MBA from Franklin University."

"She lived in northwest Columbus and regularly attended a Catholic church." Luke paused beside her. Her scent reminded him of wildflowers in the spring. Fitting.

He felt Crys stiffen. Something was definitely on her mind. What was it?

Crys sliced another piece of tape, using it to post their notes for their second victim. "Alfred Murphy was found at the reservoir February 24, fifteen days after Rita was discovered."

"They don't seem to have a connection." Luke took over the recitation. "He was born and raised in San Antonio before relocating to southeast Columbus only ten years ago. Alfred was fifty-nine, an investment banker and divorced."

"He and his ex-wife have five adult children. His ex-wife and kids still live in Texas, and he occasionally attended a Methodist church." Crys stepped back as though to study the notes from a distance. Or maybe she just needed to move. Luke had noticed his new, temporary partner had trouble staying still.

Luke stood with his arms crossed over his chest, scanning the notes and searching his mind for new avenues to connections between their first two victims. "It doesn't seem likely that Alfred's children or his ex would have flown to Columbus, knifed him, then flown home."

"No, it doesn't." Crys's tone was dry as it traveled forward to him. "And what would be their connection to Rita or to Sally Stead." She affixed the profile of their third victim to the board. "Sally was fifty-two, closer to Alfred's age. She graduated from South High School—"

Luke interrupted. "Which is in the southern part of the city."

Crys gave an abrupt nod. "She earned her accounting degree from Columbus State Community College. She worked as an accountant at OSU Medical Center. She and her husband were members of a Jewish temple near their home."

Rubbing the back of his neck, Luke broke their brief silence. "Are there any overlaps between these three victims?"

Crys gestured toward the board. "They all have college degrees. Rita has a master's. But they all also graduated years apart. Rita earned her undergrad in 1994 and her master's in 1996. Alfred got his undergrad in 1967 and Sally in 1974."

Luke turned toward his desk, stopping abruptly when he found Crys a lot closer than he'd thought. Heat radiated across his chest as though he'd stumbled against a hot oven. Crys's eyes widened as they met his. She stepped aside.

"Excuse me." Grabbing the notepad on his desk, Luke took a moment to collect his thoughts. "We should find out if Rita, Alfred or Sally belonged to professional associations or civic organizations."

"Good idea." Crys returned to her desk and jotted something into her writing tablet.

Her praise, however faint, startled him. Was she warming to the idea of working with him? *Don't get ahead of yourself, Gilchrist.* One kind word didn't make them pals. Besides he had to remain impartial for the sake of his investigation.

He shifted his attention from her notepad and got lost in her dark eyes. "I'll look into any professional connections."

"And I'll check for community groups." Crys turned back to the board. "All we need is one connection. Just one thing that links the three of them."

Luke heard the desperation in her tone. He followed her gaze. "It occurred to me that they all have high-level office jobs."

Crys stepped closer to the board, bringing her notepad with her. She studied the victim profiles as though trying to see through the words to the truth. "But they worked for different companies in different parts of the city."

"We need to see if there's a connection between those companies." Luke stopped beside her. This time, he didn't sense her muscles tense. "Perhaps they use the same vendors or served the same customer base. Maybe an employee worked at all three companies."

"Another good point. I'll follow up on that." A reluctant smile curved her full, heart-shaped lips. It dazzled him.

"Why do you sound so surprised?" Once again, Luke couldn't take his eyes off her. "I told you I could help with this case."

"Yes, you did." She returned to her desk, breaking her spell over him.

Luke took his seat. "But you still don't trust me."

His desk didn't have as many items as hers. Someone had packed up Vic's belongings. Had it been Crys? Luke was spending a few hours each morning at his office at the

BCI before coming to the department. His coffee mug was the only thing he'd brought over.

Crys spun her black, padded cloth chair to face him. She held his eyes in silence for a moment. It was disconcerting to have her focused so intently on him. Luke folded his hands on his desk and struggled not to fidget. An image of him sinking his fingers into her mass of thick, curling tresses tempted him. His skin tingled as though the vision wasn't just in his mind.

"I don't buy it." Crys seemed to be waiting for his reply.

"Excuse me?" Luke's cheeks heated with embarrassment. He wasn't sure he'd heard everything she'd said. "You don't buy what exactly?"

Crys frowned. "That you're only here to help me with my investigation. What do you really want?"

Studying her delicate features, being pulled into the challenge glinting in her eyes and tracing the curves of her heart-shaped lips, Luke chose not to answer that question. "What do you think I want?"

Crys kept her eyes on him as she settled back against her seat. She was silent for a beat before responding. "I believe you want to help find this serial killer. Don't get me wrong. I appreciate the assist. But you have another agenda. What is it?"

Either she was scary insightful, or he'd lost his poker face. "It's obvious I'll have to work harder to earn your trust. I hope you'll give me that chance."

Crys maintained her stony stare. Something inside Luke stirred as though accepting her unspoken challenge. He hadn't felt this spark of anticipation in years. Not since the last woman who'd broken his heart. But Crys's pull was stronger, harder to resist. And he'd been trying.

After a few moments, Crys grunted an unrecognizable reply, then got back to work.

Luke breathed a sigh of relief. He suspected it would be the last easy breath he took for the remainder of his investigation.

Chapter 5

"Did you make that?" Luke drew another breath of the soup Crys had heated in the cafeteria's microwave Friday afternoon. The scents of onions, peppers and turmeric made his mouth water.

She packed her lunch. Yesterday on their way back from questioning Sally Stead's widower, Crys had taken them to a fast-food drive-through. At the time, Luke thought she was trying to give him the impression of someone who was careful with their budget. But he'd seen her take her lunch from the employee refrigerator before she'd left yesterday. Would a detective on the take pack leftovers for lunch? Luke couldn't image that.

Crys paused with her spoon halfway to her mouth. Her expression was guarded. "Yes, I did. It's lentil soup."

"It smells great." His eyes dropped to her desk. She'd also packed a Honeycrisp apple. An image of a seven-year-old Crys, eating her packed lunch in her elementary school's cafeteria slid across his mind. The thought made him smile.

Crys jerked her chin toward his meal. "What did you get?"

Luke had lost his enthusiasm for the cold sandwich, pasta salad and chips he'd picked up at a nearby sandwich shop. "Turkey and cheddar on rye."

"Sounds good." She returned her attention to her computer. They were working through lunch. Again. "Have you found anything?"

"Not yet." Luke could stare at Crys's face for hours, but he needed to concentrate on both of his assignments, the serial killer case and his investigation into Crys. "I've reviewed the reports. Now I'm looking through each of our victims' professional online networks for connections between them. What about you?"

"Same." Her fingers moved across her keyboard. "I'm about halfway through their social online network. So far, no links. Rita has almost twice as many friends as Alfred and Sally. She also has more social media accounts."

Luke replayed her words in his mind, but he was still confused. "What's the significance of Rita having multiple social media accounts?"

Crys shrugged. "Maybe nothing, but it implies Rita spent a lot more time on the internet."

Luke hesitated. "Do you spend much time on social media?"

"No." Crys's smile was reluctant. "I prefer private conversations to posting my every thought and move on the internet. Especially since the only people who'd care about any of that are just a phone call away."

"Would those people be your sisters?" Luke nodded toward the photograph on her desk. "You and Vic also seemed close."

Crys's eyes dropped from her computer monitor to her keyboard. "I thought we were."

"What do you mean?" Luke noted the chill that had entered her tone. It hadn't been there when she'd discussed her deceased partner before. He waited several seconds.

Crys didn't respond. He'd started to repeat his question when she spoke.

"I might as well tell you." Her narrow shoulders shifted under her long-sleeved, cream shirt. The gesture was restless, almost angry. "Do you remember Vic's eldest daughter, Abby, gave me a package yesterday?"

"Yes, an oversize manila envelope." *Act natural. Don't press her.*

Crys's tension pounded him like a sledgehammer. Luke wanted to smooth the furrows from her brow and take hold of the hands she'd balled into fists on the desk beside her keyboard. Whatever Crys found in that packet had added a burden to her slender shoulders. It surprised Luke how desperately he wanted to bear that load for her.

"My aunt was murdered during a break-in at her home a year ago tomorrow." Crys's voice was weighted with grief.

"I'm so sorry, Crys." Luke straightened as a thought occurred to him. "Having Vic killed under similar circumstances must have brought back those painful memories. I'm really sorry."

"Thanks. And you're right. It did." She paused. Luke couldn't tell if she was collecting her thoughts or lost in them. "It also hurt because my aunt's murder remains unsolved. Part of the problem is that several critical documents from her case file had disappeared."

"How?" Luke's eyebrows launched up his forehead. "When?"

Crys sprang from her chair as though propelled by frustration. Stiff strides carried her to their mobile crime scene board. She spoke with her back to him.

"Those are the questions my sisters and I have been asking for almost a year." Her voice was rough like she was chewing glass. "How could documents from our aunt's homicide investigation case file disappear?" She waved a hand to encompass their surroundings. "This is a police department. People can't walk in off the street and steal stuff. What happened, when and why? Yesterday, we got our answers. My *partner* had accepted a bribe to destroy critical reports from my aunt's file, crime scene documents, witness interviews, photos."

Luke took a moment to catch up. "Is that what was in the envelope Abby gave you? The documents?"

"Yes, and a letter, explaining what he did. He'd stolen the files, but he hadn't destroyed them." Crys turned to face him. "I think he expected me to be grateful."

Luke didn't think she was. "In his letter, did Vic tell you who'd bribed him and why?"

She crossed her arms over her chest. "All he said was that they were powerful and dangerous, and that they had connections in very high places."

That sounded ominous. "Why didn't he destroy the files?"

Crys shook her head. "He didn't explain that, either. But that's probably what got him killed."

Luke watched her closely. "You no longer think your aunt or your partner were killed in burglaries gone bad, do you? You think both murders were staged."

"I can think of only one reason someone would want my aunt's case file destroyed: it implicates them in some way. And Vic had documents from that file so he was also a threat to them."

"Have you spoken with Jasper about this?"

"Yes. I gave him Vic's letter this morning. It wasn't the gift he would've asked for. He'll have to report Vic's violation. It's a black eye to the department."

That was an understatement. "What about the case documents?"

"Since the detectives originally assigned to the case aren't with the department any longer, I've returned the documents to my aunt's cold case." Crys took her seat behind her desk. Her mood had shifted. She seemed more determined than angry now. "But my sisters and I are going to solve our aunt's murder."

Luke leaned into his desk. "You can't share your aunt's case files with your sisters. That would be an ethics violation."

Crys frowned at him as though he'd said something ridiculous and uncalled for. "My sisters and I are aware of that. One is a prosecutor. And as you know, the other is a crime beat reporter, or at least she had been before your friend Caleb came to town."

"Is that the reason your sister's so angry with him? She blames Cal for her being laid off?"

Crys returned his look in silence.

Luke continued. "You have the wrong impression of Cal. He's a good guy. He feels bad about your sister being laid off but, Crys, that's not his fault."

"Isn't it, though?" Crys gave him a doubting look as she pulled her chair farther under her desk.

She was trying to get under his skin—and failing. He couldn't take her taunts seriously, although they didn't bode well for Cal. His friend hated the idea that his being hired at *Capital Daily News* had anything to do with someone else being let go. Knowing the person who'd been laid off blamed him would only make him feel worse.

Luke set those thoughts aside and considered Crys's confiding Vic's criminality to him. Wasn't that more evidence that she wasn't involved in corrupt activity? What was going on?

"Let's go." Crys's abrupt command wrenched Luke from his thoughts.

He stood. "Where are we going?"

She started toward the door. "To speak with Rita Gomez's family again. We don't have any indication the killing spree is done. We need to find the link between our victims to identify any future targets."

Crys's desk phone pealed late Friday afternoon. She grabbed the receiver before it screamed again. "Homicide. Detective Rashaad."

"Crys! Detective! Detective Rashaad! It's Becca—Rebecca Hansen. Hill." Rebecca Hansen-Hill was Vic's youngest child.

Crys thought she remembered Vic telling her Becca was a divorced single mother with a young daughter. She was a pharmacist with a major pharmacy chain. Right now, Becca was in panic mode. Her voice was shrill and strained, coming much too quickly over the line. Her words tumbled over each other, becoming almost incomprehensible.

Straightening in her chair, Crys pressed the phone closer to her ear. "Becca, what's wrong? What's happened?"

In her peripheral vision, she saw Luke look over at her from his seat at his desk. He seemed drawn by the urgency in her tone.

"Oh, Crys! I didn't know who else to call." Becca sounded like she was sobbing. "We've always called Daddy or Abby but now they're not here."

Crys's heart skipped, then galloped in her chest. "What do you mean Abby's not there? What's happened to her?" She met Luke's eyes. They'd darkened with concern.

Becca choked on a sob. She struggled to get the words out. "A car hit her! She was hit by a car! She's in a coma, Crys!"

"Oh, my gosh." Crys surged from her chair. "Where are you?" She paused as Becca gave her the name of the hospital.

"She's in the ICU. Gordy's here." Becca referred to Abby's husband. "But he's a mess. We all are." She stopped and Crys heard soft sobbing. "His mother took Abby's kids and my daughter to her house to get them away from the hospital."

That information gave Crys a measure of relief. "Good. I'm on my way." She cradled the phone with her right hand and grabbed her jacket with her left.

Luke circled their desks. He brushed aside her fumbling fingers and helped her get into her jacket. "What's happened?" His voice was low and measured.

Crys turned to him. "I have to leave. Vic's daughter, Abby, was hit by a car. She's been taken to the hospital. She's in a coma. I need to at least check on them and find out what happened."

"I'll come with you." Luke took his jacket from his chair.

"You don't need to." She hooked satchel onto her right shoulder. "I don't know how long I'll be."

"I want to come with you." Luke rested his palm on the small of her back and nudged her toward the door. "You're upset and I'd worry about your driving alone."

He'd worry about me? That was interesting. Crys didn't have a response for that.

Luke escorted her to his silver SUV. Crys spent the journey to the hospital worrying about Abby and her family—her husband, children, siblings—and mentally reviewing the questions she wanted answered. Yes, she was upset with Vic. His criminal actions delayed and possibly denied justice for her aunt. But she couldn't turn her back on his family when they asked for her help.

Luke kept pace with her as she rushed into the lobby, then waited for directions to the ICU where Abby was being treated. Crys located Becca in the waiting room a few paces from the elevator. The air in the midsize space was cold and heavy with the scent of disinfectants.

Becca was seated in a blue hard plastic chair beside Abby's husband in the waiting area. Her round face was drained of color and frozen in a wide-eyed expression of shock and disbelief. Abby's husband, Gordy, was bent forward on his chair. His elbows were propped on his knees. His forehead was cupped in his palms.

Crys led Luke to Becca. She had to call the other woman's name three times before gaining her attention.

Becca leaped off the chair and grabbed Crys in a hug. "I'm so glad you're here. I didn't know who else to turn to. I called Larry but he's in South Carolina. I don't know when he'll get here."

Crys returned Becca's hug, then stepped back. "It's all right, Becca. I'm glad you called me. What's Abby's condition?"

Becca glanced at Gordy before responding. "The doctor said they had to put her in a medically induced coma to protect her from additional brain damage after the accident. That's all we know. That's all they've told us."

Poor Abby. Crys offered Becca another hug. "I'm so sorry."

Releasing Becca, Crys approached Abby's husband. Her voice was gentle. "Gordy, what can I do?"

Gordy raised his head to look at her. His blue eyes were red and damp with tears. His curly red hair was tousled and sticking up in different directions as though he'd been dragging his large hands through it. His voice was strained as if every word hurt. "I need to know what happened to my wife. That driver ran her over like trash, then left her in the street like she didn't matter. The mother of my children. Like she didn't matter."

Crys squeezed his shoulder. The gesture was meant to offer comfort, but it felt inadequate. "I'll make some calls, Gordy." She stepped back to stand beside Luke. "This is… my friend Luke Gilchrist. Luke, Becca Hansen-Hill and Gordy Tiller."

Luke inclined his head. "I'm so sorry about Abby's accident."

Gordy and Becca responded with muted sobs.

Pulling her cell phone from her satchel, Crys addressed Luke. "I'm going to make a few calls to see if I can—"

"Crys? Crys Rashaad?" A male voice interrupted her.

Crys turned toward the sound. A tall, slim uniformed officer had entered the waiting room. She smiled her recognition of the youthful, tan features and ready smile.

"Marco." Crys crossed the room to greet him away from Abby's family. "It's good to see you. How've you been?"

"Living the dream." Marco spread his arms. He held a pen in one hand and a notepad in the other.

Marco Robledo had joined Crys's police precinct shortly before she'd been promoted to detective and left for her new department. She'd enjoyed working with him for those few weeks.

Crys gestured toward Luke beside her. "This is Special Agent Luke Gilchrist. He's with the BCI."

Marco's expression dimmed as he offered Luke his hand. He gave Crys a quick, curious look. "We've met. Hello again, Special Agent Gilchrist."

"Luke, please." Luke's smile seemed stiff. "It's good to see you again, Officer Robledo."

"Marco." Marco switched his attention to Crys. He gestured behind her toward Becca and Gordy. "Are you here about Abigail Hansen-Tiller's accident?"

"Yes." Crys's eyes dipped to his notepad before returning to his face. "Are you assigned to it?"

"Yes." Marco frowned. "What's your connection?"

Crys sobered. "Abby's my deceased partner's daughter. Is there anything you can tell us about what happened?"

"I'm sorry about this, Crys." Marco turned to a page in his notepad. "According to witness reports, Ms. Hansen-Tiller had been leaving the grocery store at Hilliard-Rome Road at approximately 2:00 p.m." He looked up at her, his bright brown eyes soft with sympathy. "Witnesses said as she stepped off the sidewalk to cross the parking lot, a black, low-slung sports car sped toward her. It struck her, sending her several yards across the lot. It never stopped."

Crys covered her mouth in shock. "Oh, my gosh." Her words were muffled behind her hand.

Luke shook his head. "Oh, no."

Marco looked at Luke, then away. "Eyewitnesses said it looked like a deliberate attack. Ms. Hansen-Tiller's lucky to be alive."

"Did anyone get a plate?" Luke asked.

Marco shook his head, his eyes glued to his notepad. "No. They all said it happened too fast. The sports car came out of nowhere."

Crys patted his upper arm. "Thanks for the info, Marco."

"Sure." Marco tucked his notepad into his inside jacket pocket. "It's sad. This is obviously attempted homicide, but there's not much we can do with that description and no plate. I hope she pulls through."

"So do we." Crys took a step back. "Please give your wife my best and tell her I miss her pastries."

Marco patted his flat stomach and flashed a smile. "I need to miss her pastries, or I won't be able to fit into my uniform."

Crys's smile faded as her former colleague disappeared toward the elevator and the seriousness of Abby's attack reasserted itself. A chill crawled through her.

She lowered her voice, keeping her back toward Becca and Gordy. "Why would someone want to kill Abby?"

"It could be connected to Vic's murder." Luke's voice was a whisper. "Or your aunt's homicide."

"Or both." Crys looked over her shoulder at Becca and Gordy. She didn't think they were in danger. But what about her—and her sisters?

Chapter 6

"They blame *me* for Jade being laid off from *Capital Daily*?" Caleb turned from his stove Saturday evening. His coal-black eyes were wide with surprise. "How is that *my* fault?"

His accent tagged his Chicago roots. He always sounded like he was ready for a fight.

Luke held up his left hand, palm out while his right hand secured his longneck beer bottle. "I'm just telling you that's probably the reason Crys and her sister didn't drink the beers you bought them, and why Jade poured hers into her empty salad bowl."

Caleb turned back to his stove. Sometime before Luke had arrived, his friend had changed into black warm-up pants, and a purple-and-white Northwestern University pullover.

He continued setting the baked chicken, green beans and garlic potato on their dinner plates. His Southern grandmother would be proud, not only of the meal but the surroundings. The tiny kitchen was spotless. Everything appeared to be well organized and in its place. The black-and-silver appliances sparkled. The smoke-gray tiled flooring gleamed under the fluorescent lights. An ornate plaque above the stove was obviously a gift. It read, The Kitchen is the Heart of the Home.

"Yeah, Jade said as much before she left. That's not fair, though. It wasn't my choice to lay her off. Brock made that decision before I'd arrived." Caleb shook his head.

Brock Mann was *Capital Daily News*'s editor-in-chief. He was the one who'd brought Caleb into the organization and the one who'd laid off Crys's youngest sister, Jade, and an entertainment reporter who'd been weeks away from retirement.

Luke was surprised at how defensive he felt on Crys's behalf. "Look at it from their perspective. You said the paper had never had an executive editor before. Brock hired you, then less than two months later, he cut two members of the staff. That sequence of events gives the impression the paper reduced the rank-and-file to afford your salary."

Caleb winced in reaction. "The timing could have been better. It was bound to cause resentment and hurt morale. And Brock could've warned me about his plans. He said things had been set in motion before I arrived to let go of Jade and the entertainment reporter. Still, a heads-up would've been helpful."

Luke took the plate Caleb offered him and followed him into the dining room. The area was small but comfortable with bright, hardwood flooring and a maple wood dinette set that could accommodate six people around the simple yet elegant rectangular table. Pale blue drapes framed the solitary rear window. A sheer white curtain let in the soft rays from the evening sun. Beside the window, blond-wood shelving displayed pots and baskets of leafy green plants and, inexplicably, black Northwestern University bookends. He and Caleb had graduated from the university together, but Caleb was more of a fanatic.

Luke would never have thought the newsman would leave his Chicago roots. The opportunity with *Capital*

Daily News was a good career move for him, though. And having his longtime girlfriend break up with him was an extra motivating factor.

The steam rising from his plate tempted Luke with the aroma of olive oil, oregano, paprika, brown sugar and fresh garlic. It reminded him of how hungry he was.

"Did Crys say anything else about Jade?" Caleb settled onto the seat across the table from Luke. "Has she found a new job?"

Luke heard the concern in his friend's voice. He knew without Caleb having to tell him that his former college roommate felt guilty about what happened to Jade. Luke would've felt the same way. Or was there something more to his interest? The Rashaad women were intelligent, charismatic and attractive.

He cut into the baked chicken, releasing more of the seasonings that made his mouth water. "Crys doesn't share much personal information. I can't tell whether it's because she keeps her professional and personal lives separate, or because she's focused on the case. Or maybe she doesn't trust me yet."

Caleb swallowed a forkful of his chicken. "It could be all the above. You're not exactly the most trusting person yourself."

Luke couldn't deny that. His cynicism had grown worse after his last relationship. "There's a reason for that."

"I know." Caleb's tone was somber with understanding. "Maybe Crys has her reasons as well."

"She probably does." Like him, had she had bad experiences? Or was she wary because she had something to hide?

Luke thought about the way her big brown eyes always met his without a hint of evasion. That didn't track with the accusation of her being duplicitous. Then he recalled the way she smelled like wildflowers in spring and wondered again whether his assessment of Crys was unbiased.

"So how's it working out for you, splitting your time between the murder investigation and your cases at the BCI?" Caleb took a drink of the iced tea he'd served with their dinner.

His friend's question brought Luke back from his thoughts. "It's a little tricky." Understatement. "But I'm handling it, splitting my time between the two offices."

"Hopefully, you won't have to do that for much longer, although I don't understand why you were assigned to help with the homicide investigation."

Luke's lips curved in a lopsided smile. "Neither can Crys. She's making me work hard to prove I have anything to contribute."

"That'll keep you humble." Caleb saluted him with his clear acrylic glass. "How's the investigation going?"

"Are you trying to get me fired?" Luke arched an eyebrow as he drank his iced tea. "You know I can't comment on an ongoing investigation, especially to someone in the media."

Caleb spread his hands, drawing attention to his dining room. "And I wouldn't interview someone in my home. Come on. You know me better than that. If I were going to grill you, I'd warn you first."

"That's true." Luke inclined his head. Caleb was one of the few people he could trust completely. "One of my cases with the BCI isn't going well. Or maybe it is."

"That's clear as mud," Caleb grumbled.

"What I mean is, I'm investigating a member of law enforcement on allegations of corruption." Luke was aware of the need to strip his explanation of any identifiers, including pronouns and specific details.

Caleb frowned. "I didn't realize the bureau investigated

law enforcement ethics violations. I thought that was internal affairs."

Luke started shaking his head before Caleb finished speaking. "Allegations could be submitted through any channel—internal affairs, city council—and that agency has the option to take the lead on the investigation. In this case, the complaint came into our division. My boss took it and assigned the case to me. But everything I've uncovered so far indicates the target of the investigation is innocent."

Caleb ate in thoughtful silence for a beat. "How long have you been on this investigation?"

"Just over two months." Nine weeks and five days.

That included his preliminary investigation, which consisted of reviewing Crys's files and speaking with her colleagues. Marco's cold reaction to meeting him again was one example of Crys's colleagues not taking kindly to her integrity being questioned.

"Two months?" Caleb's thick black brows stretched toward his hairline. "And you haven't uncovered anything sketchy about this person?"

Luke shook his head. "Personnel reviews have been exemplary. Colleagues have only had good things to say. My impression of this person is also positive."

Caleb was silent again, as though he was processing Luke's information. "What does Martina think?" He referred to Luke's supervisor.

"I haven't told her yet." Luke dropped his attention to his nearly empty plate. "But I will. Something's not adding up."

"What more can you tell me about the complaint against Crys Rashaad?" Luke settled into one of the visitor's chairs across from Martina's desk early Monday morning.

Martina shook her head, causing her pearl stud earrings

to glint under the fluorescent lighting. Her salon-styled hair swung above her shoulders, then settled back into place. "You have a copy of the report. What could I tell you that isn't in there?"

Luke didn't want to give his boss the impression he was grasping at straws. But he was. "The source's identity is confidential, but you spoke with them. What impression did they give you?"

Martina paused as though considering his question. "The person seemed very concerned. And also afraid."

"Afraid of what?"

Martina's pause was longer this time. "I didn't ask, but I had the sense the caller was afraid the subject would retaliate if she learned who the source of the complaint was."

Retaliation? Crys? "What did the source think Crys would do?"

Martina's voice snapped with impatience. "How would I know?" She sat back against her padded black faux leather executive chair. "As I said, I didn't ask. I'm basing what I'm telling you on the sense I got from my conversation with the complainant. Why are you asking these questions?"

Luke couldn't reconcile the idea of Crys threatening someone to protect her crimes with the image he had of her comforting a grieving widower and referring to murder victims by their names.

He mentally shook his head. "There isn't any evidence supporting these allegations of Detective Rashaad's corruption."

Martina pulled her chair under her desk and folded her hands on its surface. "Luke, you've only been working with Detective Rashaad for two days. This will be your third. In light of that, don't you think your finding that she's innocent is a bit premature?"

Luke had expected Martina would say something like that. "You know I began my inquiries into Detective Rashaad the day you assigned this case to me almost ten weeks ago. I read her personnel file and spoke with her former supervisors and colleagues at the precinct as well as other detectives in her department. I shared those findings with you. There's no evidence Detective Rashaad is corrupt."

"That's right. On paper, she seems squeaky-clean." There was a stubborn light in Martina's gray eyes. "Which is the reason I told you to observe her without letting her know she was under investigation."

Luke inclined his head. "And you convinced Kim to give me the Griggs Reservoir Killer case."

"How's that investigation going, by the way?"

Luke frowned again. "We haven't found a connection between the three victims yet, but we're checking on some other angles."

"And how are you and Detective Rashaad working together?" Martina's eyes bored into him as though she wanted to fact-check his answer against whatever she read in his mind.

"We're fine." Except Crys didn't trust him. Luke didn't think it was a good idea to share that part with Martina, though. It would make her more suspicious.

"She's a very beautiful woman." Martina gave him a narrow-eyed stare. "And she seems intelligent. That's a powerful combination."

Yes, it was. "Are you accusing me of having a bias in this investigation?"

"Do you?"

Luke felt a stirring of irritation. "No, I do not."

"Because looks can be deceiving, Luke." Her eyes held his. "You don't want to put your trust in the wrong person."

His impatience was growing. "You know I'm impartial in my investigations. I let the evidence determine my findings."

"Your natural skepticism has always been an asset in your work." Martina relaxed back into her chair.

"Nothing will change that." Although part of him wished something would. Cynicism was a heavy load to bear.

Martina hesitated a moment longer. "I'm satisfied that that's true. I'll let you continue the investigation. Don't leave any stone unturned. I can't abide corruption in our law enforcement agencies."

"Neither can I." But Luke still had his doubts about this case. "Detective Rashaad told me about an incident with her partner, Victor Hansen. Last year, he took a bribe to destroy documents in her aunt's homicide case file." Luke filled Martina in on the details as Crys had explained them to him, including the letter Vic had left for her.

Martina leaned into her desk. "But he didn't say who'd bribed him or why?"

"No, only that they were powerful and dangerous."

She searched his eyes. "Did you see the letter?"

"No, she'd given everything to her boss, Lieutenant Bright."

Martina looked dubious. "So all you have is Rashaad's word that her partner's the only one who took a bribe to tamper with a case file." Her question surprised him.

"It was her aunt's homicide case file." Luke spread his hands. "Why wouldn't she want her aunt's murder solved? What would be her incentive to obstruct the investigation?"

"Money." Martina shrugged. "Money is a very powerful incentive, Luke."

He couldn't picture it. "Stronger than bringing her aunt's killer to justice?"

Martina shrugged. "All I'm saying is that you only have Rashaad's side of the story that her partner acted alone and was the only one who took the bribe. Meanwhile, her partner is dead and unable to defend himself."

"I don't think Crys would accept a bribe to obstruct her aunt's homicide investigation and prevent the person who murdered her aunt from being arrested." In fact, Luke knew she would not have done that. He had seen the resolve in Crys's eyes. She was determined to find her aunt's killer and hold them accountable. "I'm trained in behavioral science. It's part of our investigative techniques. Detective Rashaad doesn't fit the profile of a corrupt law enforcement agent."

"And I think Rashaad gave up her partner in an effort to throw suspicion off of her." Martina held up her hands palms out. "Even if she wasn't in on destroying files from her aunt's case, it doesn't mean she hasn't accepted other bribes."

"You're basing your suspicions on one person's claims. I—"

Martina interrupted him. "We only need one complaint. We're in law enforcement. We're charged with upholding justice. As such, we have a responsibility to be above reproach. We must have zero tolerance for corruption in our ranks. Detective Rashaad must be thoroughly investigated. If there's even a shred of doubt in her innocence, she has to be held accountable. Agreed?"

Luke stood. "Agreed."

He returned to his office to collect his jacket and attaché case before meeting Crys at the police department. He'd gotten his marching orders. He had to either find proof of the allegations of corruption against Crys—or evidence to support her innocence.

Maybe Martina was right and his attraction to Crys was having a stronger influence on him than he thought. He of all people knew looks could be deceiving.

Chapter 7

"His name was Carter Wainscott." Crys took a moment to say a quick prayer for their fourth victim late Monday morning. Was he the fourth? Something felt…off.

Ignoring the small army of police officers collecting evidence from the crime scene, Crys cast her eyes around their surroundings at the Griggs Reservoir. She smelled the fresh river water from the reservoir's waterfall, the moist earth, and the budding foliage from the trees and bushes. Something scampered in the nearby undergrowth—a chipmunk, squirrel, a gopher? The scratching sound combined with the rush of the waterfall and the birdsong.

"Crys? What else does Mr. Wainscott's driver's license tell us about him?" Luke's question pulled Crys from the fairy-tale setting back to the macabre crime scene.

Carter Wainscott had been an attractive Black man a few inches shy of six feet. He'd been well-groomed with tight, ebony curls and a carefully shaped goatee. He was lean and fit, perhaps a runner? And a sharp dresser. His pin-striped black suit, gold tie and white shirt looked expensive.

Crys felt comforted by Luke addressing their victim by his name. "According to his ID, Mr. Wainscott was almost two months shy of his forty-fourth birthday. And he lived close to the Arena District."

"That's a new area." Luke straightened from his examination of Carter Wainscott's body. His charcoal-gray casual cotton pants looked really good on his slim hips and long legs. "In other words, on the surface, Mr. Wainscott didn't have anything in common with our other victims while he was alive. And maybe not in death, either."

"You noticed the discrepancies, too." Crys closed the gap between them, using his body as a shield against the cool breeze off the waterfall.

Like her, Luke wore blue latex gloves. He gestured toward their victim. "Mr. Wainscott was killed shortly before he was brought here. He doesn't have as much postmortem rigidity as Ms. Gomez, Mr. Murphy or Ms. Stead. At a rough estimate, I'd say he was killed sometime between 7:00 and 9:00 a.m."

Crys hunkered down next to Carter Wainscott. Reaching forward, she gently opened his mouth again. "Most importantly, there isn't a lure in his mouth."

"No, there isn't." Luke lowered himself beside her as though to get a closer look at Carter's tongue.

Despite his shift in stance, the angle of his body blocked the waterfall's breeze. Was he aware she was using him as a protective barrier? Crys's cheeks warmed with embarrassment. She stood and put more distance between them.

"We have a copycat killer." She spoke with her back to him, studying the ground beneath her feet. White polyethylene fiber shoe covers protected the crime scene from her black loafers.

"It seems that way." Luke's deep voice rolled like a gentle wave over her. "Someone wants us to believe the serial killer took a fourth victim, but they weren't able to mimic the signs exactly because you'd withheld information about the delay between the murders and the bodies being moved, and the detail about the fishing lure."

"Why would they want to make it look as though the suspect was responsible for Mr. Wainscott's murder as well?" Crys spread her arms. "What's the copycat's agenda? And what, if any, connection does Mr. Wainscott have to our other victims?"

Luke frowned. "What makes you think there could be a connection?"

Crys tilted her head. "What makes you think there isn't?"

"I asked you first." Luke's enigmatic eyes twinkled as though applauding her for a joke.

Crys wasn't joking. She appreciated his attempt at levity, though. When he'd arrived at the department early this morning, he'd seemed distant, almost cold toward her. His attitude made her worry something pertaining to her case—or to his secret agenda about her—was troubling him. It seemed she'd been wrong. His coldness had warmed. Something else must have been on his mind.

She swept her right hand toward Carter Wainscott. "Why go to the time and effort to match our previous crime scenes unless you think there's something about your target that will make us believe the murders are connected?"

Luke massaged the back of his neck. "Maybe you're right and there is a connection between Wainscott and the other three victims. But there's just as good a chance—if not better—that Mr. Wainscott's killer is an opportunist who's hoping to hide their crime in our investigation. They probably never imagined they were missing critical details, the guilty knowledge information."

Guilty knowledge information—the details known only to the perpetrator and the investigating detectives.

Crys felt a slight thrill at hearing him refer to the investigation as *our*. At first, she'd resented his saying that. Now, six short days later, it sounded right. How had he gotten so close so quickly?

She battled her way through the confusion. "This copycat murder could help narrow the search for our serial killer."

"*If* your premise is correct." Luke led them forward, away from the patch of grass and underbrush where Carter Wainscott's body had been found. "If *I'm* right, it adds to the confusion."

Crys followed him up the slight incline to the nearby parking area.

A high-pitched female voice called above the sound of the rushing waters, scratching underbrush and bird calls. "Special Agent Gilchrist. Special Agent."

Luke turned toward the voice and waited. A young female officer in a dark blue uniform hurried toward him. She gripped a clear plastic evidence bag in her right fist.

His eyes dropped to the bag before returning to the young woman. "What did you find, Officer?"

Crys joined them at the edge of the parking area. The officer stopped within a foot of Luke. A little close. Her name badge read A. Neat. Officer Neat's blue eyes sparkled with admiration as they roamed Luke's face. Her pale cheeks pinkened with a blush. Her slight smile seemed inappropriate for the circumstances. Crys looked at Luke in her peripheral vision. Either he didn't notice, or he was ignoring the officer's attraction. Crys followed his lead.

Officer Neat held the evidence bag aloft. "An employee ID, Special Agent Gilchrist. It's from *Capital Daily News* and it's for Brock Mann."

Brock Mann? Crys recognized the name of Jade's former

boss. Shock raced down her spine like an electric current. Luke took the bag from Officer Neat.

The plain white hard plastic was still attached to a black, cloth lanyard covered with a row of white *Capital Daily News* logos. The identification badge bore a larger *Capital Daily News* logo, as well as Brock Mann's name and picture. Crys recognized the man who'd taken her sister's job from her within months of hiring a more highly compensated executive editor.

"Brock Mann?" Luke studied the identification through the plastic bag.

Crys's eyes widened. "You know him?"

"I've heard his name. He's Cal's boss." Luke looked as stunned as Crys felt. "Could he be the copycat?"

Crys started walking toward their vehicle. "Let's ask him."

"Brock, the police want to speak with you." Brock Mann's administrative assistant's voice was heavy with curiosity as she made the announcement.

The petite, curvy redhead stepped aside to let Crys and Luke enter the spacious office. The room's dingy white walls and aged wood shelving overflowed with ego boosters: photos of the newspaper's editor-in-chief with local, state and federal officials; captains of industry; and foreign dignitaries; framed certificates of commendations for the newspaper's community coverage; and trophies for media competitions.

Seated behind a massive dark wood desk centered in the back of his office, Brock was cloaked in a bright white collared shirt, a champagne silk tie and arrogance. His short blond hair glowed beneath the fluorescent lighting. His black vinyl padded executive chair stood in front of a large picture window that framed the downtown Columbus skyline.

After a moment, he looked up from the laptop computer in front of him. His small, pale blue eyes landed on Crys. They widened in surprise and his thin lips parted. Blood drained from his sharp, white features. Brock closed the laptop and stood without releasing Crys from his attention. The editor was thin and of average height, perhaps five-nine or -ten, several inches taller than Crys's five-seven.

"That will be all, Monica." He waited in silence until his administrative assistant pulled the door behind her. Her reluctance was palpable. Brock's smile was fake. "Do you happen to know Jade Rashaad?"

Crys felt Luke's eyes on her as he and Brock waited for her response. "She's my sister. But she's not the reason Special Agent Gilchrist and I are here."

Brock's eyes flew to Luke as though he'd only just realized he and Crys were not alone. His lips parted in another, wider, but equally false smile. "Please. Forgive my manners." He circled his desk and approached Luke with an outstretched right hand. "Brock Mann."

"Special Agent Luke Gilchrist." Luke released Brock's hand.

Crys hesitated briefly before accepting the editor's outstretched hand. "Detective Crystal Rashaad."

"Ah." Luke nodded before releasing Crys and leading the way to the small dark wood conference table to the right of his desk. "Your family resemblance is very strong. How is Jade?"

Unemployed.

Crys gritted her teeth to keep the word from snapping out. "As I said, Special Agent Gilchrist and I aren't here to discuss my sister. We're investigating a murder."

"Murder?" Brock froze behind the seat at the head of the table. "Who was killed?"

"Carter Wainscott." Luke stopped behind one of the eight matching conference chairs.

Crys watched Brock's reaction. His thin blond eyebrows knitted together. He lowered his eyes as though searching his memory.

"I don't know him." Brock gestured Crys and Luke to the empty chairs in front of them before sitting.

"Are you sure?" Crys kept her eyes glued to Brock on her right. "He was a Black man in his early forties. He was fit and just shy of six-feet tall."

Brock continued shaking his head as his eyes moved between Luke and Crys on his left. "No, that name isn't familiar to me. Why are you asking?"

Luke ignored the question and pulled a notepad and pen from his inside jacket pocket. "Could you take us through your movements this morning?"

Brock's eyebrows jumped toward his hairline. "What is this about? Am I a suspect?" Panic hovered around the edges of his words. His eyes shot to Luke. "I've already told you I don't know the man. What reason would I have to kill him?"

Luke's voice was inflexible. "Please answer our questions, Mr. Mann."

Brock pressed back against his chair. "Do I need a lawyer, Special Agent?"

"You're free to consult a lawyer. That's your right." Crys started to return her notepad to her satchel. "You can have your attorney meet us at the department where we'll continue our questioning."

Brock looked at her in surprise. "Look, my letting your sister go was not personal. It was business. It was the unfortunate consequence of having to reduce our operating expenses."

Crys held on to her self-control with sheer willpower. She leaned into the table, chaining Brock with a fierce stare. "Neither are our questions personal. They're the necessary consequence of investigating a murder."

Brock's Adam's apple worked as he took a series of swallows. His eyes moved again between Crys and Luke. "All right. I'll answer your questions—without my lawyer's representation. All right?"

Luke responded before Crys could. "We appreciate your cooperation, Mr. Mann."

"Of course." Brock inclined his head. "My movements this morning. Well, I woke up early, as I usually do to work out at 5:00 a.m."

Crys interrupted him. "Where did you go?"

Brock frowned. "I have a rowing machine in my basement."

Luke wrote something in his notebook. "How long did you work out?"

Brock's sigh was long and frustrated. "About an hour. I work out for an hour every morning. Then I cleaned up, got dressed, ate breakfast and drove to work. Will you answer my questions now?"

"No." Crys enjoyed that. "What time did you leave your home to come to work?"

"Seven." Brock's tone was short. "Every Monday through Friday at seven. I have a routine, Detective."

Luke paused in his writing. "Did you drive straight to work, or did you stop off somewhere?"

"I drove straight to work, Special Agent." Brock's growing anxiety made itself heard. "I didn't stop for food, gas or anything else. I came straight here. I parked in the garage beneath this building, rode the elevator to the lobby as I do every workday, showed the security guard at the desk my ID and took the elevator to our offices. I got to my desk a few minutes before eight, as usual."

"Can anyone corroborate your schedule for today?" Luke's eyes were steady on Brock's.

Brock's narrow shoulders lifted and fell in a deep sigh. "My wife. She can verify what time I left the house. She made my breakfast. And the security guard at the desk can verify the time I arrived. I don't know her name but there aren't many female guards assigned to this building. She's short. And white."

Over the years, Jade had shared a few funny stories and anecdotes about the building's security staff. Her sister had always referred to the guards at least by their surnames. Names were important to Jade. She would've been able to tell them who'd checked her ID that morning—if she still worked for the paper.

The guard at the desk who'd signed her and Luke in when they'd arrived at *Capital Daily News* had been a young Hispanic man whose name badge had read Cabral.

Reaching into the satchel she'd set beside her chair, Crys pulled out the evidence bag with Brock Mann's employee identification.

"When you showed the guard your ID this morning, did you show her this one?" Crys laid the clear plastic bag on the table in front of her so she, Luke and Brock could see it.

Brock stiffened in shock. "Where did you get that?" His voice was breathless.

"Is this your identification?" Crys asked.

"No." Brock stood on unsteady legs. Three stiff strides carried him back to his desk. He pulled open the thin, shallow drawer at the top and retrieved an identification badge before returning to the conference table. He set the employee card beside the evidence bag. "*That's* my ID."

The badge Brock dropped onto the table beside the evidence bag was nearly identical to the one recovered at the crime scene. They were the same size, shape and material. Each used the same *Capital Daily News* logo, font and staff photo. The only visible difference between the two was that the employee badge and black, cloth lanyard Brock had pulled from his desk were worn compared to the one in the bag, which appeared brand new.

Luke leaned into the table as though to get a closer look at the two badges. "When you laid off Jade Rashaad, did you take her ID?"

What the—?

Crys's head snapped toward Luke. Her cheeks were hot with anger. Her brow tightened with her scowl. What was he implying? She knew he could feel her eyes on him. They were close enough for her to pinch him. But he ignored her.

Brock's voice was strained. "Of course, we did. We took her ID *and* her keys."

With an effort, Crys pulled her glare from her temporary—thank goodness—partner and returned her attention to Brock. "Who makes the *Capital Daily* staff IDs?"

"I have no idea." Brock waved a hand toward his door. "Monica can give you all that information."

She gestured toward his ID. "Do you always keep your card in your desk?"

His nod was less certain. "I don't need it during the day, and it distorts the lines of my suit."

Of course it did. "And is the drawer unlocked? Can anyone get into your desk?"

His blue eyes widened with surprise as they met hers.

"Well, yes, but who would want to make a copy of my badge? Where did you find the duplicate?"

Crys watched him closely. "Near Carter Wainscott's body."

The blood drained from Brock's face. "Someone planted a copy of my ID near a dead man?"

"Appears that way." Crys dropped her eyes and gave herself a mental shake.

She shouldn't find so much satisfaction in Brock's discomfort. They were questioning him as part of their homicide investigation. She needed to give Carter more respect. Besides, no matter how shook Brock was, none of this would get Jade's job back.

"Do you have any idea who would want to frame you for Mr. Wainscott's murder?" Luke asked.

Crys glared at him again. *Not my sister.* She turned back to Jade's former boss, waiting for his response.

Brock's eyes lowered to the conference table. "Of course not." But he didn't sound as certain as he wanted them to believe.

What wasn't he telling them? "Have you received any unusual or threatening messages or phone calls? Have you had any angry exchanges with anyone recently?" *Other than my sister?*

"I'm in charge of a newspaper." Brock pushed himself from the table and stood to pace his office. "Of course, I get threats. Not everyone loves our coverage. I get into arguments with readers and newsmakers almost daily."

Crys rose from her chair. "We're going to need a list of those people as soon as possible."

Brock spun to face her. Something in his expression made Crys suspect there was at least one name he was more concerned about than any others. Would he provide them with that contact information—or conveniently leave it off the list?

"Preferably before the end of the day." Luke stood beside her. "The sooner we get the list, the sooner we'll find the person who tried to frame you for murder."

Brock's cheeks grew even paler. "Yes, I can see how that would be true."

Crys hoped Luke's words would scare Brock enough to loosen his tongue.

She strode through the door, aware of Luke following close behind her. Stopping at Monica's desk, Crys asked the administrative assistant for the employee identification card vendor's contact details. Monica had the information ready. Either the admin was a mind reader or she'd been listening to their conversation through her boss's partially open door.

"You're upset I brought up your sister." Luke paced beside Crys down the hall to the suite's exit. "That's why you're speed walking toward the stairs."

Crys pushed through the Plexiglas doors before turning to confront him. Her face burned with anger. "My sister wouldn't kill someone, much less murder an innocent person just to frame her ex-boss. That's the stupidest thing I've ever heard."

"Mann laying off your sister gives her a strong motive against him." Luke pressed his hand to the small of Crys's back to guide her into the stairwell. "Revenge. We should at least interview her. If you were thinking clearly, you'd realize that yourself."

"I *am* thinking clearly." Her voice echoed in the stairwell. Crys stopped on the landing between the newspaper's third-floor suite and the second floor. She pinned Luke with a resentful glare. "Clearly enough to realize you have a hidden agenda. What is it?"

"The only agendas I have are the cases I've been assigned to." Luke circled Crys to continue down the stairs.

Crys hurried after him. "I don't believe you."

"I can't help you with that."

"Can't—or won't?"

Luke didn't respond. She hadn't expected him to. But she wasn't giving up. Luke was hiding something. She was certain of it. And she was determined to find out what it was.

"My gut's telling me there's a connection between the serial killer and the copycat." Just as her gut was telling her too many people were hiding information from her. Vic. Brock. Luke. She was in the middle of investigating multiple homicides. Could those secrets help close her case?

Luke sat at Vic's desk. He paused as though absorbing her statement. "Are you suggesting we have two serial killers now?"

"The copycat has killed one person." Crys flipped through her notes from their interview with Brock and with Carter Wainscott's widow. "So far."

Crys and Luke had broken the tragic news to Alice Trueman-Wainscott after they left the *Capital Daily News* offices. The absolute worst part of her job. It had taken a while to calm Alice down. Understandably. She'd been making plans for a surprise trip to celebrate their fifteenth wedding anniversary. Now she was being forced to change gears and plan her husband's funeral. Crys's heart shredded as she recalled the other woman's grief.

Alice hadn't known Brock Mann, nor had she ever heard Carter refer to him. Perhaps once the new widow had a moment to think clearly, she'd have more information for them.

When they'd returned to the department late Tuesday afternoon, Luke had contacted the employee identification card vendor. They were waiting for a callback from the executive in charge of business development. That could take a while. It was a small company. Crys also suspected the company believed a message from a special agent with the Ohio Bureau of Criminal Investigation merited a call to their legal counsel.

"OK, let's drill into your theory." Luke's voice was skewed with skepticism. "What information would that give us to advance our investigation?"

"If the killers know each other, the copycat would know what connects the serial's victims." Crys didn't look at Luke. He'd crossed the line by implying Jade could be a suspect in these homicides.

But he had a point. Crys clenched her fists as she made the concession. Revenge was a strong motive for murder. It seemed to be driving their serial killer. To preserve the integrity of their investigation, they had to speak with Jade. That didn't mean she had to like it.

"So you think Wainscott is somehow linked to Gomez, Murphy and Stead, even though we still don't know what connects those three?" Luke sounded as frustrated as Crys felt.

Crys closed her notepad. "The copycat didn't know about the delay between the suspect committing the murders and taking the victims to the reservoir. They also didn't know about the fishing lures."

Luke interrupted. "But they knew about the method of murder and the recovery at the reservoir, information they would've gotten from the news coverage."

"Which was the reason we withheld the time delay and the fishing lure." Crys rose from her seat and paced the few steps to the crime board. "Understandably, Alice Trueman-Wainscott wasn't able to give us much today." She stuffed her hands in the front pockets of her spruce green slacks. "We'll need to follow up with her. Carter's murder could give us our first solid lead."

"Or the copycat could be hoping to hide in plain sight, using the serial killer's victims as cover." Luke came to stand beside her.

Crys was sure he was crowding her on purpose. She kept her eyes on the crime board. It was disheartening. They had a growing number of victims and a lengthening time-line, but no credible suspects.

"We need to dig into Carter Wainscott's life." Crys pulled her hands from her front pants pockets and returned to her desk. "It could be a distraction, but that's not what my gut's telling me."

Either about the case—or about you.

Chapter 8

"I keep going straight to Mann's voicemail." Crys checked her watch again. It was just after 9:00 a.m. Wednesday. "That's the second message I've left for him this morning. He was supposed to get us his suspect list yesterday. I've left messages for Monica, too. Neither of them is getting back to me."

Crys's thumb tapped an impatient rhythm on her desk as her eyes lingered on Luke. He stood akimbo, facing the crime board. His shoulders were straight and broad under a warm blue shirt, tapering to a slim waist. His large hands were hooked on his lean hips over the tailored gray pants that covered his long legs. Despite herself, Crys's heart fluttered. She didn't trust the agent but darn it, that didn't stop her body from appreciating his.

"Let's give him a few more minutes." Luke spoke over his shoulder. "Then I'll call Cal to find out what's going on." He'd crossed his arms over his chest, pulling his shirt more tightly across his back. Crys swallowed hard before tearing her eyes from him.

The board wasn't encouraging. Just four victims—Rita Gomez, Alfred Murphy, Sally Stead and Carter Wainscott—and a bunch of questions with no answers. Yet. How were these people connected? When and why did their paths cross? Where were they murdered? Red *X*'s were scattered across the color printout of the Griggs Reservoir Park map. They marked the areas in which the four victims had been recovered.

Crys sat straighter on her chair. "I think it's suspicious that Brock didn't send us the list yesterday. And that he and Monica are dodging our calls today."

"Agreed." Luke turned to face her. His front was even more distracting than his back. "But we verified his alibis. His wife assured us he'd left the house at his usual time, seven. And the security guard confirmed he'd arrived for work a few minutes before eight as usual."

"I remember." She'd been there. Although it wouldn't have hurt her feelings to keep Brock on their suspect list a little longer. Like Jade, she was having a hard time getting past the fact he'd laid off her sister after hiring a higher-paid executive. "But if he doesn't have anything to hide, why isn't he giving us his list of people who've threatened him?"

"Maybe that's what he's hiding." Luke crossed back to Vic's desk.

Crys's eyes widened in surprise. She spun her chair to face him. "So you got the feeling he's hiding something or someone, too?"

"Yes, I did." Luke's eyes searched hers. "Someone went to a lot of trouble, duplicating Brock's ID to make him look like the serial killer. They wanted Carter Wainscott to look like another victim and they wanted Brock to take the fall for all four murders. Why?"

"Because whoever framed Brock is connected to the murders." Crys stood to pace. "There's a reason the copycat murdered Mr. Wainscott and a reason Brock Mann was targeted."

"You're saying you believe there's a direct link between our first three victims, Wainscott *and* Brock?" Luke sounded skeptical.

"Yes, I do." Crys scanned the details listed beneath each victim's photograph and the few items written under Brock's. What was she missing? "Why else would the copycat frame Brock for all four? Because framing him would put the copycat in the clear."

"We haven't even found a link between Gomez, Murphy and Stead."

"That's because we haven't gone back far enough. Yet." She returned to her desk. "You said yourself, 'Revenge is a dish best served cold.' The question is, how cold?"

They returned to their background research. Crys dug deeper into Rita Gomez and Alfred Murphy. Luke continued looking into Sarah Stead's and Carter Wainscott's pasts. Was it as painfully slow going for him as it was for her, creating the sortable lists and comparing their social media contacts, both personal and professional? Each victim had dozens of social connections and scores of professional colleagues.

After more than an hour, Crys completed the list of Rita's and Alfred's professional associates. She stood from her chair and stretched to get her circulation moving. "I'm going to try Brock again."

Luke nodded without looking up. She had the feeling he was deliberately avoiding eye contact with her. Odd.

Crys lifted her telephone receiver as she sat. She tapped in Brock's number from memory. A jolt of anticipation shook her when the call connected after two rings.

"Hello?" The woman's voice was familiar, though she didn't sound like Monica.

Crys frowned her confusion. She met Luke's eyes across her desk. "May I speak with Brock Mann, please?"

Luke narrowed his eyes at her question.

"Who's calling?" The woman sounded suspicious.

"This is Detective Rashaad. Who's this?"

"Crys? It's Wendy. Why are you calling?"

Crys blinked. Wendy Goldman had been a homicide detective for more than a decade. Rumor had it she'd started planning her retirement. A cold foreboding swept over her.

Apparently reading her expression, Luke circled his desk. He crowded her on her right and gestured for Crys to put the phone on Speaker. She did. Crys ignored Luke's scent—cedar and the sea.

"Wendy, I'm here with BCI Special Agent Luke Gilchrist. Brock Mann is connected to a case we're investigating."

There was a brief pause. "The serial killer who's leaving their victims at Griggs?"

"That's right." The intensity in Luke's deep voice sent a shiver down Crys's spine. "Detective Goldman, what's happened?"

Wendy's sigh held a hint of fatigue and a wealth of sorrow. "Brock Mann was murdered. The coroner's assistant estimates his time of death at sometime between nine and ten last night."

Crys closed her eyes in disbelief. "How? How was he killed?"

"He was shot in the chest with what looks like a small-caliber weapon. The shooter probably stood on the other side of his desk." Wendy hesitated as though she was taking in the crime scene again. "His admin found him about eight this morning."

Poor Monica. Crys didn't know whether she and Brock had a comfortable relationship. Either way, it must have been horrible to find her boss dead behind his desk.

"Did Brock often work late?" Luke's forearm brushed Crys's shoulder as he shifted his stance.

Heat spread across her chest. Had his touch been deliberate? Crys glanced up at him. His complete attention seemed to be on their phone call.

Wendy blew another breath, which carried through the speaker. "According to Monica, it wasn't unusual, but she said he didn't have any after-hours meetings on his calendar."

Crys exchanged a look with Luke. Brock had made a private, late-night meeting after speaking with them yesterday. Could that meeting have been with the person who'd framed Brock for Carter Wainscott's murder?

"I suppose it's too much to hope the visitor signed the security log when they came to the building?" Luke asked.

Crys held her breath as she waited for Wendy's answer.

"Of course, it is." Her voice was dust dry. "Last night's log is missing."

Crys clenched her fist in frustration. How could that have happened? "Wendy, since Brock was connected to our investigation, I think his murder has implications on our case."

Wendy interrupted. "I agree, and I'm way ahead of you. I'll send you my notes and transition the case over to you. If you need anything—anything at all—let me know."

"Thanks, Wendy. I appreciate you." Crys ended the call.

"Great. Thanks for handling that." Luke straightened, crossing his arms over his chest. "You realize we'll have to bring your sister in for questioning."

Crys stood. Her body heated with her rising temper. "Brock laid off my sister more than a month ago."

"It wouldn't have taken the copycat that long to plan to frame him."

Crys took a deep breath in an effort to control her emotions. Jade was an adult, but to Crys—and probably Amber, too—she'd always be their baby sister. The thought of her youngest sibling being hauled into a police interrogation room and questioned in connection with a homicide made Crys want to kick in a wall.

She narrowed her eyes on Luke's too-handsome face. "My sister had nothing to do with Brock's murder. Questioning her will be a waste of our time."

"Questioning her would address our due diligence, and we'll be able to move on with our investigation." Luke cocked his head. "I don't think it would be a good idea for you to be in the room when I meet with her. I don't think you can be objective."

Really? Two can play this game. "Fine. I don't want you in the room when I question Caleb."

Luke frowned. "Cal? Why do you want to question him?"

Crys felt a fierce rush of satisfaction. "Because Caleb is next in line for Brock's job. That gives him at least as strong a motive as you claim my sister has." She collected her car keys, satchel and jacket. "Come on. Let's get your buddy."

"The company's still in shock." Caleb sat behind his modern white-and-bronze desk in his office at the *Capital Daily News* suite.

Eyeballing it, Luke estimated the room was half the size of Brock's office. But whereas Brock used his space to advertise his standing in the community, Caleb's came across as a giant file cabinet. It was a clutter of publication style sheets, competitor newspapers and magazines, deadline reminders and company memos. His desk balanced a large disposable cup from a nearby coffeehouse as well as a generic white porcelain mug. Coffee and clutter. Nice to know some things hadn't changed since they'd been college roommates.

"What time did you leave last night?" Crys had been doing a continual scan of the office and its contents since they'd taken their gray cloth-cushioned seats in front of Caleb's desk.

Caleb looked from Crys to Luke and back. Luke worked to mask his irritation and keep his expression neutral. To suspect his friend of murder would be laughable if it wasn't so maddening, which is probably the same way Crys felt about his suspecting her sister.

The newspaperman seemed more curious than anxious over Crys's question. No doubt he was taking mental notes for a potential story. "You consider me a suspect because I worked with him."

Crys responded before Luke could. "Everyone's a suspect, Mr. Brunson."

Caleb offered her a smile. "Please call me Cal." He continued when Crys didn't respond. "I left work a little after six last night. I stopped by Brock's office to make sure there wasn't anything he needed from me and to let him know I was leaving. He said he was going to be at the office for a few more hours, which I thought was strange."

Luke interrupted. "Why did that seem strange to you?"

Caleb's mouth curved in a familiar crooked smile, indicating his friend smelled a story. "One of the candidates for secretary of state was hosting a fundraiser last night. High-profile people from all over the state were expected to make at least a brief appearance. Brock wouldn't miss a prime opportunity to get himself in front of a crowd of luminaries."

Luke made a note in his notepad. "Did he say what or whom he was waiting for?"

Caleb started shaking his head before Luke finished speaking. "No, and that was out of character, too. Brock loves—loved—to name-drop." He paused as though making an effort to move past his shock and sadness. "He got a charge out of bragging about being on a first name basis with people who had access to people with power."

Luke remembered Caleb making a similar observation about his now-deceased boss during one of their recent conversations. With whom had Brock planned to meet last night? Was it one of his powerbrokers, but he wanted to keep the meeting secret? Or was it with someone else?

He continued his questioning. "How did Brock seem when you stopped by his office yesterday evening?"

Caleb's shoulders rose and fell in a deep sigh as he seemed to search his memory for an answer. "He seemed anxious, almost apprehensive. I didn't think much about it before, but I sensed he was dreading the meeting."

Luke frowned. "What gave you that impression?"

Caleb stared into his coffee mug as though he'd found flashes of his memory in the brew. "He was fidgeting. At one point while we were talking, he left his desk to pace his office."

With whom had the editor met last night and why had he been afraid of them?

"How would you describe your relationship with Brock?" Crys's question drew Luke from his thoughts.

Caleb cocked his head as he considered Crys's inquiry. The question didn't seem to surprise his friend. "Brock and I worked well together. We didn't always agree. On those occasions when I disagreed with him, I let him know I thought he was wrong. For example, when he let your sister go, I told him he was making a mistake. Your sister was the best investigative reporter we had. But in the end, I realized as editor and publisher, Brock was in charge and his decision was final."

A ghost of a smile curved Crys's bowed lips. A cynical spark brightened her dark eyes. "That's pretty ballsy of you, bringing my sister into this investigation. Are you hoping your flattering words will give me a more favorable impression of you?"

Caleb flashed a grin. "I understand your skepticism, but I'm telling you the truth."

Crys narrowed her eyes. "Why don't you tell her this yourself?"

Caleb shrugged his thick, black eyebrows. "I think you remember what happened when I tried."

Luke saw the twinkle in Crys's eyes before she lowered them to her notepad. It was time to change the subject from Caleb's crush back to their murder investigation. "How would you describe Jade's relationship with Brock?"

In his peripheral vision, Luke caught Crys's sharp look, but she refrained from stating her objections.

Caleb dragged his hand over his close-cropped hair. "The whole newsroom was aware of the hostility between them. Jade was fearless when it came to her reporting. She was determined to investigate allegations of crime and corruption at all levels of industry and government, regardless of whom she ticked off. Brock wanted her to take a more cautious approach. They butted heads a lot. Some of Jade's targets were big advertisers."

"Do you think she'd kill someone over not being able to cover a story?" Crys's tone dripped with sarcasm. Luke could have collected it with a spoon.

Concern darkened Caleb's eyes. "No." He turned to

Luke. "Jade didn't kill Brock. She wouldn't. She'd want him to live to see her prove him wrong about her story."

"You know my sister well." Crys's tension seemed to ease a bit.

"What was she working on?" Luke asked.

"She wouldn't talk about it." Caleb shrugged. "Jade may have a temper but she wouldn't hurt anyone."

Luke had his doubts about that. If Jade Rashaad was like her sister, he could easily picture them resorting to violence to protect the people they loved. Luke felt an almost painful twist of envy. The question flashed across his mind: What was the cost of entry to that club?

He made a mental note. Don't mess with Crys's family. "Do you have any idea with whom Brock was meeting last night?"

Caleb shook his head. "Like I said, he was very secretive, unusually closemouthed about his meeting. The only thing I know is that the person he was waiting for was a man."

Luke jumped on the clue. "How do you know that?"

Caleb shrugged. "When I asked him how late he thought he'd be in the office, Brock said he hoped he wouldn't be much longer. I thought that was because he wanted to attend the fundraiser. Then he checked his watch and muttered something like, 'He's already late.' He sounded more nervous than irritated."

Luke stood to leave. "Thanks, Cal. You've been a lot of help."

Caleb pushed back his chair and got to his feet. "I don't feel as though I've been helpful." He looked between Luke and Crys. "Do you have any idea why someone would've killed Brock?"

Crys rose from her seat. "We can't comment on an open

investigation, but if you think of anything else that could help solve Brock's murder, please contact us."

Caleb nodded. "Of course."

Luke followed Crys from the office into the anteroom where the elevator banks waited. Remembering her preference for walking, he reached past her to push open the door to the stairwell. "I think I should interview your sister on my own."

"Not a chance, pal." Her response was quick and unequivocal. "You didn't wait outside while I questioned your good friend. You're not going to treat my sister any differently."

"I don't think you could remain objective during the interview." Luke jogged down the flights of stairs beside her.

Crys stopped at the second-floor landing to face him. She pinned him with her glare. "The only way you'll keep me from that room is to physically remove me. If you try that, I'll charge you with assault."

As tempting as it might be to test her threat, Luke didn't think it would be wise to push his luck. Besides, he really didn't believe Jade Rashaad was capable of murder—any more than he believed Crys Rashaad would take a bribe.

"I believe you." Luke walked around her to continue down the steps. "We'll do this your way."

"I'm glad you can be reasonable."

Luke wasn't sure he'd go that far. His feelings for the target of his investigation were anything but reasonable.

"One of my sisters is a homicide detective. The other is a prosecutor. I've covered crime in Columbus for three years. I can smell a fishing expedition."

Luke was taken aback. He'd thought after being exposed to Crys's directness, he'd be prepared for her youngest sister. He'd been wrong. Whereas Crys was direct, Jade Rashaad was blunt almost to the point of inflicting pain. She was in a category of her own. Still, he hoped interviewing her would give him greater insight into Crys for his investigation into allegations of her corruption—allegations that seemed more far-fetched with each passing day.

Jade had agreed to meet with Crys and Luke at her home in northeast Columbus late Wednesday afternoon. The cozy, two-story cottage was clean, well maintained and deceptively welcoming. After greeting her sister with a hug and warm smile, Jade had accepted Luke's handshake with a reserve that let him know his character was still being evaluated.

She'd escorted Crys and Luke to her dining room, where she'd offered them tea before taking the seat at the head of the table and firing her first salvo.

Seated on Jade's left, Luke looked across the table at Crys for her reaction to her sister's opening statement. Was she surprised, disappointed, angry, proud? He couldn't tell. She had an impressive poker face. She also wasn't speaking. Apparently, she was deferring to him for their response.

Reaching for their standard statement, Luke met and held Jade's irritated espresso eyes, so similar to Crys's. The family resemblance was very strong. "Ms. Rashaad—"

"Jade." The look on Jade's face assured Luke her invitation to address her by her first name wasn't a compliment.

He didn't take it as one. "Jade, this isn't a fishing expedition. We're investigating the murder of your former editor. Our due diligence demands we interview people who knew Mr. Mann and who might have a motive for this crime, if only to rule them out before identifying the killer."

A twinkle of amusement shone in Jade's long-lidded eyes. She lowered her mug of tea. Her cell phone, writing tablet and pen lay at her right elbow. "You think I'd kill Brock because he fired me more than a month ago?"

"Laid you off." Luke noted the clouds of suspicion growing in Jade's eyes.

She shrugged. "The result is the same. My unemployment is about to run out and my future is uncertain."

Luke cocked his head. "As you pointed out, it's been more than a month, but I can hear the anger in your voice when you talk about it."

A shadow gathered over Jade's heart-shaped face. It was as though someone had flipped a switch. He couldn't read her expression.

"I hope you never know how I feel, Special Agent Gilchrist." Her voice was low and without inflection.

The haunted sincerity in her tone gave him a chill. Luke switched his attention to Crys. A wave of pain rolled across her delicate features, poignant and tangible, before she lowered her head as though masking her reaction. When she raised her eyes to return his gaze, all signs of emotion had been wiped clear of her expression. But Luke felt her frustration and helplessness in the air between them. She was a protective older sister. Could a sense of responsibility toward her family be the motivation for her accepting bribes?

He turned back to Jade. "Luke. Please. Jade, could you tell us where you were last night between 9:00 and 10:00 p.m.?"

Again, a twinkle of humor briefly replaced the irritation in her dark eyes. "My sister must be royally ticked off with you for interrogating me as a murder suspect."

He spread his hands. "And yet we're here, speaking with you in connection with this case."

"That's because my sister's very good at her job." Jade sat back against her dark wood chair. Pride sounded in her voice. "My parents used to say if I broke the law, Crys wouldn't hesitate to arrest me and Amber would make sure I got the best defense possible, even if she wasn't representing me. My parents raised us to obey and respect the law, both the constitution and the bible." For the first time since they'd settled at the table, Jade looked to her sister. "I've got an alibi for the time of Brock's death. I was on a videoconference with some podcaster colleagues."

Crys nodded, acknowledging Jade's information, but she remained silent. It was as though she wanted to be there to witness the interview but wasn't going to risk charges of influencing the record by participating in it. Would a corrupt agent take those same preventive steps? Or perhaps she didn't want to attract closer scrutiny to her actions.

Luke made a record in his notes. "That's kind of late for a videoconference, isn't it?"

Jade returned her attention to him. Unlike Crys, she couldn't mask the temper in her eyes. "My colleagues and I are on different time zones. The others also have day jobs, unlike me."

Crys spoke up for the first time. "Jade, your podcast *is* your day job. Right now, you're building it, but you'll be launching it soon and it will be a success."

Jade nodded, but Luke felt anxiety vibrating around her. She wasn't as confident of her success as Crys was. Did she realize how fortunate she was to have someone in her corner as she started this new venture? The gratitude and love in her eyes as she exchanged another look with Crys let him know she did.

Releasing the cream porcelain mug that held her tea, Jade tore the top sheet from her writing tablet. "When Crys called to tell me Brock had been murdered and you wanted to speak with me, I had a feeling you'd want the contact information for my alibis." She extended the paper to Luke.

"These are the names and numbers of the three other people on the videoconference. You can call them now, if you'd like. I don't have anything to hide."

Luke took the information from her. Crys had called Jade while they were driving to her address. That wouldn't have given her enough time to alert all three of these people, even if she'd left messages for them.

He folded the paper and tucked it into his notepad. "Thank you for the information, but I'll follow up with your colleagues when we return to the department. I still have a few more questions. You have a very nice home."

Jade's sudden dry chuckle surprised him. "You're wondering how a newspaper reporter could afford a home like this on her own, and how I could continue making mortgage payments now that I'm no longer gainfully employed. Am I right?"

Luke's face heated with embarrassment. Across the table, Crys's displeasure battered at him like a gale force hurricane. "Yes, that's exactly what I was wondering."

As quickly as it rose, Jade's sarcastic humor drained. "What does that have to do with Brock's murder? Do you think someone paid me to kill him and I accepted the bribe to make my mortgage payments?"

"Did you?" The benefit of blunt speaking was that it enabled you to get to the point a lot faster.

Jade exchanged a look of incredulity with her sister. Crys shrugged her eyebrows before turning back to Luke with an expression of deep condemnation.

"You're ignoring one very important question, Special Agent Gilchrist." Jade folded her hands on the table in front of her. The distrust in her eyes was more pronounced. "How did Brock's killer get a gun into the building? The murderer couldn't have carried a gun past security, which

means it must have been planted somewhere in the building before Brock's time of death. And the killer doesn't
work for the paper."

Crys frowned. "How do you know it wasn't someone
who worked for the paper?"

"There's no way to carry a gun directly into our offices.
The killer would have had to arrange to deliver it in advance to another company renting offices in our building.
Now, if I were the murderer." She looked at Luke. "Which
I'm *not*, I would have hired a courier to deliver a package
to the other company's mailroom and have someone intercept it, then hide the gun." She shrugged. "Although we
can't rule out that someone from the paper could've been
working with the killer. Brock wasn't very well liked. Still,
I can't imagine any of my former colleagues shooting him.
They'd just quit."

Crys looked as impressed as Luke felt.

"Thanks for the tip, J." Crys rose, turning to Luke. Her
eyes gleamed with an unspoken told-you-so. "I think we're
done here. Would you agree?"

Luke stood. "Yes. Thank you for your time, Jade."

Jade led them to her front door. "Brock and I didn't part
on the best of terms, but I wouldn't have wished something
like this on him. I hope you catch the person who killed
him." She opened the door for them before pinning Luke
with a direct stare. "And that you found whatever else you
were looking for in this interview."

Luke caught the sharp look Crys gave her youngest sister, but Jade never broke eye contact. Was she guessing, or
did she somehow know this meeting wasn't just about their
murder investigation? Something told him he was running
out of time to wrap up his investigation into Crys.

Chapter 9

Her heart had scissor kicked her in the chest late Friday morning when she'd received the email from the detectives investigating Vic's homicide. They wanted to meet with her. Good. She wanted to meet with them, too.

But why had Luke asked to join her? What was his interest in Vic's homicide? Crys should have questioned him. Jade would have. He hadn't known Vic. Her partner's death wasn't connected to their investigation, but Brock's murder was. She was sure of it. So why was Luke invested in Vic's case when they had so much work to do on their own?

Stopping at their colleague's desk at the other end of the floor, Crys forced a smile. "Good morning." She split a look between the two older white men, one who resembled a grizzly bear and the other a penguin gone to seed. "This is BCI Special Agent Luke Gilchrist. Luke, this is Detective Sam Worchester and Detective Wyatt Snyder."

Sam and Wyatt stood to greet Luke before Wyatt turned to her. The sixty-something-year-old was tall and broad with a full graying beard that covered half his face. His shock of salt-and-pepper curls cried out for a haircut.

"Thanks for coming." Wyatt's deep voice was gruff with a hint of a Southern Ohio accent. His bright blue eyes were kind. "How're you holding up?"

"I'm managing." She was afraid they hadn't made any progress. She was afraid they had. Either way, how would that impact her aunt's case? "How's your investigation going?"

"Fair to middlin'." Wyatt leaned his hips against his desk. He waved Crys and Luke into the nearby visitor's seats.

Sam shrugged his narrow shoulders, pinching the bridge of his sharp nose. "About as well as yours, I guess, just with fewer bodies."

Wyatt sighed. "We don't have much yet, other than the information in the file Vic had returned to you."

"I still can't believe he was on the take." Sam gestured between himself and Wyatt. "We always thought of Vic as a straight arrow. We knew his wife's illness had taken a toll on the family's finances, but if you'd asked me or anyone else here, we never would have imagined Vic would turn like that."

Wyatt shook his head adamantly. "Never in a million years."

"Neither would I." Crys pulled Wyatt's guest chair toward her so she could sit facing the other two detectives. Luke arranged his seat beside hers. "Vic was my mentor. I never suspected a thing. And it was my aunt's file that he'd taken." She heard the trace of anger in her own voice.

Sam ran a hand over his already disheveled, thinning gray hair. "Your aunt's file is the only one that we know he tampered with. Bright's not thrilled that Internal Affairs is now reviewing all Vic's case files to see if he tampered with any others."

Luke frowned. "But I thought Vic hadn't been assigned to Kendra Chapel's homicide?"

Wyatt searched Luke's face. Crys sensed his suspicions stirring. "No, he hadn't been. Bright gave that case to Mayne and Taupe. Mayne's dead and Taupe's living the dolce vita in North Carolina." He looked from Luke to Crys and back. "What's the BCI's interest in all this?"

Luke shrugged. "We're just lending a hand with this serial killer case. It's not unusual for us to help departments with bigger investigations."

Wyatt grunted. "That Griggs case definitely fits the bill. It sounds like a bear." He inclined his head toward Sam. "Let us know if there's anything we can do to help."

"I appreciate that." Despite their offer, Crys probably wouldn't reach out to them for help. She'd heard the rumors that Wyatt and Sam weren't the most diligent investigators.

Sam nodded. "We wanted to ask you some questions for our investigation into Vic's murder. Standard CYA stuff, you know? The night Vic was killed, you were having dinner with a friend, right?"

"That's right." Crys wasn't offended by the question. If the situation were reversed, she'd have asked them the same thing. Family members and close friends were prime suspects in a murder investigation. She just didn't like when *her* family members and close friends came under scrutiny.

But this was like déjà vu all over again. She'd been on a date the night her aunt Kendra had been murdered as well. For someone without an active social life, was it suspicious that both murders happened when she was out for the evening? She didn't believe in coincidences, but she had to be careful not to trip over into full-on paranoia.

"Did your aunt and Vic know each other?" Wyatt asked.

Crys shook her head, glancing at Luke. "Not to my knowledge. Aunt Kendra had never mentioned Vic to me. And I wasn't aware Vic knew anything about my aunt until his daughter gave me the package he'd left for me."

Luke gestured toward Crys. "But Vic wouldn't have had to have known your aunt to take her file. Whoever paid him to tamper with the evidence probably knew about his financial struggles and hoped that would make him a convenient target for a bribe."

Wyatt gave Luke another long suspicious stare. "You're probably right."

Sam nodded his agreement.

Luke split a look between Sam and Wyatt. "It's my understanding Vic's and Kendra Chapel's crime scenes were similar."

"They were more than similar." Sam circled his desk to sit behind it. "They were identical. Both Vic's and your aunt's cases were burglaries gone wrong. They both occurred on a Friday night. And in both cases, the victims interrupted the burglary at about the same time and were shot center chest."

Crys frowned, thinking about her aunt. "How many other burglaries have you found with those characteristics?"

"Actually none." Sam's eyebrows stretched up his growing forehead. "Just Vic's and your aunt's."

Crys's suspicions grew. These were not burglaries gone wrong. But for now, she'd play along with Sam and Wyatt's premise. "But Vic and my aunt lived in different areas of the city. If the crimes were similar, it implies they're being committed by the same perpetrators. Wouldn't they focus on the same or nearby neighborhoods?"

Wyatt was nodding before Crys finished speaking. "They would, unless their targets were specific rather than random."

"Are there any other links between the cases?" Luke's eyes lingered on Crys's expression as though searching to see if she was OK. "Did you recover any prints?"

Wyatt seemed to be getting more comfortable with Luke's presence. "Only Vic's, his children's and grandchildren's."

"We did find another connection between the murders." Sam exchanged a look with Wyatt. His partner's nod was barely perceptible. "We got the ballistics on the gun used to kill Vic. According to the report in your aunt's case file, the gun used to kill Vic is a match to the one used to kill her."

Crys felt as though the breath had been sucked out of her body. The blood rushing from her head sounded like a freight train cutting through the silence of the night. Her grip tightened on the arms of the dark wood chair. She clenched her teeth, struggling to keep her composure.

Luke's eyes seemed to burn the side of her face. "The scene and setup were the same for both murders. Do you think Kendra was killed because of something she knew?"

Crys cleared the lump of emotion from her throat. "And Vic was killed because he hadn't destroyed her case file the way he was supposed to. Any doubts I may have had are gone. They were both targeted and the burglaries staged."

Frowning, Sam shook his head. "If that's the motive, why wait a year before killing Vic?"

Wyatt spread his arms. "Maybe they only just found out Vic hadn't destroyed the report. Maybe Vic told them for some reason."

The muscles in Crys's neck and shoulders were drawn so tightly, she feared they'd snap. "But what did my aunt know that would make someone want to kill them?"

"The gun used to kill Aunt K was the same gun used to kill Vic." The words felt heavy as they left Crys's chest.

She and her sisters had gathered in her family room after lunch Sunday afternoon. The scent of lentil soup had followed them from her kitchen.

It was their first official meeting to solve their aunt's murder. Crys studied Amber's and Jade's expressions. They looked as stunned and fearful at the implication of Crys's announcement as she'd felt after learning the ballistics results two days ago.

It had been four days since Brock Mann had been found dead, the fifth body that seemed to be connected to her serial killer investigation. And yet, she couldn't let her aunt's murder remain unsolved, especially since it now seemed to be connected to another case, one that had dire consequences for her department.

"What does this mean?" Amber sat beside Jade on Crys's overstuffed powder-blue, floral-patterned sofa. Her voice was thin and breathy with shock. "It can't be a coincidence that the same people who burgled Aunt Kendra's house and murdered her also broke into Vic's house and killed him."

"Why would those two murders be connected?" Jade frowned at the area rug beneath Crys's honey wood coffee table as though the answer to her question was hidden among the blue-pink-and-white floral pattern. "Aunt Kenny didn't know Vic. And you didn't know him until four months after Aunt Kenny's death."

"Remember Vic's letter?" Crys shared a look with Amber and Jade. "He knew who killed him and the people who killed him knew Aunt K." That fact sent a chill down Crys's spine. She stood from her matching overstuffed armchair and circled the coffee table to pace her family room. Her pink fuzzy socks were silent on the blond wood flooring.

Amber groaned. "Aunt Kendra, what were you involved in?"

"She wasn't involved in anything." Jade's voice seemed sharper than necessary.

Behind her, Crys heard the soft swooshing sound of cloth rubbing against cloth as though one of her sisters had shifted on the sofa. Probably Jade. Ahead of her, Crys's eyes absently scanned the view beyond her bay windows. Her street was quiet. The majority of her neighbors were retirees. Very few had young children, and most of the kids played in the nearby park.

This had been her family home, where she and her sisters had grown up. She and Jade had moved out of their separate apartments and into the house after their parents had died. By then, Amber had already bought a small cottage in a nearby community. Aunt Kendra had left her home to Jade in her will. It had taken a few months and a lot of soul searching before Jade had moved into it, which had been for the best.

As much as she loved Jade—and she knew her sister loved her, too—living together had been a bit stressful. Crys was proactive. Once she verified the pros and cons of things like home repairs and renovations, she was ready to act. Jade needed to triple check everything. That drove Crys out of her mind. She'd lost track of the number of times they'd had to call Amber to arbitrate their disagreements.

"I wasn't implying Aunt Kendra was living a secret life of crime." Amber's tone was conciliatory. "She was one of the most honest people anyone had ever met."

"That's the truth." Crys's response was reflexive. She hadn't meant to interrupt.

"But something or someone she was innocently involved with must have been shady." Amber paused. "Aunt Kendra didn't have a lot of outside interests. Other than work, she had her books and her garden, and she went swimming at her neighborhood gym."

"And she enjoyed going to the hair salon." Crys turned

away from her window and the many potted plants assembled on the blond wood ledge. Most of them had started as cuttings from her aunt's various thriving plants. "Did she mention any new interests or projects to either of you?"

Amber shook her head. "No, not anything I can think of. Something may occur to me later."

Jade hesitated. "Nothing comes to mind." She seemed distracted as though she was searching her memory for clues about their aunt.

Crys crossed back to her armchair on the far end of the sofa closest to Jade. "Whatever it takes—we need to get justice for Aunt K, not only because of what she meant to us but because her murder could be connected to other crimes." She looked from Amber to Jade. "Maybe we should review what we remember about Aunt K's last activities. Before we do that, though, there's something that's been weighing on my mind since her death."

Amber shifted on the sofa to face her. "What is it?"

Crys drew a deep breath, filling her lungs to ease the tightness in her chest. "The day Aunt K was murdered, she'd called to ask if we could have dinner. She wanted to get my input on something. I put her off. Tim had been in town for the weekend and asked me to have dinner with him."

Tim had been her college boyfriend. They'd met her sophomore year. Crys had broken up with him before graduation, but sometimes she wondered whether leaving him had been a mistake. Then she'd gotten the news Aunt K had been killed. She'd died within an hour of the time they would have met for dinner.

Jade gasped. "What?"

"Oh, no, Crys." Amber's words were muffled behind her palm. She lowered her hand. "I'd canceled on her. A couple of days earlier, we'd made plans to meet for dinner that evening. She'd wanted to discuss something with me, too. I thought I would be free, but something came up with one of my cases and I had to work late. I asked her if we could reschedule for the next day. She said it would be OK."

Jade shifted to face Amber. "You bailed on her, too?"

Amber's eyes stretched wide with surprise at Jade's attack. "I didn't bail on her. I had to work."

Jade stood from the sofa and crossed the room. "You couldn't take even one hour to have dinner with Aunt Kenny? You could have gone back to work afterward."

Crys rose from her chair. "J, that's not fair. We've all been caught in Am's situation when we need to reschedule something because of work—or other conflicts."

"Don't I know it." Jade switched her attention to Crys. Her voice trembled with temper and another unidentifiable emotion. "The two of you are always bailing on our standing Sisters Night because of your work. You both stood me up again last week. You cancel so often, we can't even call it a standing dinner anymore. And the sports bar where we meet is literally walking distance from your offices. I'm the one who has to make the half hour drive downtown."

Amber stood, hooking her hands on her slim hips above her rose cotton slacks. "You're acting like it's our fault Aunt Kendra was murdered."

"Don't be ridiculous." Jade raised her voice. "Neither of you is responsible for Aunt Kenny's death. The person who killed her is. But you both keep putting your work ahead of our family. As important as your jobs are, I've learned the hard way that jobs will come, and they will go. *Family* is forever."

Speechless, Crys watched as Jade marched on stiff legs

to the coat closet, grabbed her purse, then let herself out of Crys's home.

Amber circled the coffee table. "We need to talk with her."

"No." Crys's voice was firm. "Give her some time to calm down. She's too upset to hear anything we have to say now."

And Crys suspected at least some of Jade's anger was directed at herself. Why? Did Jade know something about their aunt's murder? If so, could her sister be in danger?

"Why do you think Rashaad was willing to let you question her sister?" Martina sat behind her desk at the BCI early Monday morning. Her smoke pearl stud earrings matched her necklace and the band of her pearl wristwatch. Was they new? "I mean, I'm aware Mann had fired her sister from the paper—"

"Jade Rashaad was laid off, not fired." Luke didn't know why Martina's error in referring to Jade as having been fired bothered him so much. It was more than the lack of accuracy. He didn't like the implication that Crys's sister had done something to deserve having her job taken from her.

"Fine. Laid off then." Martina rolled her eyes. "That would give her motive to kill Mann. Are you certain her alibi checked out?"

Luke inclined his head. "I called the three people from the videoconference. They verified the time of the meeting. They confirmed Jade logged on early and stayed until the end."

Martina made a humming sound as her eyes scanned her office. Luke had the sense she was searching her mind rather than the room.

Her brown eyes refocused and pinned him to the gray

cushioned guest chair. "What was your impression of Rashaad's sister? You're saying this is her youngest sister?"

"That's right. Crys has two siblings, both younger sisters. Jade is the youngest of the three." Luke took a deep breath as he mulled over Martina's question. The scent of her expensive perfume mingled with the aroma of his black coffee wafting to him from the coffee mug he held in his right hand. "She and Crys are very much alike. Both smart, assertive and direct. In fact, Jade may be even more confrontational than Crys."

"Really?" Martina frowned. "Could she have been using aggression as a way to get you to stop questioning her?"

"No." Luke shook his head again. "I told you she has a strong alibi. Three of them and they all checked out."

"Darn. She's such a good suspect for Mann's murder." Martina expelled a frustrated breath. "Why was Rashaad willing to let you question her sister?"

Luke couldn't hold back a smile as Martina's inquiry triggered the memory of his conflict with Crys. "I didn't say Crys was willing to let me interview Jade. I had to talk her into it. She was very much opposed to the idea."

"But she did let you talk her into it. What was your read on that?" Martina leaned forward in her seat.

Confused, Luke shook his head. "She wanted to clear her sister's name. And we interviewed my friend, Cal Brunson, the paper's executive editor. He's next in line for Mann's job."

Martina arched an eyebrow. "That's not as compelling a motive as Jade Rashaad's." Her voice was dry. "Has the sister gotten a new job?"

"She's starting her own business."

Her smile was condescending. "Really? In that case,

it's a good thing Jade Rashaad has those alibis. Otherwise she'd be at the top of my suspects list."

Luke frowned. Why was Martina fixating on Jade? "I don't think any of the Rashaad siblings are involved in corruption. I haven't found anyone who's had a negative experience with Crys. Everyone who's worked with her admires her."

Martina's eyes widened with surprise. She pressed back against her seat. "How can you be so unequivocal about the Rashaads' character? You haven't met all of them yet. Have you?"

"No, I haven't but—"

"And you only spoke with Jade briefly this one time."

"That's true, but—"

"And you've known Crys Rashaad for less than two weeks—"

Frustrated, Luke cut Martina off. "But I've been investigating her for almost three months."

Martina folded her hands on the desk in front of her. "Based on what you've learned about your target, is it possible Rashaad has been trying to throw her sister under the bus?" She shrugged her sturdy shoulders. "Perhaps Rashaad didn't know about Jade's videoconference, which means she wouldn't have known Jade had an alibi."

Luke narrowed his eyes. Crys Rashaad trying to throw one of her siblings under the bus? Ridiculous. "Absolutely not. Crys barely said a word during the interview. She left it up to me, letting me pursue the line of questioning. Besides, she and her sisters are very close. They get together for dinner weekly. There's no way she would set her siblings up for a crime."

"Are you sure of that?"

"Positive." Luke held Martina's skeptical eyes through several silent beats.

Finally, she nodded her acceptance. "Could you get invited to one of their dinners?"

Luke blinked his surprise. "You want me to crash one of their family meals?"

Martina searched his expression. "That's right. Would you have a problem with that?"

"It's a private dinner the sisters have to catch up with each other. Why would they let me join them?"

Martina shrugged. "It's worth a try."

"Why?"

Martina shrugged again. "Isn't it obvious? So you could get to know them better. It's possible the sisters could be working together with these bribes."

"What?" This was going from bad to worse.

Martina continued. "In one way or the other, they're all involved in criminal investigations. Crys Rashaad is a detective. Amber Rashaad is a prosecutor, and Jade Rashaad is, or at least was, a crime beat reporter. With their various contacts, they'd have all the angles covered."

Luke took a moment to get his irritation and frustration under control. "Why are you so certain Crys Rashaad is corrupt?"

Temper snapped in Martina's eyes. "You forget, Luke, I'm the one who took the tip. I heard the conviction in the complainant's voice."

"What makes you think the tip you received is more valid than the work I've put into this investigation? I've spoken with more than a dozen of her colleagues, people who work directly with her and people who've supervised her. They've all sung her praises."

"Luke, you generally do good work. That's why I assigned you to this investigation." Martina's voice was tightly controlled. "But I have years more experience than you. This isn't my first investigation into allegations of police corruption. If you're uncomfortable with this investigation, I'll be happy to replace you. Just let me know."

She was serious. Luke could see that in her eyes. He was confident in his investigative work. He'd been more than thorough. He'd interviewed past and present supervisors and colleagues. Unfortunately, Vic had been murdered before he'd been able to speak with him, but he'd met with her current supervisor. There was no *there*, there. But for some reason Martina was convinced of Crys's corruption. What wasn't she telling him? Why was she withholding information?

Whatever the reason, Luke didn't trust anyone else with this investigation. If Crys was indeed on the take, he wanted to be the one who took her down. But if, as he suspected, she was innocent, he wasn't going to allow anyone to railroad her.

Luke stood to leave. "Replacing me won't be necessary. I'll finish what I started."

Chapter 10

"You've been quiet today." Luke's comment broke Crys's concentration Monday afternoon. They were working through lunch again. "What's on your mind?"

She looked over at him, seated behind Vic's battered wood desk, which faced hers. "Do you mean other than our serial killer case, which has at least five victims connected to it?"

The scents of cayenne pepper, garlic, paprika, onions and cheese from her bowl of homemade chili drifted up to her.

"Other than that." Luke slid aside the remains of his sad-looking roast beef sandwich on whole grain bread. His navy-blue shirt and black tie looked crisp and fresh even halfway through the day. The colors warmed his brown skin. "You're dealing with a lot. This case." He gestured toward the pile of papers on his desk and those in front of her. "Your partner's unsolved murder. Learning Vic was the one who tampered with evidence in your aunt's cold case homicide investigation. And now you have confirmation that whoever killed your aunt is also behind Vic's murder. Do you think it might be time for you to step back?"

His question was delivered with respect and caring. It still stung.

Crys leaned into her desk and pinned him with a look.

"No, I don't. My stepping back from this case isn't going to help anyone. There are five people and their families who need justice and closure. I know how that feels. I'm not going to stop until I get that for them."

"I thought that would be your response." Luke settled back against Vic's chair, now his seat, and gave her an assessing look.

His dark eyes shone with what looked like admiration. His expression made her uncomfortable. She was doing her job, nothing more, nothing less. "Are you saying I'm predictable?"

"You know I'm not." He lowered his eyes as though masking his thoughts. "It must have been a shock to learn your aunt and partner were killed by the same person or at least the same gun."

Crys took a moment, waiting for a wave of grief to ebb. "Part of me suspected a connection. The circumstances of the murders are too similar. It's not much of a leap to think whoever killed Aunt K killed Vic to keep him quiet. Now I need to know why they targeted my aunt in the first place."

"Why do you think they waited a year before doing that, though?"

"We keep going back to that question." Sitting back against her chair, Crys crossed her arms under her chest. "Something spooked them. Either Vic asked for more money, or he threatened to tell me what he'd done."

"Or both." Luke shrugged his broad shoulders. "It could be that meeting the niece of the woman whose case he derailed made Vic have a change of heart about what he'd done." The assessing look returned to his dark eyes. "Did he ever say anything to you about your aunt?"

Crys shook her head. "No, and I never said anything to him about her. I didn't have any idea he knew I was related to Kendra Chapel. That's one of the many reasons I was so shocked to receive that package from him."

They each sank into their own thoughts. The silence was punctuated by the rustling sound of Luke reaching into his bag of chips, which had come with his sandwich combo meal.

He ate another chip. "How's your investigation of your aunt's case going?"

Crys swallowed to ease the dryness in her throat. The angry exchange with Jade had been the main cause of her sleepless night. It probably also was the reason she felt so out of sorts today. "We may have hit another snag."

Luke wiped his large, brown hands with a thin, white napkin. "What's happened? Maybe I can help."

His offer seemed sincere. Crys was so startled, she blurted out the first thing that popped into her head. "Jade's angry with me."

Her eyes widened with shock. Had she really said that? Why? She'd never shared anything so personal with her partners. But now that she had, how could she take it back?

Luke's eyebrows stretched toward his hairline. "I'm sorry. I could tell how close you and your sisters are when I saw you at the sports bar." He seemed at a loss. "Would it help to talk about it?"

Maybe. "I hate arguing with my sisters. I mean, we have our disagreements. We're each very different. But I hate it when we're angry with each other." She snorted. "Although Amber and I think anger is Jade's love language."

Luke flashed a grin that made Crys's toes curl in her black loafers.

She swallowed again before continuing. "The day my aunt was murdered, she'd called to invite me to dinner. But I said no. I had a date." Crys paused as her voice wobbled.

She shrugged her right shoulder, trying to shake loose the feeling of being self-centered and stupid. "An ex was in town for business and had asked to get together. When my sisters and I met last night, I told them I'd put off Aunt K because of him."

"Is that why Jade's angry? Because you kept your plans with your ex rather than having dinner with your aunt?" Luke's tone didn't indicate whose side he was on.

"Yes." Crys rubbed her eyes with the heels of both hands. "She accused Amber and me of always putting our plans ahead of our family."

"Oh." Luke searched her face as though trying to read her thoughts. "Is she right?"

It was a fair question. And again, Crys couldn't tell what Luke was thinking. Was he judging her like she was judging herself?

Restless, Crys pushed herself from her seat and paced the aisle in front of their crime board. "My friend was only in town for one night. I thought Aunt K and I could get together the following night."

"That's what should have happened. You couldn't have known it wouldn't." Luke's words rang true, but they didn't ease Crys's guilt. Not even a little.

She filled her lungs with a deep breath, catching the scents of her spicy chili and his roast beef sandwich. "Jade's right. I prioritize work and friends. I don't know why. My family's the most important thing in my life." She blew a frustrated breath. "I was taking them for granted." The words weren't easy but until recently they were true. "I put my ex first and my aunt was killed."

"Don't make connections where none exist." Luke's voice was firm. "Your having dinner with your ex is separate from your aunt's murder."

Crys unclenched her teeth. "She was killed at the same time that we would've been having dinner. If I'd met her as she'd asked, she wouldn't have been home. She wouldn't have been murdered."

Luke's silence was like a vice tightening across her chest. Crys flexed her shoulders, struggling to ease the constriction.

When he finally spoke, Luke's voice was like verbal tip-toeing. "This will be hard for you to hear. It's hard for me to say. Whether you had dinner with your aunt that night or the next, nothing would've changed. Whoever wanted to hurt her would've kept coming back until they completed their objective."

"Then why do I feel so guilty?"

Behind her, Luke's chair creaked as though he'd shifted on his seat. "Because you and your sisters still don't have closure on your aunt's murder. You're striking out against everyone, including yourselves, looking for someone to blame."

The imaginary rope across her chest broke. "That's very insightful of you, Special Agent Gilchrist."

"I have a degree in psychology."

That tracked.

Crys faced him.

"My sisters and I need to make amends and get back to work on our aunt's case. According to you not only will it bring justice for our aunt, it will repair our relationship."

"Mind if I help you?" Luke spread his hands. "An extra set of eyes and hands could be helpful."

"Thank you." She took her seat and found a smile for him. "Let me check with my sisters." That would be an interesting conversation.

"One more question." Luke held up his hand. "What happened with your ex?"

"It didn't work out." Crys shrugged. "He hadn't changed. Neither had I."

"I don't think you need to change." Luke looked as surprised by his comment as she felt.

Crys's appetite returned. She hid her smile behind a spoonful of chili.

"Thanks for coming." Jade secured the front door of the home she'd inherited from their aunt Kendra. She sounded distracted as she led Crys and Amber into her family room Monday night. "I should have come to you. I owe both of you an apology."

Crys glanced at the collection of manila folders on the dark wood coffee table in front of the cream faux leather sofa. She dropped onto its corner closest to Jade's armchair. Jade had texted her and Amber earlier that afternoon, asking them to meet at her home. Crys had grabbed a quick dinner. However, she hadn't had time to change out of her forest-green slacks and beige-and-green floral shirt before picking up Amber to drive to Jade's house.

She glanced at Amber beside her before continuing. "We understand, J. We're all still grieving Aunt K's death, especially since her killer hasn't been caught."

Cancer had taken both of their parents, which didn't make the pain of their loss any easier, but at least they had closure. Their maternal aunt's unsolved homicide investigation had burdened them with so many unanswered questions. Who'd killed her? Why? And when will the murderer be held accountable for their crime? Crys caught her breath at the sudden, sharp jab of grief. They owed it to Kendra, their parents and themselves to get justice for their aunt.

Sitting sideways on the sofa, Amber leaned toward Jade. "We should probably have a standing apology since this won't be the one and only time we snap at each other during this investigation. That's just the way we are."

"For real." The clouds in Jade's eyes lingered despite her brief smile. "But it's important you know I don't blame either of you for Aunt Kenny's murder. We all understand the person responsible—the only person responsible—is the killer."

Crys's brow furrowed. Why did Jade sound as though she was trying to convince herself of that fact? Her eyes drifted again to the coffee table, where a stack of folders grew in front of Jade.

"Don't worry. We know that." Amber's warm response interrupted her thoughts.

Crys inclined her head toward the neatly arranged manila mini mountain. "What are those?"

Jade seemed to force herself to look at the stack. "This is the reason I asked you to meet me here. I didn't want to transport all these files." She took a breath as though trying to collect her composure. "I think there's a strong possibility Aunt Kenny may have been killed because of an investigative report I'm working on."

"What?" Crys looked over her shoulder at Amber. She appeared as shaken as Crys. So many questions raced across her mind. She forced herself to pick one. "What report?"

"I need to start at the beginning." Jade unfolded herself from the armchair, turning her back to the room and crossing to her pale stone fireplace.

Amber shifted to the edge of the sofa. "Please do."

Jade stared into the cold fireplace. She wore a gray long-sleeved T-shirt with faded, worn blue jeans. Her feet were covered in gray slipper socks. She was fit, like Crys and Amber, but several inches shorter than her sisters' five foot seven.

"About two years ago, I met with five siblings. Both of their parents had been killed in a tragic traffic accident." Jade turned right, pacing to the bay window overlooking her front yard. Her strides were long but jerky, not her usual confident steps. "An eighteen-wheeler had skidded on some black ice and crashed into their SUV."

"How horrible." Amber's voice was thin.

"Oh, no." Crys winced, imagining the scene. When she'd been a patrol officer, she'd assisted after some heartbreaking traffic accidents.

Jade paused before continuing. "Their mother and father were in their early sixties and in good health. They'd had separate life insurance policies. All five children were listed as equal beneficiaries on both policies. Their parents had paid the insurance premiums for more than three decades. Their accounts were in good standing. However, the insurance company denied their claim."

"On what grounds?" Crys felt a surge of anger on behalf of the offspring.

To lose both parents suddenly and unexpectedly was bad enough. To have to battle unreasonable bureaucrats on top of that would make the grieving process even more painful.

Jade glanced at her as though she'd heard Crys's thoughts and agreed with them. She turned to pace toward the archway that led to her Spartan dining room. "The company based its denial on the traffic accident report, which listed the calculated speed of their parents' SUV as above the limit."

Amber frowned her confusion. "So since the parents were suspected of speeding, the company claimed they were in some way responsible for the accident?"

"That's right." Jade gave a jerky nod. "It denied the siblings' claim, because under its morality clause, deaths that occur during the commission of a crime are not eligible for life insurance benefits."

Amber's winged eyebrows leaped up her forehead. "That seems sketchy at best."

Crys's jaw dropped. "That's outrageous."

"Yes, it is. But this company has a history of denying claims for equally ridiculous reasons." Jade faced Crys and Amber. "The siblings didn't have the money or emotional bandwidth to challenge the company's determination in court. However, one of them found a chat room started by other beneficiaries whose claims this company had denied. The company had recently lost a class action lawsuit. However, instead of paying the multimillion-dollar judgment, it claimed bankruptcy and dissolved. It then reconstituted under a new name but with the same practices. It was first founded in 2022 as Mirrabarre & Shoubern, LLC. At the time I started my investigation, the company was called Stansburrie & Fisk, LLC."

Frowning, Amber glanced at Crys. "Stansburrie & Fisk? Isn't that the company Aunt Kendra worked for?"

Crys's blood went cold. Her lips were numb. She kept her eyes on Jade. "I think that's J's point."

Jade crossed back to her armchair with quick, stiff strides and collapsed into it. She dropped her head into her hands. Her voice was thick with tears. "I think Aunt Kenny was killed because I asked her to be a source for my report."

Crys dropped to her knees in front of her youngest sister and took her in her arms. Behind her, she heard Amber moving. Soon she felt her middle sister holding her and Jade.

Amber cleared her throat. "Remember what you told

us. The only person to blame for Aunt Kendra's murder is the killer."

Crys paused to swallow the lump in her throat. "We'll get through this together. Like we always do."

"You think your aunt was murdered because she was going to be your source for your investigative report?" Luke skimmed several printouts Crys had shared with him.

He and Crys were meeting with Jade in one of the department's small interview rooms Tuesday morning. The sisters had just explained their theory that the motive behind their aunt's murder was Kendra's connection to Jade's investigative report. Crys and Jade had made copies of Jade's files to share with him as evidence supporting their hypothesis.

"That's right." The strain in Jade's expression telegraphed the weight of her guilt and sorrow for whatever role she mistakenly thought she'd played in her aunt's murder. "My independent research confirmed what the families on the message board were claiming—Stansburrie & Fisk denied 30 percent more beneficiary claims than the national average. Aunt Kenny was the administrative assistant to the chief financial officer. I asked for her help with my investigation, if she could find internal memos on claim reviews and processing, anything that would shed light on financial corruption or policies that would favor the company."

"I take it your aunt found something." Luke turned his attention to Crys.

She sat beside Jade on the other side of the rectangular, worn and weathered dark wood desk. Her eyes were clouded with concern. But beyond the clouds, Luke detected a spark of hope. Jade's breakthrough signaled that perhaps this event provided motive behind Kendra Chapel's homicide. And if they had motive, they were several steps closer to solving their aunt's cold case.

"She did." Crys glanced at Jade before continuing. Her riot of ebony curls tumbled past her narrow shoulders. "Aunt K accessed the CFO's hard drive. He had a folder full of executive memos reinforcing the company's policy of incentivizing employees to deny claims. There also were email exchanges between members of the company's administration and directors, documenting the company's goal of increasing premium revenue while minimizing benefit payouts."

"Incredible." Luke shook his head in disgust.

Jade took up the recounting. "Aunt Kenny told me she was going to give me printouts of everything she'd found, but first she wanted to talk to Amber about the legal protections she would have if she were a source for my article."

Crys met Luke's eyes. "When she couldn't meet with Amber, she called me, but I didn't meet with her that night, either." Her voice was still thick with grief.

"None of you could have known Stansburrie & Fisk were aware of your aunt's activities." Luke lowered his eyes to the files in his hands before turning his attention to Jade. "She took precautions to be careful, which makes me wonder. How did they know she was working with you on your report? Your copies of your communication with her show she used her cell phone to text and email you from her personal account."

Jade shrugged restlessly. "I can only speculate that Aunt Kenny's boss somehow realized she'd accessed his hard drive and which folders she'd gone through."

"Did you tell anyone—maybe your editor—that she was your contact for this investigation?" Luke watched Jade closely as he waited for her response.

"Of course not." Jade was adamant. "I protect my sources. And I wouldn't have named her in my report. She was going to provide me with background information only."

"She never got those files to you." Luke made it a statement.

As distraught as the Rashaad sisters were over their aunt's death, Luke suspected Jade would not have allowed her grief to stop her from moving forward with her exposé. Not only would the article have exposed Stansburrie & Fisk's corruption, it also would have ensured her aunt's efforts weren't in vain.

Jade shook her head again. "I've been in her home for almost a year. I haven't come across any thumb drives or printouts with the files she described."

Crys sighed. "It's possible the person who broke into her home and killed her took the drive or printouts. After all, their purpose was to make sure the company's corrupt practices weren't exposed. They would have wanted to destroy those documents themselves."

Crys's theory was the most plausible. He was angry on their aunt's behalf. Everything she went through to try to get justice for the company's policyholders had amounted to nothing.

Luke's eyes lingered on his partner. "I think you have a strong theory for your aunt's murder. If the company suspected she was going to expose them, they may have taken steps to silence her and retrieve those files, then paid Vic to stop the homicide investigation. Have you shared this information with Worchester and Snyder?"

Crys was shaking her head before he finished speaking. "I haven't spoken with them yet. It does seem that Aunt K's and Vic's murders are connected. But Jade has information that also seems to link our serial killer case."

Luke shifted his attention to Jade. Since he and Crys were having a hard time getting traction with their investigation, he was willing to entertain the podcaster's idea. "What do you think connects our case to your aunt's murder?"

Jade glanced at Crys. It was the first time Luke had sensed uncertainty in the younger sister. "I think the victims in the serial killer case you're working may be connected to my report, too."

Luke's eyes widened with surprise. He glanced at Crys before returning his attention to Jade. "What makes you think that?"

Jade held his eyes. "Three of the victims were connected to the life insurance company."

Luke's frown deepened as he searched his memory. "No, they weren't. We did deep background checks."

Crys added her support to Jade's argument. "Remember, the company changed names multiple times over the last four years. You and I weren't aware of that. We weren't looking at the companies. We were looking at the victims."

Jade continued. "The life insurance company started in 2022 as Mirrabarre & Shoubern. After the first lawsuit, it changed its name to Stansburrie & Fisk in 2023. That's when our aunt went to work with them. Alfred Murphy was still a director. It changed its name a second time in 2025 to Shearman & Axel. Alfred Murphy left in 2026, but Sally Stead joined the board at the end of the year when it changed its name to Pieter & Marcus. Rita Gomez joined the board in early 2026 when it became Dragon & Kelp." Jade gestured toward the stack of journals beside the photocopied files. "The names are hard to keep track of, which I think was the administration's goal. But these are the annual reports for each of the company's iterations. You'll find the victims listed as members of the boards of directors at different times."

Luke felt a jolt of excitement. He recognized those names: Mirrabarre & Shoubern, Shearman & Axel and, of course, Dragon & Kelp. As Crys had said, when he'd first seen them on the victim profiles, he'd been focused on the people not the companies. Satisfaction rushed through him. They finally had a break in the case, a connection for their victims. Justice seemed within reach. Regardless of the motive, murder was never the answer.

He refocused on their meeting. "The killer could be someone whose claim was denied when those victims served on the board."

Crys's dark eyes sparkled with anticipation. "That's what we think. Gomez, Murphy and Stead overlapped with the company in 2025. We think that's the year we should focus on when reviewing the denied claims."

"What about Carter Wainscott?" Luke asked. "He was a copycat victim, but do you think he has a connection to the insurance company?"

Crys leaned into the table, reaching for one of the annual reports. She flipped to a page and pointed to Carter Wainscott's name. "He was one of the company's lawyers in 2025. It's possible he was killed to keep him silent—similar to Vic—but whoever killed him wanted us to blame the serial killer."

Luke nodded. It seemed like another solid theory, one well worth pursuing. He caught Crys's eyes. "Let's get a subpoena for those claimant files."

Chapter 11

The offices of Dragon & Kelp, LLC, the fourth revisioning of the life insurance company that seemed to be at the center of their serial killer investigation, were understated luxury. Luke paused beside Crys as they entered the nine-story, glass-and-silver metal structure Wednesday afternoon with four uniformed officers and a search warrant.

The lobby smelled of wood polish and wealth. Its air-conditioning system was set to a brisk temperature that yanked Luke back in time to late autumn, contradicting the calendar's insistence that it was early spring.

Sofas, armchairs and highly polished coffee tables offered cozy conversation spaces across the black-and-white marbled flooring. A handful of healthy potted plants lined the dark wood walls, including one on either side of the glass front doors. Money trees. Subtle. Luke struggled against the negative first-impression vibes the company kept throwing at him.

Crys's delicate features didn't provide Luke any insights. Her expression was determined and resolute as she led their group to the trio of security officers returning their attention with wary curiosity. Luke followed her, interested to see how she would handle the guards.

She inclined her head in greeting and took her badge

from the front pocket of her black cotton slacks. She displayed her identification. "We need to speak with Roland Dragon."

The officers straightened in their seats. The oldest of the three was seated behind one of the two computer monitors. His nametag read Gold.

He glanced at Luke before answering Crys. His dark gray eyes sparked with an interest he tried to mask behind a bored tone and bland fleshy tanned features. "Do you have an appointment?"

Luke raised an incredulous eyebrow. One or two of the officers who stood behind him snickered. How would Crys react to the attempted obstruction?

Her expression didn't change. "Please tell Mr. Dragon, Detective Rashaad and Special Agent Gilchrist are here with four officers to serve a subpoena in a homicide investigation."

Crys's tone was firm but polite. She didn't throw her authority around or try to intimidate the guards in any way. In other words, she didn't exhibit the stereotypical behavior of a cop who abused the public's trust to coerce bribes or solicit undue influence.

All three guard's eyes widened in surprise.

The youngest, a thin Black man whose nametag read Ray typed something into his cell.

Luke nodded toward him. "Who're you texting?"

"My friend, Mason." His hand shook as he extended his arm to show Luke his cell phone screen. The message read, Dude! 5-0's here, investigating a murder.

It could've been worse. Luke pinned the young man with cold eyes. "No more texting."

Mr. Ray gave a jerky nod and pocketed the device. "Yes, sir, Detective. I mean Agent. Special agent."

The third guard, a middle-aged woman with a messy strawberry blond ponytail, was seated in front of the second computer monitor. Her nametag read Rhoades. She pocketed her cell phone as well.

Mr. Gold picked up the telephone receiver and punched in a four-digit extension with his thick, blunt fingers. "Margot, it's Gene at the desk." He smiled, listening to Margot's response. "Well, I have a feeling it's about to get worse. The police are here. They want to speak with Mr. Dragon." He paused again, looking from Crys to Luke and back. "Well, you're gonna have to get him out of that meeting. They have a warrant." Another pause. "Thanks, Margot." Gene cradled the receiver before giving his update. "Margot is getting Mr. Dragon out of his meeting."

"Thank you, Mr. Gold, but we can't wait." Crys looked to Mr. Ray, the only guard not in front of a computer monitor. "Could you please take us to Mr. Dragon's office? Now, please."

Mr. Ray sent an uncertain look toward Gene. The older guard pushed away from his station. Standing, Gene was several inches taller and much broader than the younger guard. "I'll take the police up, Phil. Stay here with Maeve and monitor my station while I'm gone."

"Sure thing, Gene." Phil hopped onto his coworker's vacated chair. His relief was palpable.

Gene escorted Crys, Luke and the four officers to the elevators. Luke remembered Crys's aversion to the conveyers— or maybe it was a preference for stairs?—and smothered a smile. An elevator arrived as the group entered the waiting area. Gene moved aside, allowing its passengers to disembark. Luke ignored the startled looks, curious stares and urgent whispers as employees walked past him and his colleagues, presumably on their way to lunch. Gene led Crys,

Luke and the officers onto the elevator. The guard pressed the button for the ninth floor. Crys was in great shape, but Luke suspected even she was glad they hadn't taken the stairs. The elevator carried them nonstop to their destination, the benefit of arriving during the lunch hour.

Gene led them to the glass doors separating the anteroom from the executive offices. The guard swiped his identification card in front of the electronic reader. Luke heard a swoosh-clang as the lock released and Gene pushed open the door. Luke, Crys and the officers followed Gene to a large office at the end of the hallway.

An annoyed male voice carried through the open door. "And I told *you*, Margot, I'm in the middle of a *very* important meeting. The police will have to wait."

Beside him, Luke sensed Crys stiffen with irritation. He was aggravated, too.

Crys marched into the office. Ignoring the other eight men and women seated around the long, wooden, rectangular desk, she stopped beside the older gentleman at the head of the table and held up her badge. "Mr. Dragon, I presume? As much as we regret turning your day upside down, sir, five people are already dead. We're not waiting."

Luke handed Roland Dragon the warrant. "You can look that over." He tapped the top sheet. "But we'll need all rejected claimant files between 2024 and 2026 today."

A muscle jumped in Roland's jaw as his eyes swept across the warrant's first sheet. He flipped through the attached pages. "Is this some sort of April Fool's joke? If so, I'm not amused."

Luke frowned. It was the first day of April, wasn't it? He shook his head. "No. Not a joke. Murder."

Roland's tanned features flooded with angry color. "Everyone get out." He raised his voice. "Now."

The other executives jumped into action, pushing their wheeled chairs from the table, collecting their files, laptops and computer tablets. How much of their speed in complying with Roland's rude order came from their joy that the meeting was ending early? Luke recognized the look of relief in several of the executives' faces. One attendee was smiling. His expression sobered when he saw Luke watching him. Within seconds, the group was scurrying out of the office like the proverbial rats abandoning a sinking ship.

"Not you, Margot." Roland's bark froze the administrative assistant in her tracks. "Get Sy." His eyes landed on Gene. "You can leave."

"Yes, sir, Mr. Dragon." Gene sounded more tired than offended. He nodded at Crys and Luke. His eyes found Margot on his way from the room. His expression was sympathetic.

Luke had seen Sylvester "Sy" Edmund's name on the company's website, identifying him as Dragon & Kelp's acting chief legal officer. Fine. If Roland wanted to consult the company's lawyer, Luke had no problem with that. But he wasn't leaving without those claimant files. Judging by Crys's strained features, she felt the same way.

He caught Margot's startled blue eyes. "Before you do that, could you take us to where the claimant files are stored, please?"

Blood drained from Margot's round, milky cheeks. She glanced at her boss before offering a stuttering response. "Our claimant files are stored in the basement. On hard drives. We don't have paper. I mean, we don't have paper files."

Luke smiled. "Even better. Thank—"

Roland's tone was testy. "Excuse me, Officer—"

Luke's smile faded. "Special agent."

"Special agent." Roland's smile was condescending. "Don't supersede my orders to my staff."

"Mr. Dragon." Crys lifted her right hand, palm out. "We're investigating multiple homicides involving people connected with your company. In the interest of time, how about while Margot escorts the police officers to the claimant files for the dates in question—thank you, Margot—*you* call Sy and ask him to meet you here?"

Roland's eyes narrowed. "And what will you do?"

Crys circled the conference table and took the seat on Roland's left. "We have some questions for you, Mr. Dragon, starting with where you were the night of Monday, March 23."

The night Brock Mann was murdered. Luke took the seat across the table from Crys on Roland's right. "You'd better call Sy."

"Mr. Dragon didn't have anything to do with these murders, and frankly, your intimation that he did is insulting." Sylvester Edmund looked more like a professional wrestler than the acting chief legal officer of a large life insurance company. He was also the youngest corporate executive Crys could remember meeting. He couldn't be older than her thirty.

Sy seemed to have been itching for a fight since he'd hurried into the room in response to Roland's summons. His deferential reaction toward his boss in contrast to his over-the-top antagonism toward her and Luke signaled that Sy still wasn't secure in his position. Perhaps that was due to the "acting" part of his title.

Crys directed her response to Roland. "Rita Gomez, Alfred Murphy, Sally Stead and Carter Wainscott were on the board of directors of Dragon & Kelp's predecessors. Before becoming Dragon & Kelp's chief executive officer, you also were on the board. You must have known them." She searched Roland's eyes, watching for his reaction.

Seated next to Luke, Sy answered for him. "That doesn't mean Mr. Dragon killed them. Making that assumption is quite a leap."

A glance at Luke warned Crys that he was at least as exasperated as she felt. There was a tightness bracketing his onyx eyes and well-shaped lips.

Crys continued her scrutiny of Roland's body language. "How would you describe your relationship with your former colleagues?"

Roland turned hard gray eyes to hers. His tight muscles and crossed arms were evidence of his anger. "We had a cordial working relationship, Detective Rashaad. All the directors did. We may not always have agreed with every matter, but we were able to discuss things collegially."

His response piqued Crys's interest. "On what matters were you likely to disagree?"

Roland's shrug was stiff. He obviously wasn't used to being questioned. "Business matters, Detective. Operating budgets. New products. Marketing rollouts. Those types of things. Nothing nefarious."

Nothing nefarious. Was that a slip of the tongue? "Do you have any idea why someone would want to kill your colleagues?"

Roland was shaking his head before she'd finished asking her question. "None at all, but then I didn't know them well outside of the board."

Sy waved the search warrant he still clutched in his right hand. "You seem to think it has something to do with our old claims so why are you here questioning us? You should be speaking with our customers."

Luke ignored Sy. "Where were you the night of February 8, between 7:00 and 10:00 p.m.?"

Crys recognized the date as the day before Rita Gomez, their first victim, was discovered; the night she was killed. Crys didn't want to forget that date, or the dates on which they'd found the other victims she thought were connected to the serial homicides and her aunt's murder.

Sy extended his right hand, palm out, toward Roland as he scowled at Luke. "Mr. Dragon doesn't have to answer that."

"Yes, he does." Luke's tone was strained patience. His expression was unreadable. "He can either answer our questions here or accept our escort to the police station."

Roland gave a bored sigh. The sound drew everyone's attention back to him. He tapped the screen of his cell phone, then swiped his right index finger across its surface. "February 8 was a Sunday. My wife and I hosted dinner for my daughter and her family, and Jack Quarrels, the governor's chief of staff, and his family. I believe the evening ended sometime close to 9:00 p.m., but you can confirm that with my wife, if you so choose." He recited his wife's cell phone number for them.

Crys made a note of the contact information. "While you've got your calendar out, could you please also tell us your whereabouts for the evenings of February 23, March 18 and March 23?" Those were the nights Alfred, Sally and Carter were murdered.

Roland's eyes gleamed with a volatile mixture of irritation and arrogance.

Crys tilted her head in question. "I said please." In her peripheral vision, she saw Luke's lips twitch in amusement.

Roland sighed again, then swiped and tapped the face of his cell phone. "The 23rd, my wife and I attended a fundraiser for State Senator Blaire Tiernay. March 18, we were at a birthday party for Clem Slider, the state attorney general. The 22nd was a Sunday. My wife and I hosted dinner for my daughter and her family, and State Representative Conrad Kupp and his family."

Crys noted the who's who list of alibis Roland provided: the governor's chief of staff, a state senator, the state attorney general and a state representative. It was as though he'd known he'd need alibis for those dates. Who better to corroborate your whereabouts than elected public servants? "You don't have many quiet nights alone, do you?"

Roland set his cell phone face down on the table in front of him. "No, Detective Rashaad. I'm a very busy man."

"Too busy to plan much less carry out a series of murders," Sy added in a sharp tone.

"Excuse us, Special Agent Gilchrist, Detective Rashaad." Officer Alice Neat spoke from the conference room doorway. "We've collected all the portable drives with the claimant files from 2024 through 2026."

"Thank you, Officer Neat." Crys inclined her head.

"Thank you." Luke added his gratitude.

Crys continued. "We're almost done here. We should be right behind you." Officer Neat nodded. Crys waited until she and her partner disappeared from the doorway before turning to Roland. "It's possible you could be one of the intended targets. Have you received any strange or threatening messages or phone calls in the last couple of months?"

Roland scowled. "No, I haven't received any threats. If I had, I would have contacted the police."

Crys searched Roland's expression again before turning her attention to Luke, silently asking if he had follow-up questions.

He stood, handing Roland his business card. "Thanks

for your time. We'll be in contact if we have additional questions."

"As we've established, Special Agent Gilchrist, I'm a very busy man." Roland raised Luke's business card. "If you have additional questions, you can call Sy."

Crys exchanged business cards with Sy before following Luke out of Roland's office. Although they needed an ID badge to gain access to the executive suite, they didn't need one to leave.

Luke held the left-side glass door open, allowing Crys to enter the elevator lobby first. "Do you want to take the stairs?" With the lack of inflection in his voice, Crys couldn't tell if he was making fun of her preference for walking. Either way, his flippant comment was an invitation to ease the tension lingering after their encounter with Sy and Roland. Crys accepted his offer with a smile.

"Yes, I would." She pushed through the stairwell door, and her smile became a chuckle. Judging by Luke's expression, he hadn't expected her to take him seriously. Nevertheless, his footsteps were quick and confident beside her as they began the journey down the nine flights of stairs. "Roland's hiding something."

The stairwell was spacious with high ceilings and wide steps. It had been painted a pale tan—walls, steps, landings—with black metal railings and balusters. The air was as chilly as the rest of the building. Either Dragon & Kelp believed the colder climate increased productivity or the company had a tight utilities budget.

"I agree." Luke kept pace beside her as she turned to continue to the seventh-floor landing. "He didn't seem rattled or even concerned when we suggested the killer could target him."

"I know." Crys was distracted by the way Luke's thighs

flexed and relaxed in his dark blue slacks as he descended the stairs with her. *Focus!* "I realize people react to stress and threats differently, but you'd think after telling him his life could be in danger, Roland would've at least asked how close we were to finding the killer."

"Or that he'd have asked us for protection." Luke sounded distracted.

Crys glanced up at him and found him looking at her. Her cheeks warmed as she looked away. "Right."

She continued down the stairwell in silence. Luke was quiet also, as though he was mentally reviewing their interview with Roland and Sy. Crys reviewed snippets of their meeting as well, but she was still distracted by Luke's presence beside her. She caught whiffs of his cedar-and-sea-breeze scent. The warmth from his tall, muscular body reached out to her.

Ignoring these distractions, Crys pushed through the stairwell exit, perhaps with more vigor than she'd intended. Seated behind the security desk, Gene and Maeve jumped. Their heads swiveled to their left as Crys and Luke emerged from the doorway. Phil must have been on rounds.

Regretting her energetic entrance, Crys waved at the duo as she and Luke headed toward the front door. "Thank you for your help."

Maeve smiled. "No problem, Detectives."

Gene looked from Luke to Crys. "Did you get what you came for?"

Luke gave the older man a polite smile. "We'll see."

Crys swung open the glass door, holding it as Luke followed her out. She checked to make sure the parking lot was clear before stepping off the walkway in front of Dragon & Kelp.

Luke's voice carried to her. "Do you want to get something to eat on the way back to the office? Or did you pack one of your lunches that always make me jealous?"

Assured the parking lot was clear, Crys moved forward as she sent a smile at Luke over her shoulder. "I can't help it that—" In her peripheral vision, she saw a low-slung, black sports car racing toward her. Shocked, her head snapped around to face the speeding vehicle. At the same time, hands grabbed her from behind, snatching her off the ground.

"Have mercy!" Maeve's voice squeaked with fear, growing closer to Crys's left.

"That car was coming straight for you." Gene's outraged grumble came from behind Crys.

Crys felt Luke's arms tighten around her. His heart was playing a drum solo against her ear. She was shaking from a combination of her scare and the sensation of having her body pressed so tightly against Luke's. Crys took a deep breath to gather her thoughts. Instead, his scent scattered them, filling her head and making every muscle in her body weak.

She opened her eyes to see Luke's right shoulder, and Maeve and Gene standing side by side.

"Are you all right?" Luke's question rumbled from his chest and sounded above her head. His words were sharp and unsteady.

Crys made herself step away from his warmth. "Yes, thanks to you." She held his dark eyes as she conveyed her gratitude. "I thought the lot was clear."

Luke scowled. His eyes sparked with anger. "That car came out of nowhere. Gene's right. It was coming straight for you." He turned to the security guards. "Thank you for your concern. We're going back to the department."

"Sure. Sure." Gene's eyes were clouded with a doubt that contradicted his certainty. "I guess you both can file your own incident report." Thin humor traced his words.

"Yes." Maeve took a step back toward the building's entrance. "But you know where we are if you need witness statements."

"Maeve's right." Gene jerked a thumb toward his partner. "You got a better look at the car than we did, but if you need us to corroborate your claim, just call the company's main number and ask for us. We'll be glad to fill out a report."

"Thank you." Feeling steadier, Crys took another step away from Luke.

This time, she double-checked the parking lot before stepping into it. She felt Luke hovering beside her as though ready to sweep her off her feet again at the hint of trouble. Crys was grateful for his concern. She was still trying to process what happened. She was certain she'd checked both ends of the parking lot before she moved forward. Even so, that car had driven so quickly. It had been moving too fast. This was a parking lot, not Interstate 270.

She pressed the key fob to unlock the doors of their department-issued tan sedan.

Luke extended his right hand toward her, palm up. "I'll drive."

Crys turned over the key fob and changed direction, heading toward the passenger side of the car while Luke crossed behind her on his way to the driver's seat. She was sure she could've driven, but she didn't want to argue. Crys buckled her seat belt while Luke started the engine.

"Didn't Marco, Officer Robledo, say witnesses reported Vic's daughter had been struck by a black sports car?" he asked.

"That's right." The thought had just occurred to her as well. A coincidence? She didn't think so.

"Someone was targeting you." Luke's expression was grim as he guided the sedan to the lot's exit. "Crys, I think it's time you and I talked. And your sisters should join us."

"All right, but what do we need to talk about?"

"I promise I'll answer all your questions when we meet."

Crys scowled at his too-attractive, tense profile. She wasn't long on patience. After working in each other's pocket for the past almost two weeks, she would've thought he'd have noticed that. But one thing she always had a lot of were questions. And they were mounting by the moment.

Chapter 12

"**W**hy is he here?" Jade came up short as she followed her sisters into Luke's family room Wednesday evening.

The temperature took a sudden, deep drop as the three women looked at Caleb, standing at the other end of the room. Her reaction was better than Luke had expected. Judging by Caleb's more relaxed posture, he was relieved as well.

"We're going to need his help." Luke shoved his hands into the front pockets of his navy slacks. He told himself it was because of the sudden chill in the air, but he knew it was to keep from reaching for Crys's hand.

"His help with what?" Crys's expression was puzzled—and a bit impatient. "Why are you being so secretive?"

"I don't mean to be." Luke pulled his right hand from his pocket and gestured toward the sofa. "But this will take some time to explain. Why don't you make yourselves comfortable?"

The sisters' hesitation was brief but noticeable. They seemed to assess Caleb as Crys led the way to the coffee-colored mid-century modern sofa to the left of the room.

Crys's riot of brown curls bounced as she settled into the left corner. She was still wearing the hip-hugging brown slacks and the tan pullover decorated with dots of red tulips that flowed over her torso like wine. Luke noticed his sofa was almost the exact color of her hypnotic eyes. That realization would distract him every time he walked into the room in the future.

Jade sat in the middle of the sofa. Her eyes swept his great room, seeming to land on everything but Caleb. She wore tapered-leg blue jeans and a loose, lightweight, black boatneck sweater. She'd gathered her mass of brown curls and restrained them in a warm blue ponytail holder. Sterling silver earrings in the shape of a cross hung from her ears.

Amber was on Jade's right. She'd crossed her long, slender legs and angled herself toward her younger sister. Her body language was protective. The prosecutor had accessorized her gray pinstripe suit and white scoop neck blouse with a single-strand pearl necklace and matching earrings. Her heavy brown, wavy tresses framed her diamond-shaped face and streamed past her narrow shoulders.

"I'm not the enemy." Caleb straightened from the threshold dividing the family and dining rooms. His declaration shattered the tense silence. Luke had never seen his friend so confrontational.

"I can't hear that right now." Jade's voice was low. She still wouldn't look at him. "You were hired at a higher salary than mine. Two months later, a colleague who was preparing to retire and I were 'let go.'" She used air quotes. "Brock said it was because the newspaper was in financial trouble." Jade took a shuttering breath, still staring at the hardwood floor. "Do you know what that job meant to me? It *defined* me. So no, you're not the enemy, but I don't know if we can ever be friends."

Crys put her hand on Jade's left shoulder. Amber squeezed Jade's right hand.

Caleb nodded his understanding. "I hope one day we can be. I'd really like that."

The muscles in Luke's back eased. Caleb and Jade had taken a first step toward at least an uneasy truce. "Ladies, thank you for joining us. We know it's your Sisters Night, but there are too many connections between our homicide investigation and your aunt's cold case."

Crys gestured toward Jade. "My sister's already walked us through the connection between Dragon & Kelp, the serial killer's victims and Aunt K. That's why we spoke with Roland Dragon this afternoon."

Caleb carried one of the modern, gray-fabric-and-black-wood chairs from Luke's dinette set into the family room. "What did he say when you asked him about those connections?"

Luke sank onto the armchair to the right of his matching sofa. "I'll satisfy your journalistic curiosity later." He turned his attention to Crys. "I think there's even more going on."

"Something more than murders?" Amber lifted her winged eyebrows. "I see the connection with Dragon & Kelp. If they suspected Aunt Kendra was going to divulge alleged corruption in their benefits approval process, that would give them motive for her murder. If they suspected Vic was going to expose their possible involvement in our aunt's murder, that could connect them to Vic's death. What other links do you see?"

Jade shifted to better face Luke. "And what do you think was Brock's connection?"

Caleb took her question. "Brock asked you to drop your investigation into the insurance company."

"Asked?" Jade rolled her eyes. "He ordered me to stop investigating. He said there wasn't a story there, but he was wrong."

Caleb cocked his head. "What did he say when you told him that?"

"Nothing." Jade's jaw tightened briefly. "Then a week later, I was tossed out."

"I couldn't understand his decision to let you go." Caleb's attention was steady on Jade. "You're a tough investigator with multiple awards for your reporting."

Amber hummed her agreement. "You were laid off in the middle of your investigation. Then your editor was murdered by someone who was trying to frame him as the serial killer."

Luke's brow furrowed. "Did he know your aunt was providing you with information?"

"I've already told you no. Of course not." Jade's voice skipped with emotion. "I have never, nor would I ever, reveal confidential sources. That goes triple for my family."

Crys squeezed Jade's shoulder again. The gesture seemed comforting and protective at the same time. "We think her boss must have found out she'd logged into his computer."

"She reported to the chief financial officer, right?" Luke looked at each sister in turn, letting his eyes come to rest on Jade. "Who was that?"

Jade hesitated. "At the time, it was Roland Dragon, who's now the CEO." She glanced at her sisters seated on either side of her. "I verified that from my notes earlier today."

Amber rubbed her forehead. "These coincidences are piling up. Luke's right. This is too much to ignore."

Luke drew a breath to force the words past his lips. "And a black, low-slung sports car similar to the one that struck your partner's daughter almost hit you."

Color drained from Jade's face. "She told us over dinner. Thank you so much for watching out for her."

Amber's eyes were huge. "Yes, thank you. We're so grateful."

"Of course." Luke hadn't recovered from the scare. He could only imagine how rattled Crys felt.

Caleb's voice was warm with concern. "I'm glad you're safe. That must have been frightening."

Crys's eyes met and held his. "Yes, it was. Thankfully, Luke has great reflexes."

Luke's heart stopped again as he relived that moment. He remembered the pain in his chest as his heart restarted with a vengeance. He'd held her tightly to him. Perhaps too tightly. He'd been trying to comfort her and reassure himself.

He stood and paced the room. His stocking feet were silent against the maple wood flooring. His steps carried him to his gray-stone-and-maple wood fireplace. "Which brings me to what I wanted to discuss with you."

"Finally." Crys's tone was dry.

He faced her. "When that car came flying out of nowhere, heading straight toward you, the first thing that occurred to me was pulling you to safety."

"Thank God for that." Amber's words were heartfelt.

Luke exhaled. "But then, when I knew you were safe, all the connections we just talked about piled into my mind. And something else as well." The room seemed to narrow, leaving just the two of them. "About three months ago, someone filed a complaint against you alleging corruption. I was assigned to investigate you."

Crys surged to her feet. Her eyes widened. Angry color flooded her cheeks. "What?"

Luke thought he'd braced himself for Crys's reaction to his confession, but nothing could have prepared him for the look of betrayal in her eyes. He felt like he'd been sucker punched. She stood just out of his reach but close enough for him to feel the currents of anger and outrage swirling around her.

What could he say to make things right with her? For her?

"Excuse us?" Jade's voice was rough with temper, breaking his concentration.

"What are you saying?" Amber bit off the question.

Their voices were faint and faraway, but he felt the force of their combined fury rising with Crys's. He respected the loyalty and love behind their reactions, but his focus now was not on them. It was all on Crys.

Luke continued. "My boss told me she'd taken an anonymous complaint from a caller who'd alleged you and Vic were soliciting bribes from suspects and their families to tamper with evidence."

His words acted like dry kindle on the already roaring flames of the Rashaad sisters' anger.

"That's preposterous." Amber slashed her right hand across the air in front of her.

"Seriously?" Jade's voice was strained as though she struggled to keep her anger in check.

Crys balled her hands into fists at her sides. "I have never taken advantage of vulnerable people or been involved in any type of corruption. How could you even think that of me?"

Luke raised his hands, palms out. "I didn't know you then. I was given a case to investigate and that's what I did. I—"

"Was this all a game to you?" Crys cut him off. Her eyes blazed at him. "Investigation by cosplay? Did these victims mean nothing to you?"

Luke stiffened. "Of course they did. I wasn't pretending to work with you to stop this serial killer. You know that."

Still visibly angry, Crys circled his coffee table to stop

a foot from him. "Why wasn't I told I was under investigation?"

The outcome of this exchange was too important for so many reasons. The murder victims, including Crys's aunt and Vic, needed justice. Dragon & Kelp had to be held accountable for their alleged fraud. And his feelings for Crys, which grew stronger every day.

Luke braced his hands on the back of the armchair to steady himself. "Our supervisors thought it would be better to bring me in to observe you firsthand while we worked to solve these homicides."

Crys's winged eyebrows knitted. Her eyes clouded with confusion. "*Our* supervisors? Jasper knew about these allegations?"

The pain in her voice landed heavily in his chest. Luke drew a deep breath, catching a sample of her wildflower fragrance. "He did. Yes."

Crys stumbled back a step as though the revelation rocked her. "He lied to me. He said he didn't know why the BCI had assigned you to work with me."

"The alternative was for your boss to admit you were under investigation." Jade's tone was dust dry. "There was no way he was going to do that."

Amber offered a more diplomatic perspective. "In fairness, he probably couldn't have told you, you were being investigated for corruption."

Caleb spread his hands. "Luke needed to catch you in the act or get you to incriminate yourself."

"That's right." Luke had forgotten other people were in the room. "But there were signs from the start that you weren't involved in any wrongdoing. Your former supervisors and the officers in your precinct only had positive comments about you. They said you were professional, caring, determined and fearless. All things I've noticed about you myself."

His words didn't have any effect on Crys. Her features were stiff with anger. "Does this mean I'm no longer being investigated?"

Luke rubbed the tight muscles in the back of his neck. "Crys, just as I suspect Jade was laid off because she wanted to expose Dragon & Kelp, I believe someone submitted an anonymous complaint against you to get you removed from the department."

Crys's eyes widened in shock. "Removed from the department? I would've been put in jail."

Amber gasped. "You think they're willing to ruin my sister's life to escape exposure?"

Caleb stood, circling his chair to stand behind it. "If Jade and Luke are right, they killed your aunt for the same reason. Having Crys put in jail is less of a stretch."

"Easy for you to say." Jade flung the words at her former colleague. "You're not the one they're trying to destroy."

"That's true." Caleb inclined his head. "I apologize."

Turning her back to Luke, Crys paced the short distance to his fireplace. "Who could be behind this? Roland Dragon?"

Luke noted the stiffness in her movements. It bothered him knowing he'd caused it. "It's possible. Whoever's pulling our strings must be in a position of power to have you investigated, Jade laid off, and your aunt and Vic killed."

"You're right." Amber balanced her elbows on her lap and folded her hands together. "They would have to be well-connected, politically and socially, to have access to people who could help them cover the company's corruption."

Caleb straightened away from his chair. "And he'd have

to have wealth. He bribed Vic, and I'm sure he would've had to bribe Brock."

Jade stood, crossing to the opposite side of the room from Caleb. "Roland Dragon fits that profile. He's one of the wealthiest people in the Midwest. He has powerful political and social connections. And, more significantly, he's been on the board throughout each of the insurance company's iterations."

Caleb arched a thick, black eyebrow. "He's jumped to the top of my suspect list. He's been with the company a long time."

Luke sighed. "I'm also concerned my boss might be involved."

Crys stiffened. Amber gasped. Jade bit off an exclamation. The only person who didn't react was Caleb. Luke had shared his suspicions about his boss with his longtime friend before the Rashaad sisters had arrived. He'd also confided to Caleb his intent to tell Crys he'd been tasked with investigating her for corruption. Caleb had warned him about the potential perils of confessing his transgression in front of Amber and Jade. But Luke knew how close Crys and her sisters were. Because of their relationship, he wanted to make the admission in front of all of them.

Luke gestured toward Crys. "I don't have evidence, only a gut feeling. I keep telling Martina you don't fit the profile of a cop on the take. You're not living above your means. You drive an old car, and you pack homemade lunches. I also told her you'd volunteered the information about Vic's corruption and turned the documents over to Jasper to determine whether all Vic's cases should be reviewed. Despite that, Martina's determined that I continue investigating you."

As much as he enjoyed spending time with Crys, the

subterfuge made him uncomfortable, especially since he was certain she was innocent.

Crys continued to pace between the sofa and the wood-and-stone fireplace. "You're suspicious of your boss's intent. We believe Jade's boss fired her to prevent her from exposing the insurance company. Do you think Jasper could be involved? You said he knew I'd been accused of corruption. Instead of confronting me with the allegations, he let you work with me under false pretenses."

Luke winced at her summary of the situation, although she was right. "I don't know. We shouldn't take any chances by sharing our investigation with either Jasper or Martina. We'll let them know we're looking for connections between the deaths. But we shouldn't let anyone outside of this group know we've connected the murders to the insurance company. We don't know who we can trust."

"Agreed." Crys gave a curt nod, then turned to Jade. "People who were on the board of Dragon & Kelp are being murdered. Have you found any other connections with the insurance company?"

Jade shook her head. "I haven't found Aunt Kenny's files, either. I'm still looking."

"Thanks, J." Crys tilted her head as she considered Luke in a moment of silence. "I'm not corrupt."

"I know. I'm sorry." Luke realized he was holding his breath as he waited for her verdict.

Crys nodded again. "You were doing your job."

"Thanks." Luke smiled his relief. He'd been given a reprieve—hope that they could start over.

"Can I speak with you privately?" Luke touched Crys's forearm to delay her leaving his home Wednesday evening.

After he, Crys, Caleb, Amber and Jade agreed to meet

again Sunday to review any new information they'd come across, the group started toward the door. But Luke had one more thing he needed to address with Crys and this time in private.

Crys sent a look toward her sisters who'd stopped when they realized she'd been delayed. "Jade drove Amber and me here."

Luke glanced at the two women standing behind Crys before meeting her eyes. "I'll drive you home."

Crys hesitated, possibly weighing the pros and cons of giving him more of her time tonight after learning he'd been investigating her for alleged corruption for months. It was jarring, watching someone who was usually impatient to act hesitate to respond to him. It was another sign of the shift in their relationship and not in a good way.

Her sisters were also reacting to his request. Amber stared at him intently, trying to read his intentions. Jade's distrust was tangible and something he could understand since he had trust issues as well. The youngest Rashaad might be wondering whether Crys had forgiven him too soon. In the background, Caleb lingered with his hand on the doorknob, watching for the outcome of this silent stand-off.

"Sure." Crys looked at her sisters over her shoulder. "I'll be OK."

Amber gave a nod of acceptance before embracing her elder sister. "OK. We'll catch up with you later."

"Text us when you get home." Jade hugged Crys while sending Luke a warning look behind her sister's back.

Luke escorted his guests out before facing Crys. "Thanks again for understanding that I was doing my job."

"I don't like that you withheld that you were investigating me." She crossed her arms over her chest. "But I agree rooting out corruption is important, especially in agencies that are supposed to serve the public. We have to earn the trust we ask our community to give us."

"That's right." He closed the distance between them, coming to within an arm's length of her. Close enough to catch a trace of her scent, a hint of her warmth. "I'm concerned that Martina keeps pushing my investigation. After today's attempt on your life, I'm worried whoever's trying to keep you and Jade from exposing potential fraud at Dragon & Kelp has moved to a new, much deadlier tactic."

Crys rubbed her upper arms as though she felt a sudden chill. "You could be right. Thank you again for having my back."

That phrasing minimized the heart-stopping, bone-chilling fear he'd experienced as he saw her almost step into the path of the high-speed locomotive masquerading as a low-slung sports car.

Luke tried a more direct approach. "Crys, I think someone's trying to kill you, probably the same people who targeted Brock, Vic, Carter Wainscott and your aunt."

She stilled. "I got that, and I'll tell you what I told my sisters. I'll be careful and pay closer attention to my surroundings."

"That's not good enough." Luke rubbed the back of his neck. Crys wasn't taking the threat as seriously as she should. Fine. He was worried enough for both of them. "You need protection."

"I'm a detective. I provide protection." She hooked her hands on her slim hips. "I also filed a report, remember? And Jasper said he'd ask for increased patrols in my neighborhood." She lowered her arms. "Perhaps we should take his promises with a grain of salt since he also lied to me."

Luke stiffened with offense. "I didn't lie to you."

Crys tipped her head. "Lying by omission is lying."

"I was doing—" He cut himself off. "Let's stay focused. Whoever's targeting you has already killed at least four other people. They got to Brock in the newspaper's secure building. What makes you think they couldn't get to you?"

"I've got a high-quality home security system and a gun." Crys held his eyes. "I'll also have patrols in the area. Allegedly."

Frustration pushed Luke to pace away from her. "That's not good enough, Crys, and you know it." He spoke over his shoulder. "If one of your sisters were in this situation, you'd agree with me."

"Oh, come on, Luke. That isn't even analogous." From her tone of voice, Luke imagined Crys throwing her arms up behind him. "Neither of my sisters is in law enforcement. They don't have my training."

"Even if they did, you'd still think they needed protection." He turned to her again. "You wouldn't want them to be alone."

Crys frowned her confusion. "What do you want me to do, then? I'm not hiding in some safe house for who knows how long."

Luke crossed his arms over his chest. "I'll stay with you."

"What?" Crys's expression blanked with surprise. "Where?"

He shook his head. "Your house sounds safe enough for now with your security system. But you shouldn't be alone. You need someone to watch your back at least until we solve this case. Someone with training in handling dangerous situations."

"Someone like you." Her eyes moved over him in a way that made him think of firm mattresses and tangled sheets.

Focus!

He repeated all the arguments she'd just made. "I also have training and a gun. If someone's watching you, my presence in your house should dissuade them from trying to get to you there. They'd have two law enforcement professionals to deal with."

"I like those odds." She stepped back, moving toward the front door. "But I've got this covered. Thanks anyway, Luke."

Luke tried but failed to keep the strain and frustration from his voice. "Either I stay in your home with you, sleeping on your sofa, or I park my car in your driveway until we catch the serial killer, the copycat and the person who's out to get you."

"You wouldn't."

"Try me." He thought he heard her grinding her teeth.

After several long seconds, she finally relented.

"Fine." Crys threw up her arms. "It will be my incentive to find these killers even faster."

"That's hurtful." Luke crossed to his coat closet opposite his front door and pulled out his packed suitcase.

"You've already packed a bag?" Her words were heavy with disbelief. "Were you that sure I'd agree to your idea?"

"I've seen your compassionate nature." Luke opened the front door. "Even though it's spring, it would still be cold at night in your driveway. I was hoping you'd remember that and take pity on me."

Crys rolled her eyes as she walked out of his home. "My pity for your situation could be withdrawn at any time."

He was aware of that, too.

Chapter 13

"Leave your suitcase at the foot of the stairs and I'll give you the nickel tour." Crys met Luke's dark eyes over her shoulder late Wednesday evening. She led him down the short hallway from her home's entryway into her kitchen.

Crys feared she was betraying her parents by allowing an investigator who'd suspected her of corruption into their family home.

Mom, Dad, I hope you'll grant me some grace. The only reason he's here is to keep me safe.

As she took a moment to settle her nerves, she let her eyes land on sections of her entryway, family room and dining area. Memories of growing up here nurtured by love and buoyed by laughter healed her.

"Your expression tells me the memories in this house are worth much more than that nickel." Luke's eyes seemed to smile at her as they moved across her face.

Crys's cheeks grew warm. She turned away, embarrassed that she'd already given away more of herself to the man who'd been investigating her in secret. As much as she'd grown to like and even admire Luke, his subterfuge disturbed her.

She stopped at the end of the hallway and gestured to her

left. "Family room." She spread her right arm. "Kitchen. I hope you're not a slob."

An image of his immaculate and well-organized office came to mind. No one could ever accuse Luke Gilchrist of being sloppy.

"Your home is beautiful. I promise to treat it with respect." His deep voice sounded behind her. The sincerity in his words was reassuring. His eyes lingered on her bay windowsill and her plant menagerie. He glanced at the pictures and trinkets on the fireplace mantel.

She made an impartial visual sweep of the family room. Its pale hardwood flooring was well maintained. The thick floral-patterned, powder-blue sofa and matching love seat, and the polished honey wood coffee table were starting to show their age. In a year or so the warm cream walls would need a fresh coat of paint. The photos and mementos gathered on the polished dark-wood-and-black-metal shelving preserved some of her family's fondest memories.

Turning right, she crossed to the kitchen, scanning its small, circular honey wood table and matching chairs, brown-and-white tile flooring, pale yellow walls and silver appliances. Her home didn't look to her like an extortionist's residence.

Crys walked through the narrow threshold from the kitchen and gestured toward the white faux leather chairs and honey wood table in front of her. "Dining room."

She walked to the large picture window overlooking her backyard and pulled the heavy mocha curtains closed. To her left, wood-and-black metal shelving carried a variety of thriving green, leafy, potted plants. Crys gave them a quick once-over before turning Luke's attention to the living room.

Light hardwood flooring continued from the dining

room. A well-worn overstuffed rust-colored cloth sofa and matching chair-and-ottoman set stood on either side of a simple honey wood, rectangular coffee table. An abstract, jewel-toned area rug lay beneath the table. Again, the furnishings were attractive and comfortable, but no one could accuse her of living beyond her detective's salary. Did Luke agree? He'd seemed relaxed during her brief guided tour. She'd sensed his curiosity, but he'd kept his thoughts to himself.

"You really like roses and flowers." His statement was part question.

"Crime scenes are the stuff of nightmares." Crys kept her back to him. The words had been ripped from her before she could stop them. Angry with herself, she felt compelled to defend her statement. "I'm proud of what I do, working to bring justice to victims and their survivors, helping to prevent future tragedies. But when I get home, I want to remember that the beauty in the world far outnumbers the ugliness."

"That was very well said." His soft words felt like an embrace.

Crys squelched a spurt of aggravation. Why had she shared such a personal thought with him? She didn't need to give him any more information about her. She crossed to the stairs. "I'll show you to the guest room."

"Thank you." There was a wary quality to his voice as though he'd sensed her irritation.

Crys gave a mental shrug. She couldn't help the way she felt. "Of course." She tossed a hand toward the plain brown wood door beside the staircase. "Basement. That's where the laundry, exercise and workrooms are."

"Workroom?" Luke straightened from picking up his

suitcase. Standing two steps beneath her, the top of his head came to her shoulder.

"Yes, my parents were quite handy." Crys felt a slight smile trace her lips. She turned sideways on the narrow staircase and gestured toward the living room beside them. "For example, they made the tables in the living room, dining room, family room and kitchen." She heard the pride in her voice.

Luke's eyes widened with surprise. "Really? They were very talented."

"Yes, they were." Crys's voice was low as memories drew her back in time.

Her parents were amateur do-it-yourselfers. Crys recalled their enthusiasm at the start of a project, their eventual frustration with the chore and each other, their dogged determination to finish what they started, and finally their pride in their accomplishment. The memories almost made her laugh.

She continued up the steps before Luke noticed. Crys heard his footsteps following behind her easily as though the suitcase didn't hinder him. He must have packed light, which meant he didn't expect to room with her for long. That was a good thing. Right? Crys gave herself another mental shake. Of course it was.

At the top of the stairs, she turned to her right. "You can use this room. It was mine, then it was Jade's before she moved into our aunt's house."

Crys stepped aside, letting Luke enter the space first. While he took in his surroundings, she pulled towels from the nearby linen closet. "The bedsheets are clean. I'll put these towels in the guest bathroom down the hall."

"Thank you." Luke sounded distracted as his eyes toured the bright, welcoming space.

It was the second-largest bedroom in Crys's family home. On each pale gold wall hung two hand-sized plaques. Some were inscribed with prayers. The rest shared quotes from famous historical figures, including Dr. Martin Luther King Jr., Dorothy Parker and Joan Baez. Two large windows overlooked the quiet street at the front of the house. A large closet had been built into the opposite wall. Her parents had built matching honey wood nightstands that were positioned on either side of the queen-size bed to the left of the room. A honey wood dressing table with mirror stood to the right.

Luke stopped a few strides from the doorway. His eyes moved over the warm silver drapes, which were open, displaying the sheer white curtains. A matching silver coverlet spread across the thick mattress. Silver-and-black-patterned area rugs circled the hardwood flooring around the bed.

"This was your room?" His low voice made the muscles in her abdomen quiver.

"Years ago. Then Jade moved in, and I took my parents' room down the hall." Crys leaned against the threshold, crossing her arms.

"It's very comfortable." Luke nodded toward the nightstands. "Did your parents build those nightstands, too? They're similar to the furniture downstairs."

Crys smiled. "Yes, they did. They had a thing for honey wood."

"May I ask when they passed?" He faced her.

Crys's smile disappeared. "That information wasn't in my file?"

"You haven't forgiven me." Was there a hint of pain in his voice?

"Yes, I have." Crys was quick to correct him. "I understand why you were investigating me. I know your agency does important work. But, Luke, you were spying on me behind my back, pretending to help me with this case—"

"I wasn't pretending. I want to catch this serial killer, too."

"You interviewed people I work with. How does that make me look?" Crys blinked back tears, not of weakness but of rage.

Luke closed his eyes briefly as though acknowledging her discomfort. "I'll apologize as often as you need me to." He looked at her. "As often as you want me to."

She swept a hand in front of herself. "I don't need an apology. I need to figure out how to face my colleagues tomorrow and the next day and all the days after that."

"I'm so sorry, but once you're exonerated—"

"What do I do until then?" She waited, but he didn't answer. "Right. I forgive you, Luke, but I can't trust you. Not anymore."

Crys retreated to her room, pausing only to set the fresh towel set in the guest bathroom as promised. Earlier today, Luke had saved her life. She would always be grateful for that. But her gratitude was tempered by his breaking her heart.

"We've got to come up with a better system." Crys collapsed against the cushioned back of her wheeled office chair late Thursday morning. Their desks were surrounded by the cacophony of ringing phones, clacking keyboards and heated discussions.

She pinned her already tired eyes on Luke, seated behind his desk. His button-down, cool-green shirt and emerald tie contrasted with the more conservative image he had presented when they'd first met. She liked the change, even though it made it harder for her to ignore him or her physical attraction to him. It had been a struggle to keep her eyes from lingering on him during breakfast.

Jade would have called the meal the dictionary definition of awkward. Not surprising, considering the uncomfortable way they'd parted the night before. Crys didn't know how Luke had spent his first night in her family home. She'd read until she'd given up and forced herself into a restless sleep. She'd woken early to find Luke already on her treadmill. She'd taken her anger and frustration out on her freestanding, black vinyl punching bag. Afterward, they'd cleaned up, gotten dressed and made breakfast together. Like a couple—or good friends.

By unspoken agreement, they'd driven to work separately. They weren't doing anything inappropriate, but Crys didn't want her colleagues to think she'd slept her way out of an ethics complaint. The thought of their treating her with skepticism made her stomach lurch. She'd only worked in their department for a little more than eight months. In that time, her partner had been killed, and she was being investigated for allegations of corruption. With an introduction like that, could she ever gain their respect?

Luke rubbed the back of his neck. Crys could almost see the tension shimmering around him. "I agree. We need a more efficient process." He checked his expensive-looking silver metal band wristwatch. "We've been reviewing these insurance claimant files for more than two hours, and I haven't even made a dent in my half."

"And I've barely scratched the surface of my stack." Frustration left a metallic taste in her mouth. This review stage was the first step toward creating a solid list of suspects for their serial killer.

Luke tossed a hand toward the folders on his desk. "At this rate, we won't be able to start a suspect list for at least a month. Who would have thought a life insurance company would have so many rejected beneficiary claims?"

"Dragon & Kelp's denial rate is way above industry standard. That's what triggered Jade's investigation in the first place." Crys stood, wanting to stretch her legs. Her black loafers were silent as she paced across the linoleum flooring toward their crime scene board.

She heard the pride in her voice and gave a mental shrug. She had a lot to be proud of. Both her sisters were intelligent, fearless, determined people who, like her, were dedicated to the pursuit of justice.

"There are a few denials claiming premiums hadn't been paid." Luke's voice broke into her thoughts. "But most of the responses are the same, the insured didn't have a medical exam on file."

"I noticed that, too." Crys spoke over her shoulder. The calm, steady cadence of Luke's voice helped her focus. "We should dig into the beneficiaries whose claims were denied because of this."

Behind her, papers rustled as he searched through his claims. "I understand what you're saying. The insured had been paying those premiums for years—in some cases decades—and when it came time for their beneficiary to access the account, their claim was denied for a process reason. It was an issue that should have been caught before the account was approved."

"Exactly." Crys turned to face him, momentarily distracted by his intense gaze on her. "It would have really ticked me off—especially on behalf of whoever had paid into that policy—if my claim was denied because Dragon & Kelp didn't have medical reports on file for my loved one. That didn't stop the company from depositing the premiums so why would it stop them from awarding the claim?"

Luke's fingers tapped across his keyboard as he made a note in his computer. "Those circumstances could be the motivation behind the murders. We'll prioritize those beneficiaries. That still leaves us with a lot of denied claims, though."

"But we're whittling it down." Crys returned to her seat feeling more energized. She caught the scent of her cooling, dark roast coffee. "We're also looking for denied claims that Rita Gomez, Alfred Murphy and Sally Stead signed."

"Right." Luke added more notes to his computer file. "Three of the five director signatories, which implies we have at least two more potential targets."

"That's right." Crys sat back in her chair. She lifted her heavy hair away from the back of her neck, then let it fall. A spark flared in Luke's eyes before he dropped them to his desk. Heat rolled over Crys's skin, chasing away the slight chill from the room. She straightened in her seat. "There were fifteen directors on the board a year ago."

Luke spoke toward his desk. "Considering the company randomly selected directors for each claim sign-off, it's anyone's guess the combination of directors who signed off on the suspect's denied claim."

"And what about our copycat?" Crys folded her hands on the desk in front of her. "How do they fit in?"

"That's a good question." Luke met her eyes again. "What part did the lawyer, Carter Wainscott, play in this insurance fraud, because that's what it was. Your aunt, Vic, Brock and Carter were most likely murdered to protect this scam."

"Yes." Crys's gut roiled with outrage and sorrow. Her eyes landed on the crime scene board and Carter's photo. "Vic was killed even though he'd helped torpedo my aunt's homicide investigation. My aunt was murdered to prevent her from exposing the company's corrupt business practices. Brock was killed although he'd fired my sister to keep her from investigating Dragon & Kelp. What had Carter done?"

"The copycat could be someone with Dragon & Kelp who's tying up loose ends."

Crys returned her attention to Luke. "That's the best theory we have. But why change the MO? They shot my aunt, Vic and Brock. Why make Carter look like one of the serial killer's victims?"

Luke considered the crime scene board. "Maybe they're not the one who killed your aunt, Vic or Brock. Maybe this is someone else."

Crys looked at Luke with wide eyes. "You think we're looking for three murderers?"

Luke spread his hands. "What else explains it? We have to consider the shift in MO. Even Brock's death was different from your aunt's and Vic's. But Carter's death was deliberately staged so the serial killer would take the blame."

"And Brock was set up to take the fall for the killer. That was a distraction."

"A distraction from what? What did Carter's killer want to hide?"

Crys approached the board. She heard Luke following her. "Maybe Carter's killer is trying to hide the serial killer."

As she studied the images of the evidence, victims and secondary crime scenes, the crazy theory took shape in her mind. She turned to Luke and found him nodding his agreement.

"The identity of the actual serial killer and their motive." He held her eyes. "Dragon & Kelp knows who's killing their former directors and why."

The idea rattled her. "And the why is what they don't want the public to find out."

"I can feel your cold shoulder from here." Luke spoke with his back to Crys as he scrubbed the skillet they'd used to cook the seared chicken breasts for dinner Thursday evening.

The scents of the sea salt, pepper, onions and oregano lingered in the kitchen. He wondered whether the extra pepper in the chicken and spinach was part of his punishment for lying to her or if Crys preferred her food spicy.

She looked up from the dishwasher where she was shaking the powder detergent into the dispenser, giving him the stingiest glance before returning her attention to her chore. "I appreciate your willingness to watch my back until whoever's trying to harm me is caught." Her voice was colder than Columbus in January, calling the lie to her words. "My sisters do, too."

"Of cour—"

She cut him off. "And although I know you were just doing your job, I'm not happy that you've been prying into my personal life for weeks and know so much about me while I know practically nothing about you."

"I'm sorry, Crys." Luke finished drying the pan and returned it to the cupboard from which he'd seen Crys take it. "As I told you, I'm willing to apologize and keep apologizing until you forgive me."

"I don't want you to keep saying sorry." Crys straightened from the dishwasher. She pinned him with a challenging look. "I want you to tell me something personal about yourself."

Luke stiffened, immediately on guard. "What do you want to know?"

"Anything. Tell me something about you that few other people know." Crys leaned back against the kitchen counter beside the dishwasher. "I feel exposed and vulnerable knowing you've dug into my past, spoke with my coworkers and read my personnel files. I have to balance the scales. So, spill."

Rubbing the tension from the back of his neck, Luke searched the kitchen's white linoleum floor. He struggled to come up with something to share that would satisfy Crys's sense of justice. "Well, I'm not sure what to say. I'm an only child. My parents had me later in life. They passed away a few years ago."

"I'm so sorry." The compassion in her voice eased some of his discomfort.

"Thank you." His lips curved in a spontaneous smile. "I envy your relationship with your sisters. Growing up, I always wanted siblings."

Crys's dark eyebrows knitted. Her eyes probed his as though she was trying to read his mind. "I've been wondering. Why did you confess your sins in front of them? You didn't have to do that. You had plenty of opportunities to tell me privately."

Luke's cheeks heated. He felt like a twelve-year-old kid trying to talk to his crush. "As I said, I can tell how close you and your sisters are. You're very protective of each other. I wanted them to hear about the investigation from me. Then I'd be willing to answer whatever questions they had."

The frown lines eased from her brow. "Thank you. I'm sure they appreciated that."

He nodded. "Does that make us even?"

"Not even close." Her expression was inflexible.

Luke swallowed a sigh. He'd been afraid she'd want more. He inclined his head toward the archway that led to her living room. "Then could we sit down?"

She walked past him, leading the way to her living room. When they'd returned to her home, Crys had changed into a loose-fitting rose pullover, blue leggings and gray slipper socks. She settled into the armchair, extending her legs onto the ottoman and left the sofa to him. Luke chose to stand. He'd shed his pinstripe gray suit for black warm-up pants, a gray Cleveland Cavaliers jersey and black tube socks.

Crys's silver drapes were pulled over the sheer white curtains, shutting out her neighborhood's evening shadows. Her home was warm. The silence was deep. Luke felt as though they were the only people on the planet.

"My father died five years ago." His voice, tight with tension and grief, shattered the stillness. "I was twenty-six. My mother had died a few years before him. Losing him was hard. I had friends, like Cal, so I wasn't isolated. But my father was the last member of my family."

"Oh, Luke. I'm so sorry. I can only imagine how difficult it would be to lose your whole family." Her compassion gave him the courage to continue.

"I had been casually dating someone at the time. Tahlia Post. She told me she worked in Riverside Medical Center's billing department." Luke paced the length of the living room toward the adjoining dining room before retracing his path to the bay window. "I met her while my father was being treated. We'd been seeing each other for a few months. After my father died, she suggested we live together, either in her condo downtown or my family home in Bexley."

Luke stilled, grateful for Crys's silence as he worked

through the painful, shameful memories. This was vulnerability. This was exposing himself to someone else. He could better understand now why Crys said telling her he was an only child and that his parents had died wasn't enough. She'd wanted him to dig deeper.

He took a breath, easing the tightness in his chest, and pushed on. "I agreed for her to move into my family's home. We weren't wealthy, but we were pretty well-off. I'd wanted to keep the house."

"What happened?" Crys prompted.

Luke sensed her dread as he stood with his back to her. She would have realized the house he'd invited her, her sisters and Cal to Wednesday night had not been his family's Bexley home.

"At first, everything was fine." Shame tightened his vocal cords. He cleared his throat. It didn't help. "Tahlia moved in, showed respect for my family's belongings, treated our gardeners and housekeepers with courtesy. I never saw her go into my parents' room or offices without me. Then one day, a few weeks later, I got home from work and she'd cleaned out everything: jewelry, artwork, antiques, furniture, bonds. Everything."

"Oh, no, Luke. What did you do?"

Luke turned to Crys. She sat forward in her armchair with her feet planted on the hardwood flooring. Her wide-eyed look of shock pulled him back five years back to the past, reminding him of how he'd felt when he'd returned home at the end of the day to find his family home and his parents' belongings had been ransacked. It had been like having someone sucker punch him.

Luke took a breath. "I went after her. That's when I found out the real Tahlia Post was dead."

"Oh, my gosh." Crys groaned, sharing his remembered

pain. "She'd stolen Tahlia Post's identity and preyed on you. She targeted you because of your grief and took advantage of you."

"That's exactly what she did." Luke shoved his hands into the front pockets of his warm-up pants. "I'd been grieving the loss of my father, and his death had brought back the pain of losing my mother."

"I understand." Crys's coffee-colored eyes were soft with sympathy. "My sisters and I went through the same thing. I know it was harder for you, though, because you were also coming to terms with being the sole surviving member of your family."

"She marked me as being ripe for her scam." Luke shook his head. "Thank goodness for Cal. He kept me from losing my mind. He helped me stay focused."

"He's a good friend."

"He's a good person." Luke's response was deliberate.

Jade wasn't one of Cal's admirers and the Rashaad sisters stick together. He respected their loyalty to each other. He was loyal to Cal and he wanted them to know they were wrong about him.

Luke continued. "It took me three years to find the person calling herself Tahlia Post and bring her to justice. I'm grateful the system worked, but she took more from me than my mother's jewelry, my father's bonds, my family's furniture, artwork and antiques. She took my family home. I couldn't live there anymore. She cost me my self-respect and destroyed my trust."

Crys stood and crossed to him. She took his right hand in her left and held it tightly. "Luke, I'm so very sorry you had that horrible experience. I wish that had never happened to you. Thank you for sharing it with me."

Luke curved his fingers around hers. "Are we even now?"

Her voice was husky. "I believe I know you better now."

"Then can we start over?"

Crys's expression warmed as she looked up at him. "I'd like that."

"So would I." Luke felt himself sinking into her eyes and gifting her another piece of his heart.

Chapter 14

"Who filed the corruption charges against Crys Rashaad?" Luke watched Martina closely from his seat on the other side of her desk early Friday morning.

After Crys's near-death experience Wednesday, he'd started questioning everything. That included things he was starting to realize he should have questioned from the beginning, such as whether the person who'd accused Crys of corruption was associated with Dragon & Kelp.

Martina's brown eyes narrowed. Her long, gold earrings, a match for her single-strand necklace, swung as she shook her head. "Luke, I've told you before the complainant is anonymous. If we start demanding people provide their identity when they come forward with their charges, we'll seriously depress the number of reports we receive. That would compromise our justice system's ability to keep our public servants honest. Is that what you want?"

She was trying to put him on the defensive. That wasn't going to work. Not this time. He owed it to Crys to get to the bottom of this matter. He owed it to himself. "Is there something you aren't telling me, Martina? Have you worked with Detective Rashaad in the past? Do you have other complaints against her?"

"Of course I'm not withholding information." Martina

waved an impatient hand. "I've given you everything I have on the detective."

Luke had his doubts. He shook his head in equal parts confusion and frustration. "What I don't understand is why you're determined to believe an anonymous statement over the findings of an experienced investigator who's been working this case for almost three months."

Heat dusted Martina's peaches-and-cream cheeks. Her voice sharpened with outrage. "Are you questioning my judgment?"

Luke had anticipated her reaction. Martina expected people to follow her orders without hesitation. He'd been willing to do that when they'd been on the same mission. This time, he couldn't shake the feeling they weren't.

"I'm questioning the complaint's validity." He gestured toward her. "I think you should, too. You've read my reports, Martina. I've evaluated Detective Rashaad's personnel records. I've interviewed her colleagues and supervisors. No one has made a negative comment or criticism against her. Every interview, every performance review has been positive."

And accurate. Crys was dedicated, hardworking and intelligent. Her integrity was unquestionable. She'd earned the trust of other officers, detectives and supervisors. In the two weeks they'd worked together, she'd done the nearly impossible by earning his trust.

Martina's chuckle was sharp and sarcastic. "What did you expect? That the people you interviewed would say she's corrupt to the core? That she's a pathological liar lacking in integrity? Of course, they're going to make her sound like Mother Teresa with a badge because that's how she's going to present herself."

Luke didn't find anything about this case amusing, not

the growing number of unsolved homicides, the evidence Vic had stolen to prevent Kendra Chapel's murder from being solved, the derailment of Jade's career in an effort to bury the truth, or the attempt to smear Crys's reputation and take away her badge. He certainly wasn't amused by the attempt on her life, which had been intended to silence her. Permanently.

"Or Detective Rashaad could be who she appears to be, a detective with integrity." He leaned forward in his seat. "I've worked for the BCI for more than six years. For almost two of those years, I've worked for you. Why are you putting so much faith in an anonymous report over my findings?"

Maybe that's what Luke should have been asking all along. Instead, he'd allowed Martina to question his drive and objectivity. He never should have done that. He didn't have experience with ethics cases, but he'd handled scores of other investigations. Martina had never challenged their outcomes. Why was this one different?

Martina held his eyes as she sat back in her seat. Her assessment was cold, dismissive. "If you're not up for this assignment, tell me. There are other agents to whom I can give this investigation, agents who can approach it dispassionately."

Luke didn't flinch. Yes, he was attracted to Crys. It was more than her physical appearance. She was beautiful inside and out. Her empathy for the deceased whose murders she was determined to solve impressed him. He respected the care she showed the victims' families. And he envied the love she shared with her sisters. How would it feel to be on the receiving end of her attention? However, his feelings for Crys had not impacted his objectivity. Martina must know that.

He returned her regard without emotion. "I've completed the assignment. You'll have my draft report before lunch. But with all due respect, Martina, I'm not the one who's having trouble remaining objective."

Martina stiffened. "I beg your pardon?"

"You still haven't told me why you're convinced Detective Rashaad has accepted bribes."

Martina glanced at her wristwatch. "Turn in your draft report as soon as possible. I'll be the judge of whether it's as thorough as you claim it to be."

Luke's eyebrows knitted as he studied Martina's gold watch. It was new and seemed expensive. How many timepieces did she have?

He looked up at her gold earrings and matching necklace. They weren't the only costly jewelry she owned. He hadn't paid attention to them in the past, but today, they gave him pause. He considered her gray, double-breasted blazer dress. Was that wool? His eyes moved on to the diamond-and-gold brooch pinning the white-and-black patterned silk scarf around Martina's shoulders.

His supervisor made more money than Luke and a lot more than Crys, but did she make enough to afford the wardrobe and jewels she wore to work? Was she living beyond her means—or was her income being supplemented? Suspicion was like a cold bucket of water thrown in his face.

"Is there anything else?" Martina prompted when Luke remained seated and silent.

"No." He pushed himself to his feet. "I'll send my draft report to you and wait for your feedback."

Martina's response was drowned beneath the pulse pounding in Luke's ears. Someone may be taking bribes. It wasn't Crys, but it was time Luke looked into Martina.

* * *

"We think someone from Dragon & Kelp killed Brock even though he seemed to be helping them cover their fraud." Seated in her overstuffed, floral-patterned armchair, Crys looked around her family room after lunch Sunday.

She'd opened the pale blue drapes over the bay window that faced the front of her home. Natural light flooded the room, spotlighting the ceramic vase of dried wildflowers on the coffee table and the light fixtures on the warm cream walls.

It was her second official meeting with Amber and Jade with the goal of finding their aunt's killer. Since it also was her fourth day with Luke as her roommate-cum-personal-security-detail, she and her sisters had agreed to allow him and Caleb to join them.

From her position in the far-left corner of the overstuffed, matching sofa, Jade was closest to Crys. She typed into her electronic tablet as she spoke. "How high up do you think the order for the hits came from?"

Luke jumped in. He'd brought a chair from the dinette set. Crys smothered a smile, guessing her partner was probably triggered by Jade's breaking-news-journalist tone. "We can't get into the specifics of an ongoing investigation. We think the copycat murdered Brock Mann for the same reason your aunt and Vic were killed, to ensure their silence. And that the same people ordered the hit."

Amber exchanged a look with Jade on her right before turning her frown to Luke. "The circumstances of those murders are different, though. Aunt Kendra and Vic were shot in their homes. Brock was shot, yes, but in his office, which is in a secure building that people can only access with identification. There are guards and a metal detector in the lobby." She tossed a smile at Jade. "I was glad the building was so secure when J worked there."

Jade snorted. "Yeah. It felt nice having security escort me out the day I was 'let go.'" She punctuated her sarcasm with air quotes.

"Amber's right." Caleb had settled into the far-right corner of the sofa beside Amber. "I know your theory is the copycat wanted to frame Brock for the serial murders, but maybe there's another motive. Maybe someone's angry with the newspaper. That wouldn't be unusual. Or perhaps it was personal. Brock wasn't the easiest person to get along with."

Jade snorted again. "You're the master of understatement." She straightened in her seat when Luke turned his attention to her. "You've already questioned me and verified my alibis, emphasis on *alibis*, plural."

Crys drew a breath. The scents of the vinegar, olive oil and spices from the sub sandwiches they'd had for lunch drifted in from the dining room.

"You're right, Caleb." Crys balanced her elbows on the arms of her chair and linked her fingers together over her lap. "Someone could've wanted Brock dead for reasons that don't have anything to do with the serial murders. But we believe he was framed and then murdered because Dragon & Kelp doesn't want us to find the real serial killer or their motive."

Jade blinked. "Mind-blowing."

Caleb frowned, spreading his arms. "Maybe the serial killer framed Brock for helping Dragon & Kelp keep their scam buried."

Amber crossed her right, blue-jean-clad leg over her left, shifting to face Caleb. Her thin, wine-red V-neck sweater warmed her skin's gold undertones. "If the serial killer had framed Brock, he would have done it correctly. We wouldn't know there was a copycat."

Luke gestured toward Amber and Jade on the sofa as he captured Crys's attention. "Have you discussed the guilty information details of the case with them?"

"You know I didn't." Crys arched an eyebrow. "I've only shared the letter I got from Vic and the information we've released publicly."

Amber shrugged her left shoulder. "We don't know exactly what the copycat got wrong when they tried to fake the crime scene."

Jade frowned. "Besides, I've been helpful in this investigation. Admit it. I'm the one who told you Dragon & Kelp had changed their name each time they reorganized under Chapter 11 bankruptcy after they were sued."

"Jade's right." Crys gave him a pointed look. "We'd probably still be spinning our wheels if she hadn't given us Dragon & Kelp's previous company names, which finally gave us the connection between our victims."

Amber straightened in her seat. Her voice was hard, determined. "And there's strong evidence that your serial killer case is connected to our aunt's cold case."

Jade interrupted. "And we're going to solve our aunt's murder—with or without you."

"Yes, we are." Amber glanced at Jade before continuing. "We'd never ask you to violate department policies or to compromise your case. But if there's anything you can share with us, please do. Perhaps we could help each other."

Crys returned Luke's regard with a steady stare. She tightened her grip on her linked fingers and forced herself to remain silent and still. She was already under investigation for corruption although Luke knew she was innocent. Still, she wasn't going to put as much as her pinkie on the scale. She'd leave the decision of how much to tell her very trustworthy sisters to him.

Luke turned his attention back to Amber and Jade. "Do either of you know Carter Wainscott?"

Amber shook her heade.

Jade narrowed her eyes. "Carter Wainscott? He was a lawyer with Dragon & Kelp. Well, he started there when Dragon & Kelp was Pieter & Marcus. Its first iteration." She rummaged through the black-and-silver knapsack she'd tucked beside the sofa. "He worked with Aunt Kenny. They were friends. Actually, I think he had a crush on her."

Crys's thoughts scattered. She was stunned to learn how much Jade knew about their copycat victim. "He and Aunt K were friends?" She stood to pace. "You've met him?"

"Aunt Kenny introduced us." Jade glanced up briefly before continuing to search through her knapsack. "I saw him a couple of times when I met her for lunch."

"What was he like?" Luke asked.

Jade pulled a midsize gray spiral notebook from her knapsack and started flipping through it. "He was nice, polite, a little awkward." She came to a page halfway through the notebook. "Aha." Rising, she crossed to Crys and tapped the lined page she'd opened to. "I wanted to make sure I was remembering correctly before I said anything about Carter's work. Aunt Kenny said Carter was the insurance company's legal department liaison to the board of directors."

Luke had joined them, standing on Jade's other side. "He worked closely with the members of the board?"

Jade turned a page in the notebook. "Specifically, the standing subcommittee to review claims denied for medical reasons."

Crys's eyes stretched wide. Her body stiffened with shock. "This is brilliant!"

"What is?" Luke leaned closer to Jade.

Crys stabbed the notebook, then glanced at Amber, Caleb and Jade. "The members of the subcommittee Carter was assigned to, Rita Gomez, Alfred Murphy, Sally Stead, Wilma Strong and Janice Young."

Luke's eyes met hers. "Now we have the connection for our victims."

Crys nodded. "And the names of our remaining targets."

"We're coming at this the wrong way." Crys studied the pages of case notes she'd spread across her dining table Sunday night. Amber, Jade and Caleb had left hours earlier.

Luke stood beside her. His cedar scent made her want him even closer. "If you've thought of something more efficient than sifting through three years' worth of denied life insurance claims, count me in."

It was unanimous. They needed a plan of action, not one that required them to bury themselves in reams of paper that might not lead anywhere.

Crys turned to Luke—and found herself caught in his intense eyes. His cool-blue, long-sleeved T-shirt made them seem even darker. She caught her breath at the wave of awareness that rolled over her.

Breaking their connection, she forced her attention back to the piles of papers spread across her table. "That's it. Based on the information Jade gave us, we're working on the theory that the connection between Rita, Alfred and Sally is that they served on the standing claims review committee."

Luke studied the case notes. "Right. The committee managed by Carter Wainscott, your aunt's good friend."

Crys stepped to the side, putting space between them. "We agreed the serial killer is most likely a beneficiary of one of Dragon & Kelp's policyholders whose claim was denied."

Luke crossed his arms over his broad chest. His brow knitted in thought. "That denied claim could've triggered the suspect's anger and drive for revenge. Most of the claims were denied for administrative reasons: application timing, missing paperwork, improperly completed paperwork, no medical files on record."

"Exactly." Crys risked a quick glance at Luke. "Petty reasons that would trigger anyone's temper, but especially someone who's already grieving the loss of a loved one."

Luke turned sideways to face her. He propped his hip against the table. "After my father died, if some bureaucrat had told me my beneficiary claim was being denied because I submitted it outside of some arbitrary due date, I would've been livid."

"Me, too." Crys thought of her mother and the administrative hoops she and her sisters had had to jump through to settle her mother's estate.

Adrianne Chapel Rashaad had been Aunt K's older sister. Crys felt gratitude and grief each time she recalled the way Aunt K had put her sorrow on hold to help Crys, Amber and Jade through the probate process. When they'd lost Aunt K, the sisters had followed their aunt's example. They hadn't broken down until after Aunt K's affairs had been settled. But then, Crys hadn't thought the tears would ever stop. Guilt and grief were a vile mixture. Why hadn't she taken a rain check on that date with her ex and instead had dinner with Aunt K?

"But neither of us would resort to murder." Luke's comment brought Crys's attention back to their homicide investigation.

"No, we wouldn't." Crys mentally shook off her regrets

and focused on a new plan. "Unfortunately, someone else has. We agree the process of identifying our suspect from the vast number of records we took from Dragon & Kelp is taking too long—"

"It's like searching for a needle in a haystack—or in our case, a denial letter in an ocean of rejected claims."

"I think we should instead focus on the killer's next targets, Wilma Strong and Janice Young." Crys turned to take in Luke's reaction to her statement.

He paused as though weighing her proposal. "We could warn Strong and Young, but I don't know if we have the budget to assign them protective details."

"I'm iffy on whether we should tell them they're in danger." Crys paced back and forth beside the table. "And I definitely don't think we should give them bodyguards."

Luke shook his head in confusion. "You don't think we should tell them someone's trying to kill them or do anything to keep them safe? Why not?"

"You're twisting my words." Or maybe she wasn't explaining herself well. She was still formulating the idea. It was during times like this she wished she could express herself with more precision like Jade or draw images with her language like Amber. Crys stopped pacing and took a breath. "If we tell them they're in danger, they might change their routine. If we give them bodyguards, the suspect will realize we've figured out what they're doing and go to ground."

"Of course." Luke kneaded the back of his neck. "The killer has been tracking their targets' movements. That's how they know the best time and place to intercept them."

"Exactly." Crys was on a roll with her plan now. "If we're going to catch this killer, we need to maintain the status quo. They think we're stumbling around in the dark, look-

ing for connections. If they know we've caught some daylight, who knows what they'll do next. They could change
their MO and we'll be right back to square one."

"OK." Luke straightened from his perch beside the table
and shoved his hands into the front pockets of his gray
slacks. "You've made a compelling argument, but I still
think we need to do something to protect our potential victims. I'll put in a request for additional patrols around their
residences and workplaces."

"That's a good idea." Crys nodded her approval. "We've
got to do everything we can to keep these two people safe
while we try to draw the killer out." From the corner of her
eye, Crys noticed Luke's attention turn to her, felt his eyes
move over her profile.

"What do you mean draw them out? How do you pro-
pose doing that?"

Crys had been going over the evidence in her mind since
Amber, Jade and Caleb had left, role-playing scenarios,
making connections, discarding the obvious and working
through the possibilities. "I've noticed something about the
suspect's pattern. Gomez. Murphy. Stead. I think our suspect is targeting their victims alphabetically."

Luke's eyes widened. "*G. M. S.* Well, I can't contradict
your point. Based on that pattern, you think their next target is Wilma Strong?"

"I do." Crys forced herself to face him, back straight and
shoulders squared. "This part of my theory seems a little
thin. I mean a killer who chooses their victims by alphabetical order." She shrugged, letting her voice dwindle away.
"But I don't think we should discount it, either."

"Neither do I." Luke pulled his attention from the pages
on the table and settled it on her. "We don't have anything

else to go on. If we're making guesses, this one is as good as any other. Good work."

Crys was floating on air. Her first big case since she'd earned her detective's badge almost nine months earlier. Her partner had been murdered, and she'd been paired with a stranger—one with an impressive background and a ton more experience than her. Not only had he accepted her proposal, he supported it.

She smiled as she took a victory lap around her mind. "Thank you."

A light flickered in Luke's eyes. Crys felt her body respond to it.

Luke cleared his throat. "OK. We think Wilma Strong is our next target. We'll keep an eye on Janice Young just in case. You're on a roll. What are your thoughts on moving forward to draw out our suspect?"

"Right." Crys held his eyes. "I should take Wilma Strong's place."

Chapter 15

"What?" Luke couldn't have heard Crys correctly.

"I should go undercover as Wilma Strong." Crys's voice sped up as she outlined her idea. "Stay in her house. Go to her job. Act natural. That way, the killer will think we still don't have a clue. We don't know why they've chosen these victims or who their next target will be. Lull them into a false sense of security. Then, when they move in to kidnap and murder Wilma, we grab them."

Her enthusiasm was palpable—and discomforting. Luke schooled his features to mask his dismay. "That's a good plan. It has merit. I have a couple of concerns, though. First, I agree we need to protect Wilma Strong and Janice Young to the best of our ability. But we also need to protect you. Remember, someone has a target on you, too."

Crys rocked backward as though Luke's response surprised her. "I know that. But we can't suspend our investigation. Lives are at stake."

"Including yours." Luke started to reach for her before pulling his arm back. "I'm not saying we should put a pause on our investigation. I'm saying we need to think of your safety, too. We don't know anything about the suspects who are after you or the one after Wilma Strong, whether they're young or old, Black or white, male or female. We're going into this undercover op blind."

"This op benefits both cases." She spread her hands. "Whoever's after me expects me to be at my home or at work. They won't be looking for me at Wilma's house or her place of business. This could actually help keep me safe."

"Point taken." Luke inclined his head. But there was a bigger impediment to her plan. "I've seen photos of Wilma Strong online. She's about your complexion, but she's a lot older and has a fuller figure. I don't think we'll be able to mislead anyone into thinking you're her."

Crys jerked her head toward the window at the other end of the room. "It's early April, still cool enough that we'd need to bundle up. I can mask my figure with extra clothing under some of Ms. Strong's more familiar coats." She shrugged. "As for my hair, we can ask her to wear hats or scarves for a day or two until I take over as her."

Luke turned away, rubbing the muscles seizing at the back of his neck. "This is too dangerous, Crys. We don't know anything about the actual abduction. Suppose the suspect works in the building with Wilma Strong? What happens when you get to her workplace and take off your coat and hat? Your cover will be blown."

"I'm not actually going to be working there." Her voice carried from behind his back. "We just need the killer to see Wilma walk into the building in the morning, then leave at the end of the day. I can walk in, change out of her clothes, then leave the building. At the end of the day, I can walk back into the building, change back into her clothes and drive to her house."

"That all sounds great in theory." Hooking his hands on his hips, Luke turned to face her. "It's as flawless as a movie script. But this is real life. Anything can happen."

"It's a risk worth taking, Luke." Her voice was thick with equal parts pain and determination. "Too many people have died. I couldn't live with myself if I didn't do everything in my power to prevent more deaths and keep our community safe."

"And what about your safety?" *I couldn't live if anything happened to you.* "The longer we continue the charade, the riskier it gets. We don't know what the killer will do if your cover's blown."

"Waiting carries an even greater risk." Crys took a step closer to him and rested her right hand on his left bicep. Her voice was almost a whisper. "We're running out of time. We found Alfred a little more than two weeks after we found Rita, and Sally a little more than three weeks after that. It's been almost three weeks since we recovered Sally. This is a good plan. You said so yourself. But we've got to move *now*."

Luke looked into her eyes, searching for any hint of doubt or hesitation. He didn't find a single one. It didn't stop him from being at war with himself. Crys was a detective. She was well aware of the risks and responsibilities of the career she'd chosen. She'd trained for dangerous situations. She'd earned the right to make these choices for herself. It didn't make his choice any easier.

"All right." Luke forced the words through gritted teeth. He took a breath, then scowled at her. "But you'll wear a vest the entire time and I'm going to be your human shadow."

Incredibly, she grinned up at him. "Then I know I'll be in safe hands."

Luke's stress eased as he looked into her sparkling brown eyes. Her heart-shaped lips parted, showing pearl-white teeth. Her delicate features glowed with relief. Heat pooled in his gut.

His voice, raspy with need, was almost unrecognizable. "Crys, that's where I want you to be—safe in my arms."

Crys's smile faded. Her lips parted with surprise. Luke watched her dark eyes fill with heat. His heart pounded in his chest as he waited for her next move. This mattered. It mattered so much. Crys raised up on her toes. He met her halfway. His lips covered hers.

Electricity shot through his body. His muscles trembled with it. His heart punched against his chest. Luke didn't know when his arms had lifted, when they'd wrapped around Crys's waist. He felt her, warm and soft in his embrace, and drew her closer. Closer to his body. Much closer to his heart.

"Crys." Luke breathed her name as his lips moved over hers. Her touch was soft and sweet.

"Luke." Her voice was a sexy promise.

He stroked his tongue across the seam of her mouth. Crys trembled in his arms. She parted her lips for him. Her welcome caused his body to heat and his pulse to pick up. Luke had fantasized about holding Crys in his arms like this, ever since the day they'd met. She'd challenged and disconcerted him, made him laugh and kept him on his toes.

Luke slid his tongue past her lips. Crys moaned into his mouth. She trembled against him. Or had he shivered against her? Her taste was intoxicating. Luke's thoughts scattered. His head spun. He broke their kiss to catch his breath.

"You've turned me inside out." He whispered his confession against her ear.

"I did?" Crys whispered back. She slid her hands up his

torso, stroking his muscles and leaving a trail of fire over his skin. "That sounds painful."

Luke smiled and kissed her again. Crys wrapped her arms around his shoulders and arched into him. Luke drew his arm up her side, past her waist to her chest. He cupped the side of her breast, caressing it through her lightweight blouse. He stroked his thumb across her nipple and felt it pebble against his skin. His blood heated. His heart raced. His muscles shook.

He guided Crys to the sofa and gathered her onto his lap. She became his whole world. Her heat warmed him. Her scent filled him. He was lost in the feel of her. His need for her.

"Luke. Wait." Crys drew away.

He stiffened with his hands on her hips. "I'm sorry, Crys. Am I making you uncomfortable?"

Crys rolled off his lap and adjusted her blouse. "No. Yes. I mean—" She took a breath and stood to pace the room. Her curls were tousled. Her lips were swollen, and her cheeks were flushed. "I'm the one who's sorry. Things are complicated enough between your investigating me, our investigating a serial killer and people trying to kill me. We should keep things between us professional and not add to everything."

Luke rose to his feet. His body still throbbed with desire for her. "Of course. We'll keep things professional."

Crys gave him a half smile. "Thank you for understanding."

Luke watched her turn and jog up the stairs. He'd never felt this connection with anyone before. Tahlia didn't count because her feelings had been fake. He'd fallen for her act. How could he be sure Crys's feelings weren't an act as well?

She was right. They needed to keep things professional for his career and his heart. At least for now.

"When the media reported that Rita had been murdered, I was shocked." Wilma Strong sat at the head of her spacious dining table early Monday evening. "I was appalled. Who would want to kill Rita Gomez? She was a good person, a kind person. She had a sunny disposition and a way of listening to people so they felt respected and included. Her murder made no sense."

Wilma stared across the room at the closed teakwood pocket doors that ensured their privacy while she met with Crys and Luke after work early Monday evening. But her unfocused eyes seemed to signal that she was looking inward on personal thoughts and private memories.

The sixty-something-year-old investment banker wore a vibrant plum-and-black skirt suit that flattered her fuller figure. Her four-inch magenta heels lifted her average height past Crys's five-foot-seven-inches. Her still-dark hair was fashioned in an asymmetrical bob that framed her round face.

Wilma's husband, Peter, and her two adult children, Faye and Henry, watched the interview from the other end of the table. They wore business attire, signaling they'd also just returned from work. Their faces were stamped with nearly identical expressions of panic and disbelief as they struggled to comprehend what was happening. Crys had the sense they were losing the battle with reality.

"I sent her family a sympathy card," Wilma continued, still blindly absorbed in the pocket doors. "Then Al was murdered and Sally. Of course, I was devastated by their deaths. I'd worked with all of them for well over a year. I cared about them. But that's also when I really began to get scared." She rubbed her arms, trying to warm herself. "It occurred to me their deaths weren't only tragedies. Someone was targeting our claims review committee. I was even more sure of that after Carter was found killed."

Luke gave the older woman a perplexed look. "Why didn't you come forward sooner with your suspicions?"

Crys and Luke had called Wilma during the workday to request this meeting. They'd wanted to speak with her at her home for privacy reasons. Wilma had quickly agreed. Now Crys understood why. She was afraid.

Wilma looked at Luke seated on her left. She seemed to be taking his measure. "I don't really know why I didn't share my concerns with the police—"

"Or even with your family." Peter's anger was muted.

Wilma continued as though her husband hadn't spoken. "Perhaps I was afraid saying the thing out loud would make it even more real to me. Or maybe the police would think I was some kind of paranoid conspiracy theorist claiming people were trying to kill me."

"It's our lives, too, Mom." Henry fretted. He swept a thin arm around the lower end of the table to encompass his older sister and father. "If someone's trying to kill you, one of us could have been caught in the crossfire."

Wilma ignored her son's comment. "But now the police are telling me someone really is trying to kill me." She lifted her cream-and-gold-patterned porcelain teacup. Her hands were shaking.

Seated across the table from Luke, Crys's heart hurt for her. If the serial killer wanted revenge for their denied beneficiary claims, they should take their grievance to court. Murder wasn't the answer. For that reason, Crys would do everything she could to keep Wilma safe.

Although she felt a twinge of discomfort as she sat in

their host's dining room. Expensive royal-blue, gold and teakwood furnishings, pricey artwork and costly trinkets surrounded her. Yet Wilma served on the board of directors of a life insurance company that denied beneficiary claims for the flimsiest of reasons.

Crys shifted her attention back to Wilma on her left. "When you served on the claims review committee with Carter, Rita, Alfred, Sally and Janice, did you ever receive strange or threatening messages—letters, emails, phone calls or anything like that?"

Wilma slid a look first at Luke before returning her attention to Crys. "Yes. We received several over the years. More than half the claims we denied were responded to with angry and sometimes threatening letters."

Crys exchanged a look with Luke.

"More than half?" Luke's patience sounded strained. "We didn't see any angry letters in the claims files."

Wilma shrugged helplessly. "We were told that, if we received any threatening messages of any kind, we were to forward those to the chief legal officer. I don't know what he did with that information."

Luke opened his notepad to a clean page. "Who was the CLO at the time?"

Wilma took a moment to pull the name from her memory. "Andy Scheltzer. While I was on the board of directors of Shearman & Axel—now Dragon & Kelp—they'd settled at least one lawsuit. I'd wondered at the time if the threatening messages helped with their settlements."

Would the former CLO have any theories on the serial killer's identity? "What happened to Mr. Scheltzer?"

Wilma shrugged again. "After negotiating the settlement, he resigned. I lost track of him after that."

Crys looked to Peter, Faye and Henry before continuing. "We're sorry to tell you that we believe the suspect is killing members of your claims review committee in alphabetical order, according to your last names."

Luke's voice was gentle. "As you may remember, you and Janice Young are the remaining members of the committee."

The blood drained from Wilma's face. Her eyes stretched wide as she shot panicked looks at Crys and Luke on either side of her. "You think *I'm* the killer's next target. *Me*. That's why you're here." She collapsed back against the elaborately carved wooden dining chair.

After a second of silence, the room erupted in interjections, exclamations and protests. Crys looked at Luke. In silent agreement, they gave Wilma's family time to work through their emotions.

"Why are we only now hearing about this?" Faye's question was shrill with panic.

With his eyes on Wilma, Peter answered. "Because your mother chose to sit and do nothing rather than bringing her suspicions to us, her family. By doing that, she not only increased the danger to herself, but she put us all in danger."

Crys raised her hand in protest. "With respect, Mr. Strong, your wife explained her reasoning for not coming to us with her suspicions. Any other discussion you want to have about that can happen privately. For now, my partner and I would like to describe our plan to help protect Ms. Strong and, by extension, your family."

Luke inclined his head toward Crys, including her in his explanation. "We're proposing Detective Rashaad go undercover, taking your place. We're hoping the suspect will try to grab her, thinking Detective Rashaad is you. Then we'll take the suspect into custody."

Faye expelled an irritated breath. "You don't look anything like my mother."

Holding on to her patience with both fists, Crys glanced at Wilma's daughter. "We have a plan to address that."

She turned back to Wilma, reviewing what she and Luke had discussed the night before: using hats and scarves to cover their hair and obstruct clear views of their faces, bulkier clothes and coats to cover their figures. "You and your family will have to find a safe place to stay, either with relatives or at a hotel. Special Agent Gilchrist and I will stay in your home. I'll drive to your workplace in the morning dressed as you, change into my clothes before I leave, then return to your office at the end of the day and pretend to be you again."

Luke picked up the explanation. "You'll have to work remotely for the next week or so. The most important thing is that no one can see you while Detective Rashaad is acting as your decoy."

Wilma's brow knit with worry. Her voice was breathless. "Work remotely? Move out of our home?" She looked at Peter, seated at the other end of the table. "I'll have to give this some thought."

"Mother!" Faye's eye stretched wide with incredulity. Her voice soared several octaves higher. "What's there to think about?"

Wilma gave her offspring a helpless look. "This is turning my life upside down."

Faye's eyebrows leaped up her forehead. "It's protecting your life and ours."

Crys reached out, squeezing the older woman's forearm. "Ms. Strong—"

"Please call me Wilma."

"Thank you, Wilma." Crys smiled. "We can't force you

to do this, but we need your help to keep you, your family and others safe."

Wilma blinked back tears. "I just don't... I don't—"

Faye slapped her hands on the surface of the teakwood dining table, causing everyone to jump in surprise. She pushed herself to her feet. "You all can do whatever you *want*. I'm going to stay with Aunt Ursula until this is *over*."

Peter stood, blocking Faye's dramatic exit. "Wilma, maybe we should stay with your sister in Upper Arlington."

"That's actually a really good idea." Luke shifted in his seat to better face Wilma.

"I agree." Crys held the other woman's eyes, willing her to make the decision that could end this killing spree.

Wilma's deep breath trembled with fright. "All right." She looked from Crys to Luke. "When do we start?"

Luke noted the overcast sky and lengthening shadows as he drove them home from Wilma Strong's house Monday evening. He sensed a different type of shadow taking over his silver SUV. Crys sat in the black cloth bucket passenger seat, filling his vehicle with the soft scent of wildflowers in the rain. He glanced toward her with his peripheral vision in time to see her shiver.

He pressed a button on his climate control panel to turn up the heat. "Is that better?"

She hummed. "Thanks."

That wasn't much of an answer. Luke returned his right hand to the steering wheel and his attention to Interstate 270 North, Columbus's outerbelt freeway. "What's wrong, Crys?"

She hesitated a beat. "I was thinking of Aunt K." Her soft sigh stole into his heart. "Subconsciously, I've linked the four cases: Aunt K's murder, Vic's death, the serial killer investigation and the copycat. I didn't even realize I was doing it. But I've got to prepare myself. Finding the serial killer isn't going to solve my aunt's cold case. It may not even bring us any closer to a suspect."

Luke's heart broke for Crys and her sisters. There had been days, weeks, months when he'd thought he'd never find Tahlia much less bring her to justice. When he did, it felt like the weight of a building had been lifted from his chest. He wanted to help bring that same sense of relief and fairness to the Rashaad sisters.

"You're right." Luke checked his blind spot before switching into the right-hand lane. "Finding the serial killer won't help us identify your aunt's killer, but it will bring justice for Rita Gomez, Alfred Murphy, Sally Stead and their families."

"I know. And I'm happy about that." Her voice was small. "Still, I feel like I've failed my aunt."

Luke felt Crys's pain in the pit of his stomach. "No, you didn't. The only way you could do that is by giving up on finding her killer, and I know you'd never do that. Neither will your sisters. And neither will I." In his peripheral vision, Luke saw Crys's head snap toward him.

"Thank you." She sounded both grateful and surprised.

"No thanks needed." Luke signaled to take the Cemetery Road exit. "The serial killer won't give us the answers we need, but I have a feeling the copycat will."

"So do I." Crys's resolve had returned. "My aunt, Vic, Carter Wainscott and Brock were killed to protect Dragon & Kelp. It makes sense that the same person ordered those murders."

"We still have to keep our minds open to other possible motives." Luke turned east off the freeway before stopping at a red light. He looked at Crys. "Brock's murder may not have had anything to do with Dragon & Kelp. According to both Cal and Jade, Brock wasn't well liked."

"I get your point. We shouldn't get ahead of ourselves. But, Luke, what other reason could there be? *Everything* goes back to Dragon & Kelp."

A car horn sounded behind Luke, urging him to proceed through the intersection. "I'm just cautioning us both not to get our hopes up. Catching the copycat may not lead us to your aunt's murderer."

"It's been more than a year. Right now, I'm running on fumes. Some optimism would give me a boost."

The rustling sound from the passenger side of his SUV told Luke Crys had once again shifted on her seat.

"I understand." There were times during the three years he'd searched for Tahlia that Luke had needed an injection of hope. He shouldn't deny Crys the same encouragement.

He navigated his vehicle over the gently rolling, serpentine roads of Crys's northwest Columbus neighborhood. It was the first week of April. The naked trees and bare bushes that lined the residential streets and populated the front lawns exhibited signs of trauma from the hard winter. The sidewalks were eerily silent. He suspected any children who lived in these houses were being kept inside more because of the chilly, wet weather than the gathering dusk.

"Vic's letter warned that the people behind Aunt K's murder were powerful, dangerous and had connections in very high places." Crys repeated the words as though she'd memorized them. She probably had.

"Columbus is the state capital." Luke tapped his wiper control to clear the mist of rain from his windshield. "There are a lot of people who are here primarily to be close to people in positions of power: the governor, state attorney general, senate and house leaders, lobbyists."

"I had the sense Vic was referring to rich people, people the politicians are trying to kiss up to, not the other way around. Those who'd bribe people like Brock and Vic on behalf of the politicians to ensure those officials were loyal to them."

Luke stopped his vehicle at another red light. This time, he kept his eyes on the traffic signal. "That description seems to match the executives and directors involved with Dragon & Kelp. The investors' business model, for want of a better term, is based on collecting premiums and avoiding beneficiary awards."

"And lawsuits," Crys added. "Every time they're sued, they file for bankruptcy. And they've been getting away with it."

"It's a lack of industry oversight." Luke eased his SUV through the green light. "They follow just enough of the law to stay in the industry's good graces. When they cross the line, it's into a gray area where the rules aren't as clear."

Luke turned into Crys's neighborhood from the southeast, which allowed them to approach her address from the back of her home. His muscles tightened as he went on alert for anything that looked suspicious or out of place. He sensed Crys's strain as she sat beside him, taking in everything. The need for these extra precautions angered him. No one should be made to feel unsafe in their own home. How much longer would she have to feel this way? When would they be able to cancel the additional patrols past her residence? Could things return to normal for her—for them? Because Luke would never have her go through this alone.

The strain in his back and shoulders increased as they drew closer to her home. Crys was acquainted with the few pedestrians walking their dogs and taking after-dinner jogs in the brisk evening air. She also was familiar with the handful of cars parked on her street and around the corner. They belonged to her neighbors or people who regularly visited them. After spending the past five days in her neighborhood, Luke recognized the cars and people, too.

Before leaving to meet with Wilma Strong and her family, Crys had turned on the front and rear exterior house light in case they returned after the sun had set. They still had a few minutes of daylight. Luke pulled his SUV into her sloped driveway in front of her two-car garage. Crys had claimed to have too much junk in her garage to fit another automobile. Besides, Luke liked the idea of having his car parked where it could be a deterrent. Potential bad actors would know Crys wasn't alone.

Her neighborhood seemed to be asleep. Everything looked as peaceful as a greeting card illustration. However, Luke wouldn't relax until his protectee was behind locked doors. He turned off the engine and made a slow, careful visual scan of their surroundings before getting out of the vehicle. Crys did the same.

Using his body to shield her, Luke followed Crys up her porch steps. While she unlocked her door, he sent his eyes up and down the area in the immediate vicinity of her house. He was looking for shadows where they didn't belong, movements behind nearby bushes. Anything that felt out of place.

Luke followed her into her home and secured the front door. The skin on the back of his neck chilled in warning. His pulse kicked up. He hurried after Crys, following her around the corner of the entryway toward the kitchen. And froze. Crys had stopped in the short hallway.

Standing in the kitchen, less than two feet away, a masked intruder pointed a gun at her chest. Close. Too close.

Chapter 16

Crys stopped. In that second, she inventoried the intruder. Black ski mask; baggy, black sweatsuit; short, stocky build; big, black tennis shoes; tiny hands; expensive, black suede gloves. Very large gun. She filed that information. Then instinct took over.

She dropped into a kickboxing stance: arms up, knees soft, left leg forward. She swung her right leg up, aiming for her attacker's gun. The weapon sailed left into her family room. The intruder spun, racing out the back door. Crys charged after them, Luke's running steps sounding behind her.

The assailant leaped off her back deck, rushing through her yard and her neighbors' mulch beds to gain the sidewalk. Crys followed, lengthening her strides, desperate to catch up to them. Thankfully, the streets were empty. Not a soul in sight. The rain was heavier now, playing across her forehead, cheeks and chin forming puddles in the uneven ground.

Who was the intruder? Who'd sent them? Or had they come on their own? What was their intent? Were they the serial killer, trying to stop the investigation? Were they the copycat, intent on protecting Dragon & Kelp? Or were they connected to the person or people who'd murdered Aunt K and Vic?

Crys freed her weapon on the run. Releasing the safety, she fired a shot in the air. "Police! Stop!"

The intruder ignored her warning, instead leading Crys across the street. Luke ran past her. Their target was slowing, getting winded, even as they crossed another quiet street.

Crys tried again, this time without the warning shot. "Stop! Police!"

She added power to her strides. If she and Luke reached the attacker together, they could bring the intruder back to the department for questioning.

The assailant had other plans. Halfway up the block, under the faint glow of her neighbors' porchlights, Crys noted a car door being flung open. *Oh, no.*

The intruder dove into the passenger seat, then slammed the door shut. The low-slung, dark sports car sped out of the quiet residential area and disappeared into the dark. Crys chased after it for several seconds, squinting to read the license plate. Luke kept pace beside her. She managed to get the first three characters: HRS.

Anger and frustration sucked her remaining oxygen. The cold, wet evening seeped into her cargo coat to her bones. Crys wanted to scream, kick a fence, punch a tree. Instead, she put a lid on her temper. Now was not the time to lose control. Shivering, she bent forward, resting her hands on her knees, to catch her breath.

"Let's call it in." Luke was breathless but calm. His palm was warm on the small of her back as though offering support, both physical and emotional.

Crys straightened and jogged beside him back to her home.

"Detective!" A man's voice carried from one of the nearby houses. "Are you all right?"

Crys stopped. She hoped her stiff smile was reassuring. "I'm fine, Keyshawn. Thank you. Make sure to lock all your doors and windows."

"I will." Keyshawn glanced at Luke before returning his attention to Crys. "When I heard the gunshot and your shouts, I called 9-1-1. I gave them your name and address."

That was one task off her list. "Thank you. I'll head back to meet them now."

She wondered whether her neighbor would also be willing to call Amber and Jade. That was not a conversation she was looking forward to. Her sisters were already anxious about the threats against her. Learning an armed intruder had been waiting for her in her home would probably prompt them to camp out on her front lawn.

Crys rejoined Luke. Several other concerned citizens asked for explanations during their jog back to her home. She must have repeated, "Everything's fine. Lock your doors and windows," a dozen times.

"Do you know all your neighbors?" Luke followed her into her home.

"A lot of them. My sisters and I grew up in this neighborhood." Crys paused to lock the front door, although she'd lost trust in its security.

How had the intruder made it past her alarm system? She felt a fissure of fear as well as anger. She'd have to change the code tonight.

Two uniformed police officers arrived minutes after Crys and Luke had reentered her home. Together, they walked the officers through the break-in. The police took their separate statements, as well as photos of the internal and external areas of her home involved in the break-in. Since the assailant had worn gloves, the officers didn't dust for prints. They did, however, take measurements and pictures of the muddy footprints the intruder had left on her kitchen's white-and-gray linoleum flooring. Afterward, Crys used a wet wipe to clean up. The tangible evidence of a stranger's invasion of her personal space was galling. The officers also collected the gun to ensure proper chain of command.

It took hours for the police to complete their examination, including retracing the route the assailant had taken for their getaway. It was an odd feeling being both the victim and the investigator of their case. Crys was drained by the time the officers left. Her body was exhausted, but her mind wouldn't rest. Luke seemed to have the same reaction. Hot showers and dry clothes helped them, but not much.

"What were they after?" Luke's voice was rough as though he was still grappling with residual anger and fear.

They were drinking tea in the living room. It was after 10:00 p.m. Luke was seated on the sofa. The red-blue-and-white logo of the Cleveland Guardians Major League Baseball team stretched across the broad chest of his navy-blue sweatshirt.

Crys was sprawled on her armchair and ottoman. Her black sweatpants were loose and comfortable. Her white sweatshirt was covered in images of daffodils. "I'm pretty sure the objective was to kill me the same way they'd killed Aunt K and Vic." She clenched her teeth to stop their chattering.

Luke flinched. "I'm sorry. I can't imagine what you were feeling or what you're going through now. When you saw that gun, you must have flashed back to your aunt's murder." He stopped as though he was channeling her fear. "Would you rather pick this up later?"

Crys searched Luke's chiseled features. He really was a good person, despite his investigating her without her knowledge. "Thank you for offering, but no. I wouldn't be able to stop thinking about the attack anyway."

"All right." Luke still sounded uncertain. "I realize the suspect wanted to harm you but if that was the goal, why did he hesitate?"

Crys had wondered that herself as she stood under the shower, letting the hot water beat on her shoulders and upper back. "I think your being here surprised her. I had the feeling she got nervous when she saw you. She was expecting me to be alone. I took advantage of her reaction to disarm her."

"You were impressive."

"Thank you." Crys inclined her head. "My sisters and I took kickboxing classes, first for exercise and then for self-defense."

"You keep referring to the attacker as she. The perp was short—five-five or six—but what makes you so sure it was a woman?"

Crys's eyebrows knitted as she brought back images of the confrontation. "I told Officer Singh that I had the impression the intruder was female because her hands seemed small, even in those expensive-looking black suede gloves."

Luke frowned his confusion. "But the officers measured the shoes at a size ten."

Crys gave a stiff shrug. "Maybe she got larger shoes and stuffed them to mask her identity. But the suspect seemed female to me. As she jumped off the deck, she sort of gasped like she was afraid she wasn't going to land safely. It was kind of light and high-pitched. It sounded feminine."

Luke was silent for several seconds as he considered her words. Crys was caught in her own thoughts, primarily the fact that she'd have to break the news about the failed attack to her sisters in the morning. She didn't want to field their questions tonight, especially the ones she knew they'd ask about her security system. That would take more energy than she had. A lot more.

"A female perp with expensive tastes." Luke's comment distracted her.

She couldn't read his expression. "What are you thinking?"

"I'm thinking that's an important description to have."

Crys stiffened. Her blood chilled. Why did she have the feeling Luke was withholding information from her? He'd said during his investigation, he'd realized he could trust her, but could she trust him?

Luke stood in the upstairs hallway, staring at Crys's closed bedroom door. Every few seconds, he heard the creaking of one of the floorboards as she paced over it again—and again. It was that faint noise that had drawn him from his bed at midnight. Like Crys, he'd been unable to sleep. Instead, he'd stared at the ceiling for what had felt like hours. It had served as a screen for his thoughts as he'd projected images of tonight's events, their previous victims, and possible suspects.

A woman of average height, full figure and expensive tastes. Martina Monaco? His boss? Was it possible?

No!

She wasn't the only woman in Columbus—or even in Franklin County—who fit that description. She was in law enforcement. Vic had been in law enforcement, too. What would be her motive? Money. Just like Vic.

But she was his boss. He'd reported to her for more than two years. He'd trusted her. He would know if she were on the take.

An image of Tahlia formed in his mind. Her fair skin

had been flawless. Her gray eyes seemed to notice only him. And her full, red lips had made him believe her lies. Self-disgust was a sour taste in his throat.

No. Not again. He wasn't being duped again.

Was he?

Luke had wrestled with disbelief, dread and shame for more than an hour. Then he'd heard the floorboard in the room down the hall creak again and again like someone kept pressing on the same worn spot in need of repairs. He'd tossed off the lightweight quilt and pulled on the orange-and-brown Cleveland Browns T-shirt he'd grabbed from the closet. He didn't want to wander over to Crys's bedroom wearing nothing but baggy black cotton shorts and a smile.

The creaking floorboard led him to her door. He wasn't the only one struggling to place the puzzle pieces of this case. Maybe if they put their heads together, they could develop a plan for identifying who was trying to kill her—and their connection to the copycat killer.

Luke squared his shoulders, and gathered a breath and his courage before knocking on the door. "Crys? May I come in?"

The creaking stopped. His request was met with complete silence. Luke took a step back, preparing to leave. If she wanted to be alone, he'd respect that.

Her response stopped him. "One sec."

Luke released the breath he hadn't realized he'd been holding. Seconds that felt like hours passed before Crys opened the door to him. She'd wrapped herself in an ankle-length burgundy nightgown covered in images of pale pink, long-stemmed roses. Her narrow feet were bare and as beautiful as the rest of her. Her explosion of long, brown curls tumbled past her shoulders. The top of her head came to his lips. Tempting.

Perhaps this late-night visit was a poor idea.

"Do you need something?" Crys prompted him with a soft question.

She'd had the same shuttered look in her eyes when she'd wished him good night almost an hour earlier. It was an expression that said she regretted letting him get as close as she had and wasn't certain she should let him get any closer. What had he done to lose the ground he'd struggled to regain? What had he done to lose her trust?

Luke swallowed the lump of uncertainty that blocked his throat. "I heard you moving around and thought you might need to talk."

Twin dustings of pink highlighted her delicate cheekbones. "I'm sorry. I didn't realize I was making so much noise. Pacing helps me think, but I didn't mean to disturb you."

"There's no need to apologize." Luke smiled at her dismay. "I know you pace when you're thinking. And when you're impatient, angry, excited. Actually, in the almost three weeks we've been working together, I've rarely seen you sitting still."

Crys arched an eyebrow. "All right. There's no need to oversell it. I'll stop pacing."

"I'm sorry." Luke raised both hands, palms out, but his smile stayed in place. "The truth is I couldn't sleep, either." He lowered his arms. "I thought if we were both still working out the case, perhaps we could talk it through together."

Crys locked her eyes on his. He read the hesitation in her expression, felt her debating the pros and cons of sharing her thoughts with him. Luke fought against the invisible bonds holding him in place and once again prepared to go back to his room.

Crys stepped back, pulling her bedroom door wider. "Sure. That could be helpful. We're both awake anyway."

Luke stepped into her room and felt transported into a flower garden. Crys's scent, wildflowers after a gentle rain, swept over him. Glass vases of dried flowers sat on every surface: both nightstands, the dressing table, chest of drawers and the vanity table in the far-left corner of the space near her bathroom. Luke was certain the padded, rose-pink chair in front of the table never got any use. He wondered whether her parents had made the matching honey wood furnishings in this room. If so, they'd been amazingly talented.

The bedroom's pale pink walls displayed framed watercolor images of daisies, sunflowers and tulips. Her queen-size sleigh bed was still made, evidence she hadn't even tried to sleep. It was covered with a lightweight quilt similar to the one on his mattress. But while his quilt was a simple blue-and-silver pattern, hers was an explosion of wildflowers. It matched the accent rugs that circled her bedframe on the honey wood flooring.

"Have a seat." Crys gestured toward a rose-pink armchair and matching ottoman. The set stood near the window on the right of her room beside a small bookcase.

"Thank you." Luke felt himself sinking into the thick, soft cushions. "What was on your mind as you were pacing?"

"I was wondering how long the intruder had been waiting in my home." Crys pulled the top edges of her robe closer together as though she felt chilled. But the room was warm. Luke felt comfortable in his T-shirt and shorts.

He sat forward, resting his elbows on his bare knees and linking his fingers together. "We left your house to meet with Wilma Strong and her family around five thirty. So they—she—must have arrived after that."

"I think you're right. She could've been in my house—alone—for as long as two hours before we returned." She wrapped her arms around her waist and paced to the opposite side of the bed. "But what had she been doing here—besides waiting to shoot me."

Luke heard the edge in Crys's voice, part anger, part unease. The same emotions he was grappling with. "Coming here was a big risk. She must have thought eliminating you was worth it."

He couldn't bring himself to use the term "killing" in connection with Crys. Thinking about it made his blood run cold.

"Possibly." She marched to her bedroom door before turning to pace back to her bed. "But you and I are working the serial and copycat killer cases together. If her goal is to stop those investigations in an effort to protect Dragon & Kelp, why is she only targeting me? She made her getaway in the same sports car that tried to run me over."

Luke had noticed that, too. "I don't know why she hasn't come after me." *Unless she believes Crys has information that could damage Dragon & Kelp, like Vic's files.*

All roads kept taking him back to Martina. He wasn't ready to share those concerns with Crys, though. Not yet. He wanted more than the cold feeling in the pit of his stomach on which to base his suspicions. If he was wrong—and he hoped he was—he would be maligning the reputation of an innocent and respected law enforcement official.

"We checked my house from top to bottom. She didn't take anything, and she didn't leave anything behind." Crys's eyes swept the room, seemingly looking for clues. "Maybe she did wait two hours to kill me. She must really want me dead." She shivered as though she was caught in the middle of a storm.

Luke watched her standing mere yards away, separated by a bed. The loose-fitting burgundy robe flowed over her slender figure. Her wide brown eyes were clouded. He could imagine the thoughts that burdened her were as dark as the ones that tormented him.

"It wrecked me to see that gun pointed at your chest. I don't think I've ever been so afraid." The admission escaped his lips before he could stop it. But he was glad he'd shared his feelings. It eased a little of the fear from that memory.

Blood drained from Crys's face. "Neither have I. But I thought, if I was about to die, I was going out fighting."

Luke rounded Crys's queen-size bed, and took her hands. They were so cold, but her touch reassured him she was well, safe and standing in front of him. Stepping closer, he hoped his heat would bring her some comfort.

"I admire your bravery." His voice was rough. He didn't recognize it. "You're an amazing combination of courage and compassion."

She gave him a crooked smile. "I'm lucky you were there with me. It's easier to be brave when you're not alone."

Her expression shifted from distance to warmth, from distress to desire. Luke's body heated in response. But he was cautious. Did she want to escape from tonight's events, or did she want him?

"I'm sorry about everything that's happened tonight. You've been through a lot. Confronting an intruder in your home. Having that person point a gun at you, and chasing her down only to have her get away. I want to do whatever I can to help you feel safe again and stop whoever's threatening you. But, Crys, I don't want to *forget* tonight with you. If we spend the night together, I want both of us to remember. Everything."

Crys closed the gap between them. Her scent wrapped around him, scattering his thoughts to the wind. The heat in her eyes told him more clearly than words that she wanted the same thing. Luke's knees went weak. He couldn't walk away from her now even if he wanted to. And walking away became the furthest thing from his mind.

She laid her right hand on his chest above his heart. Her voice was a whisper. "No one could forget you, Luke. Ever."

He lowered his head to hers. She lifted herself to him. Luke covered her mouth with his and felt the strange, familiar current arc between them. Crys's right hand continued up his chest, leaving a trail of fire to his shoulder. Luke wrapped his arms around her waist and felt her embrace him.

Opening his mouth, he invited her in. Deepening their connection. Crys's tongue swept across his. Her taste was an addictive combination of sweet, hot and spicy. He couldn't get enough of it. Enough of her. Luke drew her tongue deeper. She moaned at his caress. His body throbbed in response.

Crys broke their kiss. "My head's spinning." She whispered the words against his ear. "I need to catch my breath."

"You take my breath away, too. And I love it." He trailed kisses down her long, elegant neck.

Luke brought her with him onto her bed. They removed each other's clothing with long, slow caresses and deep, lingering kisses. Whispers of praise and sighs of satisfaction urged them on. Crys's hands stroked his arms, his shoulders. Her fingers traced his torso. Each touch feeding his desire.

She straddled his hips and kissed him deeply, making

his body burn. Luke stopped thinking. He could only feel her and what she was doing to him. Need took over. His need to touch her as she was touching him. To make her feel what he was feeling. To make her want him as much as he wanted her. To make her remember and never forget.

He rolled over with her, swallowing her gasp of surprise. Luke tucked her slender body beneath his without releasing her lips. His hands swept over her body, burning at the feel of her curves and dips.

Crys sighed at the weight of Luke's long, lean body pressing her into the mattress. She arched into him as her hunger built, growing wilder, taking over. Luke moved down her body. His lips caressed her breasts, making her nipples pebble. Her breath hitched as his tongue lingered at her navel. His teeth grazed her hips. Her back arched. Her heart raced. She could hear her blood rushing in her head.

"Luke, I want you."

"And I need you, Crys. So badly." His breath was hot over the juncture of her thighs.

Crys's legs moved restlessly. "Come into me, Luke. I want you now."

"Where, Crys?" His fingertips trailed over her thigh. "Here?" His fingers slipped inside her.

Crys gasped. She pressed her head back against the pillow. Moisture pooled in her as Luke's fingers moved. Her desire took over, her body moving to the rhythm he set. Her back arched. Luke's mouth closed over her breast. Crys cried out as pure pleasure exploded in her, rocking her body. Her muscles shaking in reaction.

Luke raised himself, wrapping his arms around her as her body continued to shake. He swept his tongue into her mouth as he entered her with one, long, deep thrust.

Crys gasped as the pleasure built again. He moved in her. Rocking her. Loving her. Crys twined her arms around his shoulders and pressed herself tighter to him. He moved faster. Crys locked her legs around his hips and matched his rhythm.

She tightened her arms around him. His body stiffened. His muscles tensed. Crys lifted herself, taking in more of him. Luke buried his face in the curve of her neck. The tension snapped inside her and she cried out as they fell together.

Chapter 17

"Martina, have you read my report on the Rashaad investigation? I wanted your feedback to finalize it." Luke sat in the department-issued sedan early Tuesday morning. Between his surveillance of the Buckeye State Capitol Investment's employee parking lot and this phone call to Martina, tension had taken residence in his neck and shoulders. He didn't anticipate it moving anytime soon.

Luke had parked at a shopping center across the street from the investment company's rear parking lot. Wilma Strong had a reserved space for her luxury sedan. This was Crys's first day as Wilma's decoy.

Luke had followed her from Wilma's home, where her undercover work had begun. From his position across the street, he had a clear line of sight to observe Crys as she entered the ten-story, tinted-glass-and-silver-metal structure. A handful of Buckeye State Capitol Investment's employees had entered the building with her. None of them had seemed threatening; no one had tried to speak with her. A few had given Crys curious looks as though they'd noticed something different between the person who'd emerged from Wilma Strong's car and the Wilma they knew. Luckily, they'd walked on without blowing her cover. If the serial killer were watching, had they noticed any changes in Wilma's appearance as well? Luke's anxiety rose another notch.

Crys had estimated it would take thirty minutes for her to get to Wilma's office on the top floor, do a reconnaissance of the executive suite and then change into her own clothes before joining him. However, last evening's break-in was a stark reminder of the dangers of this case. For that reason, Luke was only willing to wait twenty-five minutes before going in after her. She had eighteen minutes left.

While he waited for Crys, Luke had called Martina and put her on speakerphone.

"Your draft is unacceptable." Martina's tone was dismissive.

That stung. Luke took a calming breath, inhaling the scent of fresh pastries from the shopping center's doughnut shop. "Why?"

Martina sniffed. "It records the praise Detective Rashaad's friends heaped on her ad nauseum. You don't provide a single context either in support of or opposition to the veracity of their statements. It lacks balance. Are you a stenographer or an investigator?"

Luke struggled with his temper. "Martina, you're deliberately misinterpreting my report. Did you read my evaluation of whether Detective Rashaad fits the profile of a corrupt law enforcement officer?" Leaning forward, Luke stared at the tinted windows of the executive suite on the tenth floor. What was Crys doing now? What she safe? Had her cover been blown? Luke's palms were sweating.

Martina expelled an irritated breath. "That profile is a generalization, a rule of thumb. It's not meant to be taken literally. It's subject to interpretation. You should know that."

The clicking noise in the background sounded like she

was typing into her computer. Luke realized he didn't have his boss's full attention. His frustration grew on a pace with his stress.

"And as the investigator on this ethics case, my interpretation is that Crystal Rashaad doesn't match the profile of a corrupt officer of the law." Luke continued to scan the parking lot and the surrounding area. He leaned forward in his driver's seat again, looking for suspicious people waiting alone in their cars—other than him. He didn't find any. "She drives a seven-year-old Toyota, packs her lunch and uses a free app to find cheap gas, even for her department-issued car. That's not typical behavior for someone who's on the take. *You* have more expensive tastes than she does."

A faint gasp rocketed down their satellite connection. He'd caught Martina off guard. Luke felt equal parts satisfaction and shame. Was his boss corrupt? Had she been using him to further an agenda to hurt an innocent woman?

"What are you implying?" Martina flung the words at him like a blade.

"I'm not implying anything." He scanned the surroundings again.

He pictured Martina's jewelry and designer clothes all on a public servant's salary. Why hadn't he questioned those things before? Had he turned a blind eye to corruption right in front of him while Martina had sent him on a hit job against an honest person—like her errand boy? Luke saw red. He squeezed his eyes shut to clear his vision.

"Perhaps it seems expensive to you." Martina was dismissive. "But we're not discussing me. We're discussing Crystal Rashaad."

Luke checked his watch. Crys had fourteen minutes before he went into the building after her.

"Martina, I strongly suspect someone's framing her."
Perhaps you.

"*Framing* her?" Martina barked a laugh. "Why would
anyone do that? What's the motive?"

"The usual, money." Luke remembered the photos in
Martina's office. She'd posed with community leaders, government officials and corporate executives. She was well-
connected. That characteristic was a warning echoed in
Vic's note to Crys. "You have one anonymous source who
made an accusation without any evidence. I have nearly a
dozen interviews with colleagues who, based on their firsthand experience with her, assessed Detective Rashaad as
honest, trustworthy and dedicated." He'd attested to the
same thing in his report.

Luke surveyed the parking lot as Martina's displeasure
poured down their satellite connection. The tapping sound
from her end of the call shifted. It had morphed into a
rhythmic clicking, giving the impression she was drumming her fingernails against her desk. Her well-manicured
nails. Was she nervous? She should be.

"I was afraid of this." She finally spoke. "You've fallen
in love with the target of your investigation. You've com-
promised yourself by having a personal relationship with
Detective Rashaad."

Martina's words stunned him. They brought back the
experience of having Crys in his arms last night, her touch,
her taste, her scent. The memory of being with her warmed
his blood. Luke shook his head, trying to free himself from
those vivid recollections.

"My investigation is completely unbiased." Luke voice
was strained with anger. "My findings are impartial and
based on fact."

"You've been spending a lot of time with her."

"We're working two homicide cases, one of which involves a serial killer."

"It's not all work, Luke. I don't think—"

Luke cut off Martina's response. "Someone tried to kill Detective Rashaad last night."

"What?" Martina's voice was breathy with surprise.

"That was the second attempt on her life." Luke swallowed, easing the lump of very real fear in his throat. Suddenly, the interior of the car was too warm and stuffy. He glanced at the clock on the dashboard. Ten minutes left. In ten minutes he was going in after Crys. He stared at Buckeye State Capitol Investment, willing her to emerge from the building safe and sound. "Doesn't that concern you? Between the false charge of corruption—"

"Who said the charge is false?"

"—and the attempts to kill her, it's obvious someone considers her a threat and is trying to get her out of the way, permanently, if necessary. I think that's what we should be investigating, don't you?"

Say yes, Martina. Don't give me another reason to suspect you.

"OK, I'll play along, Luke." Martina's irritation crackled through the connection. "Let's say someone *is* trying to kill Detective Rashaad. What makes you think it isn't someone who wants revenge for her extorting money from them? Crystal Rashaad may not be the girl scout you seem to think she is."

"What makes you so certain she's corrupt?" Luke briefly closed his eyes. "You may not be convinced, but I am. To me, the attempts against Crys's life confirm her innocence. Something else is going on. I'm closing my investigation. As my report states, there's no evidence to support the allegations of corruption against Detective Rashaad."

"I'm not approving your report." Martina's voice was stiff with displeasure. "You've obviously allowed personal feelings to affect your judgment."

Luke unclenched his teeth. "If you want to assign the case to another agent, that's your call. But I stand by my report."

Martina hung up. Luke gritted his teeth. His skin burned with anger. *What are you involved in, Martina, and with whom?*

His temper cooled when he caught sight of Crys exiting the investment company. His eyes dropped to the clock on the dashboard. She had six minutes to spare.

Luke's eyes moved over her. From this distance, she appeared unharmed. She walked down the three steps at the building's rear entrance as though it was an ordinary day—as though no one had tried to murder her last night.

As though she wasn't a decoy for a serial killer's target.

Luke still couldn't believe she'd managed to subdue her thick riot of brown curls into a knot on the crown of her head. Dark sunglasses masked half of her delicate features. She'd paired plain black slacks with a dark gray scoop neck shirt instead of her usual floral blouse. If her goal was to blend in, she could never hope to achieve that. Crys Rashaad commanded attention. It wasn't only her beauty. It was her energy, which drew people to her.

Crys wheeled a small, black suitcase as she strode with confidence, purpose and grace out of the parking lot toward the sidewalk on her way to him. Luke scanned the cars and pedestrians near her. Was anyone approaching her? Was anyone looking at her? No and no. Still, Luke couldn't relax. Someone was targeting Crys, the woman he was falling in love with. He'd do whatever it took to keep her safe.

* * *

Crys opened the car door to the backseat of the department-issued sedan early Tuesday morning. "I suppose it was too much to hope our suspect would have grabbed me—or rather Wilma—on the first morning of our undercover assignment so we could get this over with." She wedged the suitcase with Wilma's clothes, shoes, briefcase and accessories onto the floor, then slammed the back door shut.

"Their MO is to grab their victims at the end of the day." Luke had raised his voice to be heard from the driver's seat."

"I know." Crys sank into the gray cloth passenger seat and expelled a sigh of disappointment. "Did you see anyone or anything suspicious while I was inside?"

Her hands shook as she secured her seatbelt, the effects of nerves and adrenaline from her assignment as Wilma Strong's decoy.

"No." Luke backed their vehicle out of the parking space and turned toward the shopping center's exit. "I didn't pick up any tails while you were driving in, either."

"Neither did I." Crys's eyebrows knitted in concentration. "Hopefully, they'll show up at the end of the day, as you said. I don't want this to drag on."

"I hope we haven't miscalculated who the next target will be."

Crys was confident her theory of the suspect's pattern was correct. "It's not a coincidence the first three victims were in alphabetical order. Wilma Strong is the next target."

"We've also warned Janice Young and her family just in case. Extra patrols have been assigned to her residence and place of employment." Luke merged the sedan into the dwindling morning rush-hour traffic. "How do you think it went on your end?"

Crys surveyed the sidewalks on either side of the street

and the passenger-side-view mirror, paying close attention to the pedestrians and especially the cars around them. She didn't register any familiar faces or suspicious behavior. Everyone seemed focused on getting to work.

"I think it went well. I checked the floors, stairwells and restrooms for security weaknesses. There aren't many." Crys took another breath, then shifted in her seat to face Luke. Her nerves were finally settling after last night's break in and this morning's undercover assignment. "I took the elevator up to the executive suite just like Wilma does."

"That must have been hard for you." Luke's lips curved into a half smile. "I know how much you hate elevators."

Crys gave him a sharp look. His teasing seemed muted. She studied his profile, his high forehead, broad nose, sharp cheekbones and square chin. He really was an attractive man. An attractive man with a lot on his mind. Was all the tension she sensed caused by this investigation? Or had something happened in his other case, the one investigating her? Crys felt herself pull back.

"For the record, I don't hate elevators, but I do prefer stairs." She pulled her attention from Luke's compelling features and stared through the windshield at the bars, restaurants, clubs and cafés of Columbus's Arena District. The investment company wasn't far from the police department. "Wilma's really well organized. I did a quick search of her office since she said that would be OK. No one approached me, which I thought was odd."

Luke glanced at her before returning his attention to the traffic. "She told her boss about our plan. If someone reported your presence on the floor, I'm sure he handled it."

Wilma had assured Crys and Luke that she'd stuck to the script they'd given her, hitting the high points and leaving out details that would compromise their mission.

"Let's hope he didn't handle it by telling other people what was going on. Our suspect might have someone on the inside helping them." Crys turned back to the windshield in time to glimpse the Nationwide Arena where the city's professional hockey team, the Columbus Blue Jackets, played. "Still, you'd think someone would have confronted me. My disguise wasn't that good. It just made me wonder if someone grabbed her off the floor, would anyone notice?"

"I'm sure someone would."

Crys snorted. "Anyway, it's a pretty big floor. A couple of conference rooms, offices, a large cubicle farm. But again, you need a key card to gain access and there are cameras in the hall, which makes me think our suspect waits for their target in the parking lot."

"That makes sense. When you return to the building this afternoon, you'll have to be even more alert." Luke's tone conveyed his concern, which made Crys feel somehow safer. Maybe watching her back was more than an assignment for him.

"Copy that." She slid a look at him, then turned away. "According to interviews with victims' families and friends, Rita, Alfred and Sally had made it into work the morning they disappeared, which confirms our theory that they were taken at the end of the workday."

"For the kidnapping, we have the why, and good leads on the when and where." Luke pulled into the police department's parking lot. "We still don't know the how. Is there more than one abductor? Is there a direct attack or is subterfuge involved? This evening, when you return to Buckeye State Capitol, you've got to be aware of everything and everyone around you."

Crys let her eyes roam over his profile again. "I have a feeling that's not the only thing on your mind."

Luke found a parking space toward the back of the crowded, crumbling asphalt lot. He stopped the engine, then sat staring through the windshield. Crys gave him time to work through his thoughts, but he wasn't leaving without giving her the answers she deserved.

"I didn't want to say anything earlier because I don't have evidence. All I have is a feeling in my gut."

"I know that feeling well." Her frustration was building as he doled out his information in stingy portions.

Luke's chest expanded with a deep breath. "I think Martina is involved in one of these cases."

Crys frowned. Luke suspected his boss at the BCI was involved in criminal activity? She struggled to process that. "Which case?"

Luke seemed to force himself to face her. "Your aunt's cold case."

Her blood froze. "What makes you think *your boss* had anything to do with my aunt's murder?"

Luke pressed back against the driver's seat. He never broke eye contact. "She's been aggressively pushing for me to find evidence of your corruption even though everything I've learned about you shows you have integrity and honor. Based on her wardrobe alone, I suspect she's living beyond her means."

Crys's cheeks warmed from Luke's compliment even as his announcement about Martina chilled her to the bone. "You're right. Those two things aren't much to go on. They could mean she has an axe to grind against me and a lot of debt."

"But why would she have anything against you? You don't know each other."

Crys shook her head. "Not that I'm aware of."

"Yet she perceives you as a threat." Luke straightened in

his seat. "What are you involved in that could threaten her? The only possibility is your aunt's homicide investigation."

Crys stared through the windshield again. This time, her mind filled it with images of her aunt. "Everything seems to lead back to Aunt K's murder."

"I know, Crys, and I'm sorry." Luke's voice was rough. "I think my investigation was created to discredit you. If during the course of your investigation, you found an inconvenient link between Dragon & Kelp and your aunt's death, Martina would point to the open investigation accusing you of corruption. But when I wouldn't be her good soldier, she threatened your life."

Crys's eyes flew back to his. "You think Martina is the woman who broke into my home last night?"

Luke nodded. "While you were doing your reconnaissance of Buckeye State Capitol Investment, I called Martina to tell her I was wrapping up my report and exonerating you. She accused me of spending a lot of personal time with you."

"As though she'd seen you in my house." Crys went numb at the thought that the assailant who'd broken into her home and pointed a gun at her chest was a trusted, high-ranking, law enforcement agent.

"But I don't have concrete evidence. All I have are suspicions."

Crys needed to think. Her mind worked best when she was moving. She shoved open the car door and climbed out. Luke joined her.

"We don't need evidence, concrete or otherwise. Not yet." Crys strode across the parking lot, dodging potholes. "What we need is a plan, and it starts with Jade."

"Why does it start with your sister?"

Crys glanced at him as he kept pace beside her. "Jade

has developed a great network of contacts on the crime beat over the years. They might be able to give us a deep background on Martina Monaco, whereas if either of us tried to use our contacts, it could get back to her."

"That's a good point."

She mounted the stairs to the rear entrance. "I'll call Amber and Jade now. I have to tell them about last night's break-in anyway. I can use this assignment for Jade as a distraction to keep them from moving in with me until the assailant is caught."

Don't fidget!

Crys held her hands at her sides Tuesday evening to keep from tweaking her appearance yet again. Wilma Strong's scarf covered her hair and the wireless earbud. Oversize dark glasses masked her features. A bulletproof vest and Wilma's loose-fitting coat obscured her figure and her weapon. Her fingernails dug into her palms. There was nothing else she could do. Showtime.

"I'm coming out."

"I'm watching." Luke's low baritone in her ear caused the pulse at the base of her throat to flutter.

Act naturally. Or at least as naturally as you think a wealthy executive with an investment firm would act.

Crys closed her eyes and tried to control her adrenaline rush. She took a breath and pushed through the tinted glass doors. Pausing on the top of the steps, she adjusted the strap of her briefcase on her shoulder. Crys used the hesitation to do a visual scan of the parking lot. She recognized several of the employees who were climbing into their cars or lingering on the sidewalk. She'd seen them that morning. A couple of them again gave her curious looks. Most of them didn't seem to notice her at all.

Would any of them notice if I were abducted from the lot?

She'd started to descend the steps when her eyes landed on Wilma's luxury sedan. Warning bells sounded in her mind. Something was off. Was the car crooked? Or was she imagining it? Crys's eyes dropped to the wheels. Her teeth clenched. Both tires on the driver's side of the vehicle were flat, and more than just a little bit. It was as though something—or someone—had punctured them in the morning, allowing them to deflate all day.

"They're here." Crys spoke without moving her lips. She hoped.

"On my way." Luke's tone was urgent.

Crys walked down the steps, Wilma's coat billowing around her. She pressed her left hand to her chest as though she were surprised and distressed to find her tires flat. As she bent over beside the car to examine the front driver's side tire, Crys angled her body away from the parking lot. She unholstered her gun under cover of Wilma's flowing coat. She'd just taken hold of the weapon when a low female voice spoke from behind her.

"Turn around and don't make a sound."

Her weapon in her hand, Crys turned to face the serial killer she'd been tracking for almost two months. She blinked. Her shoulders stiffened with surprise. It was Maeve Rhoades, one of the three security guards she'd met the day she and Luke had served the search warrant on Dragon & Kelp. Crys recognized the middle-aged woman's messy auburn ponytail and narrow gray eyes.

Maeve wore a black warm-up suit with two thin white stripes down the sides of the jacket sleeves and pant legs. Black-and-white tennis shoes completed the casual look meant to mask her criminal intent.

The Dragon & Kelp security guard was either pointing

a gun through one of her jacket pockets or she wanted Crys to think she was. But she stiffened in shock at the sight of the gun in Crys's hand. Blood drained from Maeve's milk-white face. She stepped back.

"Police! Everybody down!" Crys yelled at the top of her lungs.

Gasps, shouts and screams slashed through the air as people realized what was happening so close to them. In her peripheral vision, Crys saw bodies drop to the parking lot and sidewalk. Fear replaced the smell of traffic fumes and asphalt.

Maeve turned to run. Luke was waiting for her, gun drawn.

"Drop your weapon." His words were clear, cold and concise. His appearance was intimidating as he stood, long, lean and rock-solid in a cream shirt and coffee-colored pants. He'd loosened his navy tie and left his suit jacket in his car.

Maeve stepped back. "I've seen you before. Special Agent Gilchrist."

"Drop it." Luke's voice cooled another ten degrees as he repeated the order.

Maeve took another step back as she raised her empty left hand above her head. Bending sideways, she laid her gun on the ground, then glanced over her shoulder. "That must mean you're Detective Rashaad. Crystal Rashaad. I know you."

What did that mean? Crys frowned. She hadn't given Dragon & Kelp's security guards her first name. How had Maeve Rhoades learned it?

"Kick the gun toward me," Luke demanded.

Maeve faced forward and took another step back.

Crys tightened her grip on her gun. "Stop."

Maeve threw her right shoulder into Crys, slamming her into Wilma's car. Without stopping, she jumped onto the sidewalk and raced out of the parking lot.

"Dammit." Crys shed Wilma's voluminous coat.

"Are you all right?" Luke holstered Maeve's gun. His eyes, dark with worry, slid over her.

"Of course." Crys raced from the parking lot, stripping off Wilma's scarf. Anger and embarrassment fueled her. Maeve had caught her off guard as though she were a rookie.

She reached the sidewalk outside of the lot in time to see their suspect rounding the corner onto Broad Street. "Stop! Police!"

Luke sprinted past her. Crys followed close behind, weaving a path through the forest of pedestrians on the crowded commercial street. Crys longed for her loafers. The four-inch pumps she wore for her decoy assignment slowed her down.

"Police! Police! Stop!" Most of the civilians moved out of the way as they heard Crys's shouts. A few seemed oblivious to what was going on. "Get out of the way!"

In front of her, Luke echoed her command for Maeve to stop. The security guard ignored them both as she pushed her way through the crowd. She looked over her shoulder, checking their progress. Crys and Luke were gaining on her. Facing forward, Maeve jumped into High Street, ignoring the red pedestrian light. Luke dived after her. Crys followed his lead. Squealing tires, blaring horns and angry shouts added to the tension and confusion. "Give me a—"

Maeve glanced back again. They were so close.

"Maeve! Stop!" Crys shouted from behind Luke.

Maeve didn't heed. Instead, she grabbed a civilian, a small, older white woman, and shoved her back toward

Luke. Crys's eyes widened, and her lips parted in concern as she watched the woman drop her bags and windmill her arms in an effort to regain her balance. Luke stretched forward to catch her. Crisis averted, Crys dodged the pair. She dug into her reserves of speed to make up the ground Maeve's dangerous distraction had cost.

Crys raced on, lengthening her strides, pumping her elbows, gritting her teeth until she was within an arm's length of her target. Straining forward, she wrapped her fingers around the collar of the other woman's warm-up jacket and jerked her to a stop.

Luke came up beside Crys. "Put your hands behind your back." He pulled his handcuffs from the back of his duty belt and exchanged a look with Crys.

Releasing Maeve into Luke's hold, Crys stepped around the other woman to face her. "Maeve Rhoades, you're under arrest for attempted kidnapping and assaulting a law enforcement officer."

With deep satisfaction, Crys read Maeve her Miranda rights as she and Luke took her into custody. But she knew this case was nowhere near being over. And Aunt K's killer continued to escape justice.

Chapter 18

"Maeve lawyered up." Crys looked at her sisters and Luke seated around her dining table Tuesday night.

She'd turned on almost every light in her home. It was her weak attempt to beat back the darkness after the stressful experiences of the past week: the near hit-and-run, the break-in and chasing a serial killer through the crowded downtown streets. She'd also served mugs of hot chamomile tea. The drink always relaxed her. Its sweet, herbal scent floated out of her large, yellow porcelain mug.

Amber and Jade had come over after she'd told them she and Luke had the serial killer in custody. They'd said they wanted to congratulate her in person and hear as many details as she could share with them. She knew their priority was to make sure she was all right. She loved them for that.

"She was a security guard at Dragon & Kelp?" Seated to Crys's right, Amber shook her head. Her wavy brown tresses slid forward over her shoulder. Her topaz blouse warmed her skin's gold undertones. "She was right under their noses. That's incredible."

Jade was across the table from Amber. She wore navy slacks and a cream, long-sleeved cotton blouse. "It's genius. As a security guard, she pretty much had the run of the building. She could go through their archives and get information on past claims, personnel files, whatever she needed to plot her revenge."

"Those are all good points." Seated at the opposite end of the table, Luke stroked his fingers over the side of his mug in a way Crys found hypnotic. "Crys and I are sure we'll find copies of Maeve Rhoades's denied benefits claim among Dragon & Kelp's files. That, plus her attempt to kidnap the person she thought was Wilma Strong should be enough for us to get a search warrant for her home."

"You said 'Crys and I.'" Jade tilted her head toward Luke. "Does that mean you're staying on this case?"

Crys held her breath. Did she want him to continue the investigation with her? Or would it be better for her heart for them to say goodbye sooner rather than later?

Luke tossed a look toward her before responding to Jade's question. "As long as my boss doesn't object, I want to continue with this assignment. We still need to gather evidence against Maeve."

Jade considered Luke's expression, then exchanged a silent look with Amber. Crys wished she knew what her sister had been searching for and what she'd found.

She filed the question away. "When we confronted Maeve, she said she knew me. She called me Crystal. I hadn't given the guards my full name."

Jade's eyebrows rose up her forehead. "Well, that's creepy."

Crys shivered. "I thought so, too."

Jade blinked. "Do you think she knew Aunt Kenny? They both worked in that building."

Crys's eyes flew to Luke's. Her blood chilled. "That's possible."

Jade shook her head. "That makes this situation even creepier."

"I'm so glad you're both safe." Amber looked from Luke, diagonally across the table from her, to Crys beside her. "You took a big risk, especially since someone's already targeting you."

Jade drank her tea. "Am's right. That was dangerous. I know it's part of your job, but I also know thinking about you acting as a decoy's going to give me nightmares for a while."

Crys sipped her tea, letting it warm the chill that seemed to have taken permanent residence in her bones. "It's not an assignment to take lightly. But I have training, and I had backup." She nodded toward Luke. "Whoever's trying to harm me wants it to look like an accident, a hit-and-run, a robbery-gone-wrong. They're not going to do something that will raise suspicions."

Jade took another drink of her tea. "Speaking of your safety, I've heard back from my contacts." She looked at Luke. "Your gut's on the right track. Apparently, Martina has a shady history. It tracks back to about five years ago when her very wealthy husband left her for a younger woman."

Crys scowled. Resentment was a vile taste in her mouth. "She wants to ruin my life because her husband left her?"

Amber crossed her arms. Her movements were stiff with temper. "It sounds more like her motive is money."

"Right the first time." Unfazed by her sisters' interruption, Jade continued her report. "Martina had signed a brutal prenup. She left the marriage with exactly what she had when she entered it, which was pretty much nothing."

Amber looked at Crys. "She was framing you to pay for her lavish lifestyle."

Jade's voice was rough with temper. "According to my contacts, Martina's resignation from her previous agency was abrupt. They suspected she got wind that the agency's ethics committee was opening an inquiry into her, so she left *before* that could happen but *after* making allegations of corruption against one of her subordinates. That person was subsequently cleared of all charges."

Surprise prompted Crys to fall back against her honey wood chair. "She'd set up her subordinate to take the fall for her crimes?"

Jade nodded. "That's what it looks like."

Luke's eyebrows rose. "Your contacts have an incredible wealth of information."

Jade wagged her index finger at him. "Don't give me that look. I protect all my sources. Remember?"

"Fair enough." Luke turned to Crys. "It wouldn't be a stretch to think she fabricated the anonymous source who filed the ethics complaint against you."

"No, it wouldn't." Crys expelled a breath. "And I'm convinced the attacker was a woman." She stood, maneuvering past Amber's chair and wandering into the adjoining family room. "I still can't wrap my mind around her going to those lengths to discredit me. To set me up to take the fall in case her corruption was discovered."

"That's just a theory. I—" Luke's voice was close as though he'd followed Crys into the room.

Jade interrupted. "But it's a good theory. It appears she may have a history of doing that. It's also the only lead we have that has a snowball's chance of keeping our sister safe."

"I agree it's a plausible hypothesis. We can work with it." Amber followed Jade and Luke into the family room.

Her expression was pensive. Crys wondered if the prosecutor in her was considering how to strengthen their theory into a charge that would lead to a conviction.

"Something else we need to factor into this." Crys wrapped her arms around her waist and turned to face the group. "My stalker isn't working alone." She looked at Luke. "When we chased her, she got into the *passenger* side of a getaway vehicle."

"What type of vehicle?" Amber asked.

Luke rubbed the back of his neck. "It was late at night. We can't be sure. But it looked like a dark, low-slung sports car."

Jade caught her breath. "Like the car that nearly ran you over in front of Dragon & Kelp? And the one that struck Abby Hansen-Tiller?"

Her stomach dipped when she thought about Vic's eldest child. She and Becca had been texting every other day about Abby's condition. She was still in a coma, but her vitals were getting stronger. For that reason, the doctors were hopeful about her prognosis.

Crys dropped her arms. "It's another connection that links the break-ins—the one here, and the ones at Aunt K's and Vic's homes—to the attacks against me and Abby."

Jade spread her hands. "A flashy car like that is a cry for attention. Why use it to commit a crime?"

Amber wrapped her hands around her mug. "It draws attention to the car and not the criminal."

That was as good a theory as any for now. Crys began pacing the width of her family room. "We need evidence against Martina so we can turn our suspicions into a chargeable offense. Arresting her could get us closer to Aunt K's and Vic's killers, whoever's behind the threats against me, and to our copycat killer."

Luke crossed his arms over his broad chest. He still wore his cream shirt, navy tie and coffee-colored pants.

He looked good. "Unlike Martina, we aren't going to fabricate a complaint so we can open a bogus investigation."

Cry stood straighter. Pieces of an idea formed in her mind. She smiled at him. "I think you gave me a plan."

"This could work." Luke stood away from the wall and dropped his arms to his sides.

Crys had spent the better part of the last half hour Tuesday night going over the outline of her plan, incorporating Luke's feedback into the framework and answering Amber's and Jade's many questions.

"It's too risky." Jade's expression was stubborn.

Amber looked from Crys to Luke. "I'm not especially comfortable with it, either."

Crys arched an eyebrow. "Would you be comfortable with it if I weren't your sister?"

"Yes," Amber and Jade answered in unison.

Crys swallowed a sigh. Her sisters could be so frustrating. "Look, this is my job. I can't spend hours reassuring you every time I go to work. With this plan, I'll have a vest, a wire and my gun."

"And I'll have her back," Luke added.

Crys paced forward to the chair at the foot of the table and gripped its back with both hands. She faced her sisters, seated across from each other. "This is going to happen in a public place, and I won't take unnecessary risks."

Jade's shoulders rose and fell with a deep sigh. "Fine." She avoided looking at Crys.

Amber held Crys's eyes. "You were a great police officer and you're becoming an amazing detective. But you'll always be our sister first and we're always going to worry about you."

Jade snorted. "And there's nothing you can do about that."

Crys rolled her eyes.

Luke checked his watch. "I'd better get going." He jerked his thumb over his shoulder toward the staircase. "I want to review a couple of my SIU projects. Amber, Jade, it's always great to see you. I hope one day, we can talk about something that doesn't involve danger and dead bodies."

Amber smiled. "Good night, Luke. And thank you for watching out for our sister."

"Yeah. Keep up the good work." Jade gave him a thumbs-up.

Luke laughed over his shoulder as he crossed to the staircase. "I'll do my best, but your sister is capable of taking care of herself."

Crys watched Luke disappear up the stairs. With his vote of confidence, he took yet another piece of her heart. Dammit.

"It's nice when someone believes in you and lifts you up like that." Amber's voice held both wistfulness and regret. "That's how Trent made me feel, until I realized he didn't believe in me. He was just using my professional reputation to help get him into the right social circles."

Crys took the seat at the foot of the table. She squeezed Amber's hand where it lay on the table next to her. "I'm so sorry."

Amber waved a dismissive hand. "Luke doesn't have an ulterior motive."

Jade lowered her voice. "How are things going between the two of you?"

Crys gave a restless shrug. "He's smart. He's kind. He's brave."

"He's easy to look at." Jade's voice was dust dry.

Crys didn't respond to that understated truth. "We've been busy with these cases. I never expected this investigation to become so complicated with a serial killer, a copycat and connections to Aunt K's murder. I need to stay focused."

Amber propped her chin in her palm. "You and Luke have arrested a suspect for the serial killings and you're close to catching the copycat. So what happens after you close these cases?"

Crys lowered her voice to a whisper. "Look, the fact is I could fall in love with him. I think I already have."

"Have you told him how you feel?" Amber asked.

Crys shook her head. "Am, I don't have the bandwidth for a relationship right now. I've just been promoted to detective. I'm trying to get up to speed in this new role. I have to prove myself. And the three of us are trying to find Aunt K's killer. That's going to take a lot of time, too. How am I supposed to handle all that and make room for a romantic relationship?"

Jade's eyes probed hers in a way that made Crys wonder again if her youngest sister was a human lie detector. "Is that the real reason you're keeping Luke at arm's length? Or are you still punishing yourself for Aunt Kenny's death?"

Crys glanced toward the stairs. Could Luke hear them? She turned back to Jade. "Punishing myself how?"

Jade leaned into the table, bringing herself closer to Crys. "Of the three of us, you're the one who's always been the most interested in getting married and raising a family. You haven't dated anyone since Aunt Kenny died more than a year ago. You haven't even talked about guys you'd be interested in going out with. You've been all about work. It's as though you're afraid that if you put yourself first something horrible will happen—like the night you canceled dinner with Aunt Kenny to go out with your ex."

Crys's lips parted in shock. How had Jade seen so clearly the cause of her reservations against having a relationship with Luke when she hadn't understood the reason she was holding back?

Amber took Crys's left hand in both of hers. "Crys, Aunt Kendra's death was *not* your fault. It just wasn't. It wasn't J's fault, either. It was the killer's fault." She lowered her voice. "If you're falling in love with Luke, tell him how you feel. Give him *and yourself* a chance to be happy."

Her sister's words were tempting. Despite her own heartbreak with Trent, Amber made falling in love sound like it was worth the risk. Crys looked over her shoulder toward the staircase again. Could she take the risk of giving her heart to Luke?

"Crys doesn't trust me." Luke reclined on the bed in the guest room Crys had given him.

"Well, you were secretly investigating her based on bogus allegations of ethics violations. So there's that." Caleb's response, though accurate, felt like a betrayal.

Luke had told Crys, Amber and Jade that he had work to do. That wasn't true, a fact that Caleb would use as additional evidence of the reasons Crys had to not trust him. He'd left the sisters alone Tuesday night because he thought they'd want to catch up, and he didn't want to be in the way. He'd thought a conversation with Caleb would be a pleasant way to pass the time. He was reconsidering that.

"She said she forgave me for that and understood I was doing my job." Luke stared at the closed bedroom door. He hoped it at least muffled his conversation with Caleb. He wouldn't want Crys to know he was talking about her much less what he was saying.

Just as he'd feared, after they made love Monday night,

Luke had woken Tuesday morning to find Crys had erected a virtual wall between them. He imaged he could read the word "Regrets" spraypainted across it. Luke had gathered the shattered pieces of his heart and prioritized the job. After all, it was the search for a serial killer that had brought them together.

"You also told me she said she could forgive you, but she couldn't forget what you did." A faint whirring sound beneath Caleb's voice made Luke think his friend was pouring a glass of water from his refrigerator dispenser. "It's sort of like that biblical verse about forgiving the sinner but not the sin."

"How am I supposed to fix this?" Luke pressed back against the headboard. He stared at the ceiling, searching for the answer.

"You've fallen hard for her, haven't you?"

"What's not to fall for?" Luke brought to mind images of Crys kicking the gun from her attacker's hand, chasing down their serial killer suspect, hugging Becca Hansen at the hospital. "She's smart. She's kind. And she's courageous. She's amazing. And I want the chance to get to know her better."

"Rebuilding trust isn't something you can do overnight. These things take time, young Padawan."

Luke closed his eyes and shook his head. "No more *Star Wars* references. This isn't the time."

There was a moment of silence on the other end of the call as though Caleb was taking a drink. "Notice I've never told you I was your father. Is Jade there?"

It took a second for Luke to catch up with his friend's change of topic. "Yes, both of Crys's sisters are here. I told you that."

"I suppose it's too late for me to stop by, pretending to

have been in the neighborhood?" Caleb's voice was hesitant. He seemed to be weighing the pros and cons of his idea.

Luke shared his friend's pain. "I'm afraid so, pal. It's pretty late. Crys's sisters will probably be leaving soon."

"Yeah. You're right." A smile, and a hint of bravado, returned to Caleb's voice. "I just thought if Jade sees me often enough, I'll eventually wear her down."

Luke chuckled. The statement personified his friend, determination in the face of adversity. "Fortunately, you're a patient guy."

"Very patient, especially when the goal is worth it." Caleb paused. "It's worth it for you, too, my friend. Talk with your lady."

"She's not my lady." Disappointment was a heavy weight.

"Yet. I have faith in you."

Luke sighed. "I appreciate that, brother." But he wished those words had come from Crys.

Chapter 19

"You were right." Luke sat on the other side of Martina's desk early Wednesday morning. He almost choked on the words but he needed the lie to keep Crys alive. Martina's office smelled of strong coffee and expensive perfume.

Luke focused on getting into the character of a repentant subordinate who had absolute trust in their manager's integrity. It was the cover he, Crys, Amber and Jade had agreed on last night as best suited to Crys's plan. Because of his suspicions about Martina, the role was a stretch, but he'd turn in an Oscar-worthy performance to protect the woman he loved.

"About Rashaad? I knew it!" Martina slapped the palm of her well-manicured right hand on the surface of her desk. Her sapphire-and-gold ring sparkled under the fluorescent office lighting. Her brown eyes glinted with victory. "What have you learned?"

For this to work, he and Crys had to keep the details simple and consistent. "Detective Rashaad claims she's found documents among her aunt's homicide cold case files with information connecting Dragon & Kelp to the order to destroy policyholders' medical records, then deny beneficiaries' claims on the grounds that medical examinations were never provided."

Luke's muscles were tight with anger. This was their first big bluff. Crys had not found any such documents. They were acting on a hunch about the paperwork Crys's aunt may have discovered.

"Did *she* tell you that?" Martina's voice was sharp with incredulity.

"No." Luke feigned surprise and disbelief at her question. "You know there have been two attempts on Detective Rashaad's life—"

Martina interrupted. "I know she *claims* someone's out to get her."

"I believe her." Luke held up his hands, palms out. "I was with her during both attempts. The first was a near hit-and-run outside of Dragon & Kelp's offices. The driver had a black, low-slung sports car. The second was a break-in at her home. The armed intruder was a woman. She escaped in an identical vehicle."

Luke watched Martina closely for her reaction to his description of the car and his assertion that the intruder had been female. Was she a little paler than when he'd entered her office?

"Fine. Fine." Martina waved an impatient hand. "You're backing up her allegations, but what do those alleged attacks have to do with the documents she supposedly found?"

Luke glanced at the framed pictures lining the walls and bookcases in Martina's office with a new perspective. Were these images of her socializing with politicians, celebrities, captains of industry and local, state, federal and international dignitaries supposed to be a virtual slap-in-the-face aimed at her ex-husband. Was this her way of telling herself that he'd rejected her, but she was capable of achieving this type of access on her own?

"Detective Rashaad asked me to protect her, to watch

her back." It had been the other way around, but everyone had agreed Martina would be less suspicious if Crys were drawn as the instigator. "She asked me to move into her guest room until her assailant could be caught."

Martina lowered her eyebrows in disapproval. "I trust you kept everything professional."

"Yes, ma'am." The lie rolled off Luke's tongue. "While I was in her home last night, I overheard her speaking with her sisters. She said the documents also connect Dragon & Kelp to Carter Wainscott's killer."

Martina raised her right hand, palm out. A thin gold bracelet slid past her wrist. "You told me she'd given Jasper—Lieutenant Bright—the files she'd received from Victor Hansen's daughter."

"That's what she told me." Luke shrugged, acting the part of innocent messenger. "And I believe that's what she told Lieutenant Bright. But obviously she lied."

Martina's narrowed eyes glittered with disdain. "And you trusted her. I told you, you were blinded by her beauty."

Luke sighed, playing along. "You're right. She duped me. Instead of handing everything over, she withheld critical documents, copied the rest of the files and is even now devising a plan to blackmail Carter Wainscott's killer. She told her sisters she'd give the suspect the incriminating documents but only in exchange for fifteen million dollars."

"*Fifteen million dollars?*" Martina's jaw dropped. Her eyes bulged.

"Each sister would get five million dollars."

"They certainly have high expectations." Martina's eyes were wide with shock, disbelief and anger. Was she imagining herself writing that check? "And I thought you said you caught the serial killer yesterday? The same monster who killed the others killed Carter Wainscott."

Luke assessed Martina's body language. She was avoiding his eyes. A thin layer of perspiration collected on her upper lip and forehead.

He felt a surge of satisfaction, but he had to stay in character. "The person who murdered Carter Wainscott wasn't the serial killer. It was a copycat. Remember?"

"Oh, yes, that's right." Martina was distracted. What was she thinking? Was she trying to figure out how to come up with fifteen million dollars?

He hoped Crys's plan was working. The sooner they caught the person who was trying to harm her, the sooner he'd get a good night's sleep, knowing she was safe, preferably in his arms.

"Based on the crime scene evidence, Detective Rashaad and I believe the same person killed Rita Gomez, Alfred Murphy and Sally Stead. And we believe we have that suspect in custody. However, due to discrepancies, we think someone else killed Carter Wainscott." Luke watched for Martina's reaction. "Detective Rashaad claims she's found proof that links Wainscott's killer to Dragon & Kelp. She also thinks she can connect that person to the murders of her aunt, Victor Hansen and Brock Mann."

The blood drained from Martina's face. "And how does she think she can do that?"

The more he kept Martina talking, the more she revealed herself. Luke straightened in the visitor's chair. "I don't know if I can tell you that. I may have already shared too much info—"

"I am your supervisor." Martina's powder-white skin flushed an angry red. She was on the edge of shouting. "I have a right to that information. You cannot withhold information from me."

Luke nodded, trying to appear subdued. "All right. Detective Rashaad believes the person who killed Carter Wainscott framed Brock Mann for the murder, then shot Brock with the same small-caliber gun used to kill her aunt and her partner."

Martina coughed as though something had become stuck in her throat. Fear? She took a sip of cooling coffee, and the obstruction seemed to ease.

"Excuse me." She stared at her desk as though it could provide an escape route from this situation. "Does she have a name?"

Luke had been prepared for that question. "I heard her tell her sisters, she thinks the killer's name is among the notes her aunt left for her. She has the report on the gun and, according to the documents, the killer is a corrupt law enforcement agent." The irony wasn't lost on Luke. It turned his stomach.

Martina's face stiffened in shock. Blood drained from her face.

Got you. The first part of their plan had been successful. Luke lowered his eyes to hide his triumph.

Martina took a breath and released it with her response. "Well, Luke, thank you for this information. It's very helpful. I'm sure we can now both agree that, as I said before, your investigation into allegations of corruption against Detective Rashaad must continue."

Luke inclined his head. "I'm sorry I didn't listen to you sooner."

She narrowed her eyes as though in disappointment. "You obviously put your trust in the wrong person."

Luke held Martina's eyes. "That's right. It's a mistake I won't make again."

"See that you don't." Martina's command was sharp.

"How do you think I should proceed?" Luke spread his

hands. "I thought I should tell Detective Rashaad that I overheard her conversation with her sisters and demand she turn over the doc—"

"No." Martina extended both arms, palms out. "If we do that, it will shut down the investigation. We have to wait until she offers the bribe to Wainscott's killer. Then we might be able to arrest her sisters, too."

"All right. You're in charge."

Martina pinned him with her eyes. He thought he found a trace of fear in them. "Does Rashaad know you overheard their conversation?"

Luke shook his head. "I stayed out of sight."

Martina once again appeared distracted. "Good."

Luke stood to leave. "I'll give you updates on my investigation."

He could tell Martina's mind had shifted to something else. He left her to her thoughts and drove his SUV to a parking lot a few blocks away. He tapped the preprogrammed number on his cell phone that would connect him to Crys. She picked up on the first ring.

"It's done." Luke scanned his surroundings in case someone was watching him.

"What do you think?" Crys's tone hinted at both dread and excitement. Wherever she was taking his call, Luke imagined she was pacing.

"She's part of this. If she didn't kill your aunt, Vic, Carter and Brock, she knows who did. I'm sure of it."

"All right. Now we wait." Crys's words were edged with anger.

"Remember you're not in this alone. I've got your back."

"I know." Some of her anger eased from her voice.

The fact Crys trusted him enough to include him in this plan to expose his boss made a future with her seem within reach. But because of the danger they were preparing to confront, he knew that future wasn't promised.

I heard you're looking for me.

The text had sent a chill down Crys's spine when it appeared on her personal cell phone late Thursday morning, a little more than twenty-four hours after Luke's meeting with Martina Wednesday. It had come from a blocked number, of course, and included a map with instructions to meet at the Polaris Fashion Place food court precisely at noon.

She'd shown it to Luke. It was proof of Martina's involvement in the criminal activity. The text may have come from Martina herself.

Crys had responded with a barrage of questions in an effort to sell the setup's legitimacy: Who were they? How did they know she was looking for them? How would she identify them *if* she agreed to the meeting? She wanted fifteen million dollars.

Their answers were frustratingly vague, but they assured her they would give her fifteen million dollars if she met them alone at the mall. Crys and Luke doubted they'd had time to collect such a large sum. But the important thing was taking the suspect into custody. That's how Crys found herself seated alone at a table for two at the Polaris Fashion Place food court. She'd arrived a little before noon.

She was surrounded by a medley of mouthwatering scents: spicy Thai food, cheesy pizza, salty fries and the sweet, buttery aroma of fresh pastries.

"Are you in position?" Luke's question was tense and rushed as his voice carried through her earbud.

The music blasting from the sound system, and the

laughter and loud conversations at the nearby tables made it hard to hear him.

Crys tightened her grip on the thick manila envelope that was serving as a decoy for the incriminating documents. "Yes. What's wr—"

"Crys, I need you to trust me." He was scaring her.

"What's going—" The line went dead. "Luke?" She hissed his name. "Luke!"

Was he kidding *her right now?* She was minutes from meeting a suspected serial killer—perhaps the person who killed Aunt K—and she had no backup. Her stomach muscles were cold and knotted. She'd trusted him to have her six. What in the—

"Hello, Rashaad." The scratchy voice held a hint of a Southern Ohio accent.

Crys looked up into her supervisor's familiar face. "Lieutenant?" He looked like a gracefully aging actor in a slim, smoke-gray Italian suit, snow-white shirt and plum tie. "What are you doing here?" But she knew.

"I heard you're looking for me." His thin smile didn't reach his cold gray eyes. He nodded toward the envelope in her hands. "Is that mine?"

A massive array of emotions slammed into her like a tsunami: shock, confusion, anger, fear, sorrow, betrayal. She clung to anger.

Crys surged from her chair. Her eyes stung with unshed tears. Her throat burned with them. "Did you kill—"

Jasper pulled one hand from his pants pocket and waved it in front of her face. "Shh. Shh."

He was shushing her? Her head was so hot, she thought it would explode.

"You. Monster." Crys stepped back and took several calming breaths. She had to control her emotions. She needed his confession. Justice for Aunt K would come after. "Where's my money?"

His voice was warm, but his eyes remained frigid. "You didn't expect me to conduct my business in a food court, did you?"

"I didn't expect *you*." Crys curled her hands into fists at her side.

Jasper swept his right arm toward one of the hallways off the food court. "Do you want your money or not, Rashaad?"

Crys glared at him before marching into the hallway. Jasper took her arm, but she shrugged him off. She didn't want her aunt's killer to touch her. What she wanted was to knock his head from his shoulders.

"This way." Jasper's voice ended her violent fantasies. He gestured toward an institutional gray door marked Facilities.

Crys pinned him with another glare. "You'd better not try anything, *Jasper*."

He arched a thick dark brown eyebrow at her childish taunt with his name. "Or what, *Rashaad*? You may think you have the upper hand, but you don't. You're a rookie detective. I'm a thirty-year veteran. I know more about covering up crimes than you'll ever know about solving them."

Crys forced her words through gritted teeth. "Did. You. Kill. My. Aunt?"

He gave her another fake smile. "Martina told me you'd figured it all out. It was the gun, wasn't it? Once Vic gave you the missing papers from your aunt's file, you were able to connect his murder to your aunt's and Mann's."

"Why?" The question emerged as a whisper.

Jasper shrugged. "The pay was a lot better than what I made with the force."

She couldn't believe what was happening. Her lieutenant

was a criminal. Her boss for the past almost nine months had killed her aunt, her partner, her sister's former editor and a stranger.

Crys had to swallow twice before she could speak. "I guess you don't know as much about covering up crimes as you thought, since this rookie detective solved yours."

Anger flashed in his eyes. He pushed open the Facilities room door. "After you, Rashaad."

Crys gave him a direct stare. "You brought me here to kill me, didn't you?"

Jasper's smile touched his eyes this time. "I don't have fifteen million dollars."

Crys locked her knees to keep them from buckling. "I'm not going in there." She called his bluff. "If you're going to kill me, you'll have to do it out here."

"All right." He pushed the door open and motioned to whoever had been waiting inside.

Crys blinked when the new arrival joined them. "Luke?" Her eyes dropped to the small-caliber gun in his right hand.

"Did you get it?" he asked.

Crys, I need you to trust me. Those words sounded in her ear as though he'd spoken them again.

She reminded herself to breathe. Pulling the mini recorder from the manila envelope, she held it up so he could see it. "Yes."

Jasper frowned at Luke. "What are you doing?"

Luke turned the gun on him. "We're arresting you for the murders of Kendra Chapel, Victor Hansen, Carter Wainscott and Brock Mann. You have the right to remain silent, but I really hope you'll keep talking."

As Luke read Jasper the rest of his Miranda rights, Crys put the handcuffs on him. Finally, after more than a year of waiting, she was arresting one of the people who'd killed her aunt.

Blinking back tears, she found Luke. Her voice was husky. "Thank you."

His smile was a little tired, but it was real and it was warm. Her heart melted. Maybe Amber and Jade were right. Maybe nothing horrible would happen if she gave love another chance. Perhaps something wonderful would happen if she took that chance with Luke.

"Martina had called as I was getting into position at Polaris." Luke sat in a corner of Crys's sofa Thursday evening. He and Crys had changed into more comfortable clothing and were sharing with Amber, Jade and Caleb the details of their arrests of Jasper Bright and Martina Monaco. "She gave me an ultimatum: help them get rid of Crys or be framed for murdering the Rashaad sisters."

"What?" Amber's and Jade's voices rose several octaves as they spoke in chorus.

Luke had already told Crys the circumstances that had led to him waiting for her in the Facilities room with a gun. She'd been furious and frightened. She'd also thanked him for putting himself in danger to protect her and her sisters. Luke hadn't considered the danger. His only thought had been protecting her and her family.

Crys had curled up in her armchair. She looked comfortable in her rose leggings and white, floral-patterned pullover. She concluded her description of the events by telling her sisters and Caleb about recording Jasper's confession and his implication of Martina. "As we suspected, Jasper and Martina lawyered up just like Maeve Rhoades had."

Amber sat on the sofa between Luke and Caleb. "I'd love to be a fly on the wall when their lawyers hear that tape."

"I wish I'd known your aunt Kendra." Luke hadn't meant to say that aloud. As soon as the words left his mouth, he regretted his impulse. The atmosphere in the room became heavy with heartache.

"I wish you'd known her, too." Jade had carried in a chair from the dining room and set it beside Crys. She wore black, tapered-leg jeans and a cobalt-blue, long-sleeved T-shirt.

Crys's eyes were somber as she held his. "She would've liked you."

The compliment went straight to Luke's heart. "I'm sure I would've liked her, too." But how does her niece feel about him? Luke clenched his teeth to keep from asking.

Amber smoothed her garnet, ankle-length skirt over her lap. "Aunt Kendra always said friends in need are the best." She looked at him, her eyes damp with unshed tears. "Thank you so much for being there when my family needed you."

Luke was overwhelmed. He swallowed the lump of emotion in his throat. "It was my pleasure."

"You're both amazing." Caleb sat sideways on the sofa, keeping Luke and Crys in his line of sight. Luke suspected his friend also had an eye on Jade. "That was a dangerous assignment, and you never flinched."

Crys turned to Luke. "It's easier to be brave when you're not alone."

Luke stilled. Her words brought back memories of their night together, a night he would always treasure, regardless of what the future held.

Crys locked the door after wishing Amber, Jade and Caleb good night and cautioning them to drive carefully. Was the danger really over? Was her family finally safe?

Her hand lingered on the doorknob as she collected the courage to face Luke.

His voice carried from behind her. "It's getting late. I'm going to pack, then get on the road."

"No." Crys hadn't meant to shout, but she'd panicked.

Luke halted with one foot on the bottom step. He looked back at her. "No? What are you saying? Do you want me to come back for my things tomorrow?"

Oh, no, no, no. She didn't want to say goodbye in stages. She didn't want to say goodbye at all.

Crys straightened her shoulders and took a breath. She felt as though she were preparing for battle. "I realize that, with Jasper and Martina in custody, I'm not in danger anymore. I don't *need* protecting. Or extra protection. You said you know I can take care of myself—"

"Yes, you can. You've proven that many times during this case."

"Thank you." Crys cleared her throat. "But, Luke, even though I don't *need* you to stay, I *want* you to stay." Her nerve started to crack when Luke remained silent. She dug deep and found the courage to push on. "I know there may not be a reason to stay—but maybe there is?"

Luke looked as though she'd sucker punched him. "What are you saying, Crys?"

"I'm saying I want to give us a chance." Crys clenched her hands at her sides. "I know falling in love is a risk, and risks can be scary. But isn't it easier to be brave when you're not alone?"

Two long strides carried Luke to her before she realized he'd moved. He lifted her from the floor and pressed his lips to hers. His kiss was firm and warm, deep. Her toes curled in her slipper socks. Crys tightened her arms around him, holding him closer. Happiness swelled in her heart. Luke lowered her to her feet.

She smiled up at him. "Is that a yes?"

He laughed, laying his forehead on hers. "I thought you didn't trust me."

Crys put her palms on his chest. "You've had my back from the beginning. You moved into my home when you realized I was in danger. You put your life in jeopardy for my family. Someone who does that has more than earned my trust."

He took her hands. His were large and rough, warm and strong. "I want to earn more than your trust. I've fallen in love with you, Crys. I want to make you happy."

Luke's chiseled features were blurry through her tears. "You've already made me happy, Luke. I know with you, love is worth the risk." She rose up on her toes and pressed her lips to his.

* * * * *

Get up to 4 Free Books!

We'll send you 2 free books from each series you try PLUS a free Mystery Gift.

FREE
Value Over
$25

Both the **Harlequin Intrigue®** and **Harlequin® Romantic Suspense** series feature compelling novels filled with heart-racing action-packed romance that will keep you on the edge of your seat.

YES! Please send me 2 FREE novels from the Harlequin Intrigue or Harlequin Romantic Suspense series and my FREE gift (gift is worth about $10 retail). After receiving them, if I don't wish to receive any more books, I can return the shipping statement marked "cancel." If I don't cancel, I will receive 6 brand-new Harlequin Intrigue Larger-Print books every month and be billed just $7.19 each in the U.S. or $7.99 each in Canada, or 4 brand-new Harlequin Romantic Suspense books every month and be billed just $6.39 each in the U.S. or $7.19 each in Canada, a savings of 20% off the cover price. It's quite a bargain! Shipping and handling is just 50¢ per book in the U.S. and $1.25 per book in Canada.* I understand that accepting the 2 free books and gift places me under no obligation to buy anything. I can always return a shipment and cancel at any time by calling the number below. The free books and gift are mine to keep no matter what I decide.

Choose one: ☐ **Harlequin Intrigue Larger-Print** (199/399 BPA G36Y)   ☐ **Harlequin Romantic Suspense** (240/340 BPA G36Y)   ☐ **Or Try Both!** (199/399 & 240/340 BPA G36Z)

Name (please print)

Address   Apt. #

City   State/Province   Zip/Postal Code

Email: Please check this box ☐ if you would like to receive newsletters and promotional emails from Harlequin Enterprises ULC and its affiliates. You can unsubscribe anytime.

> Mail to the **Harlequin Reader Service:**
> **IN U.S.A.:** P.O. Box 1341, Buffalo, NY 14240-8531
> **IN CANADA:** P.O. Box 603, Fort Erie, Ontario L2A 5X3

Want to explore our other series or interested in ebooks? Visit www.ReaderService.com or call 1-800-873-8635.

---

*Terms and prices subject to change without notice. Prices do not include sales taxes, which will be charged (if applicable) based on your state or country of residence. Canadian residents will be charged applicable taxes. Offer not valid in Quebec. This offer is limited to one order per household. Books received may not be as shown. Not valid for current subscribers to the Harlequin Intrigue or Harlequin Romantic Suspense series. All orders subject to approval. Credit or debit balances in a customer's account(s) may be offset by any other outstanding balance owed by or to the customer. Please allow 4 to 6 weeks for delivery. Offer available while quantities last.

Your Privacy—Your information is being collected by Harlequin Enterprises ULC, operating as Harlequin Reader Service. For a complete summary of the information we collect, how we use this information and to whom it is disclosed, please visit our privacy notice located at https://corporate.harlequin.com/privacy-notice. Notice to California Residents – Under California law, you have specific rights to control and access your data. For more information on these rights and how to exercise them, visit https://corporate.harlequin.com/california-privacy. For additional information for residents of other U.S. states that provide their residents with certain rights with respect to personal data, visit https://corporate.harlequin.com/other-state-residents-privacy-rights/.

HIHRS25